Fair Tomorrow

Fair Tomorrow

By
EMILIE LORING

GROSSET & DUNLAP
Publishers   *New York*

To

LOUISE GORDON HALLET

WHOSE FRIENDSHIP HAS GLOWED WITH
A LOVELY LIGHT DOWN THROUGH THE
YEARS SINCE WE MET ON CAPE COD

Fair Tomorrow

Chapter I

*C*OATLESS, immaculate white shirt sleeves rolled above his elbows, red-headed Terrence Leigh scowled thoughtfully at the gate-legged table set for two in the sunny window, ceased his muted whistling to shout:

"Hi! Pam! Which side of the plate shall I put the cranberry jell?"

In answer a door swung into the room with an agonized squeak. The sound startled the green and red parrot dozing on a gilded perch. He lost his balance, righted himself with a strident:

"Gosh!"

With the opening door came a potpourri of savory scent: roasting turkey, sage, oyster stuffing, crisping sausage, onions, spicy mincemeat. Came also a girl's head with a suggestion of black hair edging a white Dutch cap, a hint of anxiety in brilliant dark eyes, a flush from kitchen heat on satin-soft skin.

"Jelly at the right, Terry." Slender, graceful,

her yellow linen frock almost obscured by a snowy apron cloud, Pamela Leigh followed her voice into the dining room. The door swung shut behind her.

"Ooch! That squeak sets my teeth on edge. Wait a minute!" She dashed into the kitchen, returned with a cake of soap. "Rub that on the hinges. The jelly stands up well, doesn't it?"

"Like soldiers."

Terrence soaped the hinges. His boyish smile was humorously one-sided as he swung the door experimentally. "That's all right. Table looks like a million dollars, what?"

His sister's eyes followed his to the maple gate-legged table in front of the long French window which framed a view of a russet-tinged lawn enclosed by a picket fence, guarded by an iron dog whose black and white nose sniffed the salty air. Beyond it blue water stretched to the purple haze of the horizon like a sea of sparkling sapphires streaked with malachite, above it thin filaments of fleecy cloud striped a turquoise sky. Pamela appraisingly regarded the glossy damask, Chinese medallion plates, crystal goblets, molds of cranberry jelly like huge cabochon rubies. Her glance traveled on to the lowboy with its load of cracked nuts, figs, board of cheeses, jug of cider, came back to the table. She rearranged the russet Beau Belle pears, Banana apples, gold and sunburned to a dusky pink, purple and white grapes, in the choice old comport as she agreed thoughtfully:

"It does look well, Terry. I hope that we have provided the right setting. The ad distinctly stated:

"'Wanted: by two persons, old-fashioned Thanksgiving dinner. Anywhere on Cape Cod.' Nature has obligingly furnished the Cape. The dinner is as much like the one Grandmother Leigh used to serve as I could make it."

"Except the price. Five per! You have the nerve of a robber chieftain."

Pamela's lovely eyes, her ardent mobile mouth widened in a laugh. "My instincts are kind but my necessities are urgent. Perhaps the price is a hold-up, Terry, but when Madge Jarvis sent the ad she had clipped from a newspaper, she wrote:

"'Don't give away the dinner, Pam. That advertiser is out for sentiment. Sentiment is the most expensive luxury in which one may indulge, it ought to be taxed. Charge five dollars a cover at least. That might be high for shredded wheat and milk, but it isn't high for a cooked to order meal.'"

Terrence whistled and pulled down his sleeves. "Dinner for two in the wilds of Cape Cod. In the language of Hitty Betts, 'I guess them advertisers like privacy.'" He hummed and cut adolescent antics as he set chairs at the gateleg table. The green and red parrot blinked lidless yellow eyes, jabbered:

"Look who's here!"

Terrence shouted with boyish laughter. "Attaboy! Old Mephisto will add the modern touch.

Cabaret stuff. Hope he doesn't croak, ' Goo'-bye!
Goo'-bye!' in the middle of the dinner. The advertisers might leave without settling. Five dollars
per! Zowie! For a hard-boiled female lead me to
a college grad and an ex-reporter.''

Lightning slashed Pamela's eyes, eyes as dark as
eyes may be. "I was never a reporter, Terry Leigh.
I did features. That is why I get such a thrill out
of the Silver Moon Chowder House. Grandmother
called this place The Cottage. Too prosaic. A
business like ours needs something with a lift. Silver Moon somehow sets my imagination a-tiptoe.
To me each patron means a story. In our English
course at college we made diagrams of plots. Mr.
A starts for B at the other end of a straight line.
Half way he meets C. That contact sidetracks him
to D. Contacts represented by dots. Sometimes
my Mr. A never reached B.''

"You can put that over in a story but it doesn't
click in real life.''

"Doesn't it? What happened when Father, A,
started to visit you, B, at school? Half way he met
an actress, C, whose car had broken down. Took
her to her home, D. Married her the next month.
Never reached you at school, B. What did that
meeting with C do to our lives? Tangled them into
a snarl, messed them tragically, didn't it?''

"I guess you're right. We'll be in a great old
jumble if every person who orders chowder dots our
lifelines.''

"Let's make a plot diagram for today, Terry. We will call the advertiser who is coming, A, and his friend, B. C is their objective, the house to which they return from here. Perhaps I'll get a story germ. As for my being hard-boiled — somebody must be with Father sick, and those creditors of his sending threatening letters and calling on the telephone — and you having to leave prep school your last year and go to this country academy when you were leading your class in studies and were being groomed for a pitcher, — . Life is just a hideous nightmare."

Terrence cleared his throat. "Brace up, Pam. We'll get out of the woods yet. Remember that poem of Holman Day's I came across the other day about the two frogs in the pail of milk? One gave up and was drowned, the other kicked till he churned an island of butter and hopped out." He patted her shoulder. "Kick, frog, kick! Don't you worry about me. I like the Academy, honest. If you lose courage, 'twill be a cockeyed world." He swallowed hard, brushed his hand over his eyes. "Make that advertiser plank down the cash. Remember the last cheque we took in payment for five chowder dinners?"

Pamela laughed. Not too steadily, not too convincingly, but it passed. Terrence's eyes cleared.

"Remember it? If ever my heart is X-rayed, seared into its jacket will be found the two words written on that returned cheque, 'No Funds.' Hitty

Betts is coming to help clear up. We don't even know the gender of our plot germs. Perhaps A and B are men. If they are, I hope they won't be like the two who dropped in for chowder last week. Their eyes were like gimlets boring into our lovely old pieces of furniture and the Sandwich glass, till I expected to find the maple full of holes and the glass cracked after their departure."

"Perhaps they were antique dealers and knew the real thing when they saw it. A guy wouldn't need a Rhodes scholarship mind to realize that old John Leigh isn't of 20th century vintage."

Terrence and his sister looked up at the portrait above the maple lowboy. A long-gone Leigh as Thomas Sully had seen him. Black coat, white stock, snowy hair, sparse on top, thick and waving over the ears. Speculative blue eyes under bushy gray brows, florid complexion, a hawk nose, which almost met the thin line of clamped lips. A fine hand holding an open letter.

"Goo'-bye! Goo'-bye!" croaked the parrot irritably as he swung head down.

Pamela started for the door. "Thanks for the reminder, Mephisto. One would think I had nothing to do. I hope, Terry dear, that they give you a good tip. If the plot germs, A and B, are men, they will. I'm not so sure about women."

"No two of a kind in it if it's a matter of sentiment, I'll bet my hat."

√ "I can stand this mess we are in but it seems as if

I couldn't bear it for Terry," Pamela told herself as she entered the big sunny kitchen. The floor was covered with a gray and white linoleum, patterned like tiles. Chairs and tables repeated the color of the pale green walls. The girl flinched mentally even as she approved the charming effect. She had bought the paint and floor covering before she had known of the flock of bills which came flying home to roost soon after the family had moved into the old Leigh homestead.

She shook off the depression which thought of the indebtedness wrapped round her spirit like a smothering cloak and tried to be just. Why shouldn't the creditors clamor for their money? They had supplied the goods. If only she could pay them.

She beat potatoes to swansdown delicacy, added rich cream and seasoning and fluffed again. She struggled valiantly against bitterness as she remembered her last Thanksgiving. Terry had come from school to join her in the city. They had had a grand and glorious time. Twice to the theatre. Lunch and dinner at gay restaurants. She mashed copper-golden squash to delectable lightness as her thoughts trooped on. The financial crash had swept away not only her father's fortune but the money their mother had left to her children. He had gone to pieces physically — so characteristic of him not to brace with all his force to see a difficult situation through. Young Mrs. Leigh had sent for her, had furiously condemned her husband for his lack of judgment; had declared that it was the duty of his two children whom he had expensively brought up — just as if all parents didn't spend money on their children when they could — to look after him now that he was a physical wreck, that she would return to the stage. That night she had departed with all available cash, leaving hotel bill, doctors, nurses unpaid. Pamela's throat contracted as she remembered her dazed bewilderment. Her father had quarreled furiously with Phineas Carr, the lawyer who had been his mother's adviser, who had settled the estate. She couldn't go to him. She had sent for Terrence. Together they had worked out the plan to take their father to the Cape Cod farm house which Grandmother Leigh had left to her with all its contents, with acres of shore land, a short time before. She had given up newspaper work to become home-maker and nurse. The legacy had included fine diamonds. Those had been sold to pay hotel, nurses and doctors. How it had hurt. She adored jewels. She had been glad to get away from the city, with its reminding shop windows glittering with gems.

An automobile! Stopping? She slipped a pan of oysters — with pink strips of bacon between their rough shells — into the oven. Excitement rouged her cheeks. If she made good this time the two advertisers would recommend the Silver Moon, and its fame would spread and spread and spread. Once established, she would make a specialty of chowders,

lobster, clam, fish, corn, egg, the variety was end-
less. Pies for dessert. Her friend Madge Jarvis
had put the idea into her mind.

"Of course you can earn money at home. Think
up something different for people to eat and your
fortune's made, Pam. The path worn bare to the
door of the mythical mousetrap man won't be in it
with the path to yours. Grandmother Leigh en-
dowed you with something of infinitely more value
than house and lands and jewels, when she taught
you to cook. Your lobster chowder would make
the mouth of that iron dog on your lawn water;
as to your pie-crust—"

Terrence banged open the door. His eyes
sparkled with excitement. "They've come!"

Spoon in hand Pamela tiptoed forward. Whispered in her turn: "What are they like?"

"Man and girl. Classy roadster. Black with
wide brilliant red stripe, stainless steel wheels, red
morocco upholstery. It's a bird! She's little and
blonde, swanky fur coat. He's big and strong."

"Young?"

"So-so. Ready?"

"Will be when the glasses are filled."

Pamela pulled the pan from the oven. Big,
plump oysters with crisp curls of bacon, sizzled
in their own juices as she arranged six of the hot
shells around a frilled half of lemon rosy with paprika, on a doily covered plate. She sniffed. Done
to a turn. Luscious smell.

Would A and B be too absorbed in one another

to notice the maple chest, the Sully over the lowboy, the Queen Anne mirror, the Sandwich glass in the corner cupboard, the Lowestoft punchbowl? She still had those. She would work her fingers to the bone before she sold them. To what extent was she morally responsible for her father's debts? Good grief, wasn't serving the dinner enough without getting those on her mind?

"Let's go, Pam!"

Terrence in a white coat followed his excited whisper into the sunny kitchen. He picked up the plates of oysters from the porcelain-top table, kicked open the door and disappeared. Pamela listened, caught the murmur of voices, a laugh that sent a faint vibration through her heart which had seemed numb these last nightmarish months.

What sort of girl would a man with a laugh like that care for, she wondered as she surrounded the delectably browned turkey with crisp sausages, sunk cranberries deep in the curled greenness of garnishing parsley for a bit of color.

"Hi!"

The sepulchral whisper came from the other side of the swing door. She pulled it open, admitted Terrence with a plate in each hand.

"Crazy about the oysters, A, the man, is. Take it from me, B, the girl couldn't be crazy about anything. She's a snappy number, though," he admitted before he disappeared with the hot dinner plates.

He was back in a moment for the turkey. As Pamela held the door wide for him she glanced at the dining room mirror to glimpse the paying guests. She gazed straight into reflected amused eyes, a man's eyes. They set her heart, which she had thought numb, to quick-stepping. She let the door swing shut with a suddenness which caught Ter-rence in the heels with a bang. She heard Me-phisto's explosive,

"Gosh!"

"A's as pleased as a kid with an all-day sucker, that he has a turkey to carve," Terrence confided, as he picked up a dish of fluffy potato and one heaped with squash of feathery lightness.

"He can't get any come-back from the girl, though," he continued when he returned from serv-ing the onions, white, bursting from tenderness in the yellow of melted butter — the giblet gravy, smooth, brown, piping hot in its silver boat. "First she found fault because there wasn't any soup. I explained in the grand manner that we never served soup before turkey, thought it killed the hanker for the national bird. Then she fussed because he hadn't provided cocktails. If you ask me, I'll say he has a rocky road ahead if he has that ball and chain fastened to him for life."

"Cocktails! Grandmother Leigh always served sweet cider! Thought that was as important with a Thanksgiving dinner as the turkey," Pamela pro-tested. She whisked French dressing with the eggbeater before pouring it on the salad, pale green lettuce and perfect segments of chilled grapefruit, with a fig stuffed with a fluffy mixture of cheeses on the side of the plate. As she added a pink flush of paprika to its delicate yellowness she glanced at the clock. Mehitable Betts would arrive soon to help with the dishes. After Terry had taken in the dessert and coffee she would carry her father's dinner up to him. She dreaded his caustic comments. He was bitterly opposed to the Silver Moon idea, though he had no constructive money-producing plan to offer in its place.

She marked the pies in generous portions. Apple, baked in an oblong tin, the four corners lusciously candied with molasses which had been used for sweetening in place of sugar; mince pie; pumpkin pie. She stopped to look at the world outside. Two snow birds were busily pecking for their Thanksgiving dinner in the rusty grass, in front of the cottage which had once housed the farmer and his family. Purple shadows from drifting clouds cast curious patterns on the sand dunes. A rising breeze was kicking up white caps, which looked as if the sparkling blue and green sea had acquired a passion for lace ruffles. Marvelous afternoon. The dining room door swung under the urge of a vigorous kick. Terrence dodged in holding the pewter platter. He deposited it on the table, whispered:

"B's name is Hilda. Hilda Crane."

"Tender?"

He reached for a tempting sliver of white meat. "Hilda? Anything but—"

"Silly, I mean the turkey."

"I'll say it was. The joint fell away almost as the knife touched it. Made my mouth water. A said, ' Cooked to a turn!' She didn't eat fifty cents', let alone five dollars', worth, glory be." He returned to the dining room. When he came back with the plates he whispered:

"A's name is Scott Mallory."

"Mallory! His letter was signed, ' Cryder.' "

"Secretary, maybe."

With the dishes of vegetables, he contributed: "She's all excited because he insisted upon 'dragging' her to the country for Thanksgiving, she thought she was going where there would be music and dancing. She said: 'I hate sentiment—' then he crashed in, explaining that he hadn't had a real old-fashioned dinner since he went to South America, two years ago, that all the while he was away he kept dreaming about one. He's been back a month. Wanted a Thanksgiving dinner on the Cape. Advertised. Can't make out whether they're engaged or he's teetering on the brink of a proposal. He'd better Stop! Look! Listen! before he plunges. She's the kind who'll try to make him sit up, roll over and play dead dog. Salad looks grand," he approved as he picked up the green crystal plates.

When he came back with them empty he encouraged: "The snooty Hilda made no crack at that."

"Thank heaven, she has liked something. Clear the table. Put on the dessert plates and come back for the pies."

"Boy! Those smell good!" Terrence sniffed upon his return. He munched a flaky bit of crust. "A's getting colder and colder. That B has taken the fun out of his party. He was jolly and talkative when he came. She makes me think of the second Mrs. Leigh."

Pamela stood on one foot and then the other, to relieve the tired ache in them, as she poured steaming, dark amber coffee into a squat silver pot.

"That's the type which catches the big strong men. They like 'em little and grafting."

She prepared a tray for her father. Slipped a pan of oysters into the oven. Terrence came out with the pie-plates.

"B wouldn't touch hers. A's white with fury. He was saying something when I went in about intending to see this dinner through. He stopped short. And she said hateful like — wanted me to hear, I'll bet — 'See it through then! I shan't.' How I hate rows. Just as if life in this house wasn't enough of a trail of conflict with Father upstairs seeing things battle-ship gray, without having 'em brought in by our customers."

"Clientele, Terry. Clientele, it is less commercial," Pamela corrected with an attempt at gaiety.

"Bring out the pies. Then put the nuts and raisins on the table. Let the snappy Hilda pour the coffee. I will get Father's dinner ready."

As she removed the oysters from the oven she struck her hand against the door. The contact left an angry red burn across her fingers.

"Ooch! That smarts!"

She covered the turkey and vegetables with a hot plate, added crisp celery and cranberry jelly to the tray.

Harold Leigh, in a deep chair by the sunny window, frowned as his daughter entered his room. A table in front of him was strewn with postage stamps and a loose-leaf book. Sunshine accentuated the whiteness of his hair, turned his skin to the color of old wax. How old he looked, yet he was only fifty-five, Pamela reminded herself. His nose seemed about to hook into his upper lip. His resemblance to the portrait in the dining room was startling. He tapped the arm of his chair impatiently.

"Always the last one to be thought of. It's an hour past my usual dinner time."

"Sorry, but I couldn't bring it before." She pushed the stamp-laden table aside and pulled up another for the tray. Eagerly he lifted the top of one of the shells. Plump, juicy, the oyster yielded an appetizing aroma. He frowned, picked up a strip of bacon.

"I hope what you served downstairs was crisper than this. I suppose anything will do for me."

Pamela opened her lips, closed them. Why retort? She would say something for which she would be sorry later and this was Thanksgiving Day. Why take away his grievance? He would have nothing to talk about. She swallowed the lump which always rose in her throat at his irritation with her. With the assurance that she would bring the dessert later she left the room.

Curious that her father still had power to hurt her, she thought, as she went slowly down the stairs. As a child she had adored him; he had been gallant and gay, her Prince Charming. One look of affection, one tender word from him, would set little wings on her feet as she ran about to serve him. As the years passed he had grown more and more indifferent to his children; she had been rebuffed whenever her love for him had bubbled to the surface — she had been such a buoyant, bubbly sort of person in those days. His indifference had hardened her toward all men. If she hadn't laughed, she had shrugged at protestations of love. A mental hygienist, doubtless, could explain in scientific terms just what had happened to her heart; she knew only that her father's indifference had smothered something beautiful within her which had glowed.

As she entered the kitchen Terrence burst in from the dining room. His eyes, so like his sister's snapped with excitement; his red hair was rampant; his hoarse voice choked:

"Your plot germs have skipped!"

"Skipped! Terry! Not without—"

"You've said it! Without paying. That girl, Hilda, was opening up, high, wide and handsome because Scott Mallory wouldn't take her home at once. I guess I went goggle-eyed—I'm not used to women who row—for he told me to bring more coffee. Had to heat it a little. When I went back they had gone."

Chapter II

PAMELA crushed down the memory of the amused eyes which had met hers in the mirror. She laughed, a bitter little laugh.

"Managing the Silver Moon is just one disillusioning experience after another, isn't it? Dash after them in the fliv, Terry. If you catch them hang on until you get our money. If—"

Terrence was out of the room before she could finish the sentence. As she collected the plates, wherever she looked the clear, darkly gray eyes with the light of laughter in their depths seemed to meet hers. Never before had she met a man whose eyes had plunged into her heart and warmed it. And now he had run away! Of course, a person such as she had thought him wouldn't chance into the threatening, terrifying world of debt and disillusionment in which she was living.

A resounding knock shook the old door of the kitchen. Pamela glanced at the clock. Too early for Mehitable. Creditors? Their shadows were ever at the heels of her imagination. They couldn't be so inhuman as to come collecting on Thanksgiving! A yellow Ford station wagon had stopped outside. She opened the door. One of the men who had bored into her maple furniture with his gimlet eyes the other day confronted her. He touched his hat as if grudging the courtesy, scowled, demanded truculently:

"Does Harold Leigh live here?"

"Yes. But you can't see him. He is ill."

He called over his shoulder: "All right! This is the house!"

He pushed by Pamela into the kitchen. His hat on the back of his head revealed a forehead which appeared to have no terminal.

"What do you want?"

With cocky condescension he thrust one hand deep into his trousers pocket, waved a sheaf of bills in the other.

"I've come to collect on these."

"Don't shout. You will disturb Mr. Leigh."

"Oh, I will! Well, take it from me, that's what I'm here for. He hasn't answered letters, I'll see if I can get action this way."

He sniffed. His eyes dilated, his nostrils quivered like a rabbit's as he sighted the tempting remains of the turkey, one appetizingly browned side uncut. He stretched out a not too clean hand, seized a piece of white meat with a dangling strip of crisp skin. He had the succulent morsel half way to his mouth when Pamela rapped his knuckles smartly with the silver serving spoon.

"Drop it!"

He dropped it. Her eyes were brilliantly, angrily black, her face colorless as she picked up the scrap between thumb and forefinger, lifted a range lid, flung the white meat into the heart of the red-hot wood embers. The intolerable smart of her burned fingers added fuel to the flame of her fury. The man blustered:

"Treat me like that, will you? Now you'll get what's coming to you. The county sheriff is on the truck outside. I have orders to seize all the antique furniture in this house on account of these bills. See this?"

He threw back the lapel of his coat and revealed a badge of sorts. Pamela looked from it to the man at the wheel of the yellow truck. He was a stranger. She remembered now that the new sheriff was from a town at the other end of the county. No help from him. The collector laughed. Pamela restrained a furious desire to crack his knuckles again. As he took a purposeful step toward the dining room she backed against the swing door.

"You can't go in there."

He stuck his repulsive face close to hers. Shouted, "Can't I?"

The door behind her was jerked open. She fell back against someone, caught a coat lapel, steadied herself.

"He has come to seize the antiques for the creditors. Don't let him take them, Terry! Don't let him take them!"

"Not a chance of his taking them," assured a strange voice.

With a gasp of amazement Pamela looked up into the fine, lean face of a man, into the eyes she had met in the mirror, not amused now, but keen, determined. A! The advertiser! He had returned. Had Terry dragged him back? She didn't care. He had come. He stood behind her like a rock, broad of shoulders, bronzed of face. The rich green of his tie accented the soft grayness of his suit. He was a man one could take on trust, a man one could like immensely, she decided. Doubtless, by the same token, a man about whom many girls and women had thought the same. He stepped into the kitchen. The door swung shut behind him.

"What's going on here?"

The collector swept his finger along the sheaf of papers, thrust out an aggressive chin. "Got a sheriff outside to attach the antique furniture here on these bills. I know it's genuine, brought an expert here for chowder last week and he gave it the once-over. You can take it from me I'm going to get it."

"What's your name?"

"S. Linsky."

"Where's your writ, Slinsky?"

"S. Linsky! S. Linsky!"

"Well, S. Linsky, where is your writ?"

"Here. Think I'd come without it? Take me for a boob?"

"I wouldn't take you on any terms." A—Ter-

rence had said that his name was Scott Mallory,
Pamela remembered — examined the writ. "You
are attaching the furniture in this house on account
of bills owed by Harold Leigh and his wife, Cecile?"

The door behind him swung. Framed in the
opening stood almost the prettiest blonde Pamela
ever had seen in quite the most stunning fur coat.
The girl was gowned with exceeding smartness in
blue with a matching hat. With her came a faint
scent. *Nuit de Noel. Parfums Caron.* Paris.
Pamela recognized it. In the dear dead on-her-own
days, she had plunged recklessly to the extent of an
ounce of the perfume. The "snappy Hilda" of
course, who else? Curling ends of fair hair gleamed
from beneath the brim of her hat. Her lips were a
brilliant bow, an undertone of angry red flushed her
rose-leaf skin, her violet eyes were set in delicately
blackened lashes, her arched brows met in a deep line
of annoyance. She demanded petulantly:

"Scott! What are you doing? Surely it hasn't
taken all this time to pay your bill. You dragged
me back when you remembered it although I told
you that a mailed check would do just as well."
She frowned at Pamela, drawled with acid innuendo:
"Perhaps you really came back to say 'au revoir'
to the cook. I understand now why you brought
me to Cape Cod. It wasn't entirely because of
Thanksgiving dinners you had had here as a boy, as
you so carefully explained. Cut the farewell short.
I want to go home."

Pamela marvelled at Scott Mallory's self-control. Only his darkening eyes and loss of color betrayed his emotions as he apologized:

"Don't mind Miss Crane. She is apt to forget her manners when she loses her temper." He pulled open the swing door. "Wait in the dining room until I come, Hilda."

The girl flushed furiously at his reproof, set her head at a supercilious angle.

"I won't wait a moment. You are to come at once or I go — at once."

Pamela caught Scott Mallory's arm. "Please go. Don't bother about my affairs. I'm not afraid of Slinsky, really I'm not."

"S. Linsky!" The collector growled correction.

Mallory looked down at the angry burn which streaked the fingers on his sleeve, at the bald-headed man smirking satisfaction at the situation. His face was a mask as he demanded:

"Let me get this right, S. Linsky. You are attaching the furniture in this house on account of bills owed by Harold Leigh and his wife?"

Hilda Crane stood like a girl of stone. There was an instant of prickling tension before Mallory repeated his question. Was he as unaware as he seemed of the vicious bang of the swing door behind her as she dashed from the room? Linsky swelled with gratified importance, like a puff pig when its stomach is scratched.

"That's the stuff."

"You are sure that it is his furniture?"

"Sure. Didn't she say he was upstairs too sick to come down?"

Mallory looked at the papers in his hand. Demanded of Pamela:

"Are you Cecile Leigh? Wife of Harold?"

"No! I am his daughter."

"Does the furniture in this house belong to Harold Leigh or his wife?"

The side door opened. Pamela's heart thumped madly. The sheriff? Come for her old maple and the Lowestoft bowl? She sighed relief. It was Mehitable Betts looking more like a gaunt grey wolf than ever. Darn! She would spread the news of the sheriff's visit all over town before night. Mallory reminded:

"You haven't answered my question. To whom does the furniture belong?"

"To me. Every piece of it."

He held out the writ. "That settles that, S. Linsky."

The collector bristled like a hedgehog charging. "Settles it! How do you get that way! Of course she'd say it belonged to her. That girl wasn't born yesterday." He rubbed one hand over the reddened knuckles of the other.

"Well, then, I say it's hers!" Mehitable Betts, skin and thin hair as drab as her skimpy dress, jerked her steel bowed spectacles back to the bridge of her nose before she folded her arms across her flat breast. Bony hands gripping her elbows, she belligerently confronted the doubter. " I lived with old M's Leigh goin' on twenty years, on and off. I signed my name at the bottom of her will a few days before she died. And when lawyer Carr carried it away she says to me, ' Hitty,' she says, ' I'm leavin' this house and everything in it to Pamela,' she says. ' That hoity-toity stage woman Hal's married is not our kind of folks, she wouldn't know old maple from pine kindlin',' she says, ' she'd sell it. Pamela'll hold on to it for her children and her children's children.' "

Scott Mallory suggested : " That's all, S. Linsky. There isn't any more."

The collector's already high color took on a purplish tinge. " Ain't there? Perhaps not just now but I'll be back for that fake sick man upstairs."

" Better get after his attorney."

" Do you think we haven't tried? He hasn't one and his wife's skipped. I knew the girl wasn't her. He couldn't pay the price of an attorney."

Mallory presented a business card. " I am his attorney. I am acting for Miss Leigh, too. You will find me at that address."

Linsky scowled at the bit of pasteboard. There was more than a hint of awe in his voice as he inquired :

" Are you the Mallory who's trying that big case against those South American fellas?"

" The same Mallory."

With an inarticulate growl S. Linsky slouched

out. Pamela watched him climb aboard the Ford truck. He was gesticulating angrily as it turned down the road. She looked up at the man beside her.

"I can't begin to thank you for saving my lovely old maple. Knowing absolutely nothing of legal procedure, I might have bitten and scratched to keep it and in the end let it go to pay my father's debts."

"Don't let anything go. I owe you an apology for tearing off without paying my bill. I was so boiling mad that not until I reached the village did I remember. Then, in spite of — well, I came back."

"You didn't meet Terry?"

"Terry? Is that your brother's name? No, I didn't meet him. Was he after me to collect?"

His smile lighted even the closed garden of her heart into which she had locked her ambition to make good in her profession. He suggested:

"Come into the dining room. I am sure that I can help. You will let me, won't you?"

The impatient tinkle of a bell came from the floor above. "Good grief, I've forgotten Father's dessert." Pamela seized a plate. Mehitable Betts grabbed it.

"Give me that! Had any dinner?" The girl shook her head. "Hmp! Thought not. Go right into the dining room and set. You're beat out doing the cooking. Ought to have put vinegar on your burned fingers. I'll bring you something to eat and then I'll tend to your Pa. I'm not afraid of any man living. Folks is sayin' he'd be a sight better if you didn't coddle him, if he got out and found a job 'stead of hivin' up in his room licking his wounds. You and your beau go into the dining room."

Pamela snatched off her white cap, slipped out of the voluminous apron. She pulled down the sleeves of her yellow frock as Mallory pushed open the swing door. As they entered the sunny room she put a hand to her flushed cheek.

"Don't mind Hitty's conclusions. To her, every man is a potential beau; that is her word, not mine. Why — where is Miss Crane? S. Linsky was so upsetting, I forgot about her. She must be waiting in the living room. Please, please don't bother about me any more."

Hands in his gray coat pockets Mallory stood at the window. "I suspect that Miss Crane is now speeding toward home in my roadster. It's gone."

"Gone to C!"

He swung round to face her. "Gone to sea in a roadster?"

"C, the letter, not s-e-a. It is part of a plot diagram Terry and I imagined. You, the advertiser, were A. Your friend was B. C was your objective when you left the Silver Moon. My affairs dotted your life-lines and sent each of you off at a tangent. I'm sorry. Miss Crane hated everything about the place, didn't she?"

Mallory shook his head, explained slowly as if he were thinking the situation through: "It was not the place, it was the man. Curious how a person can change. Perhaps it isn't the person, perhaps it is one's point of view. Hilda Crane was on the boat coming up from B. A. She was the first American girl I had played round with in two years. She was good fun. Gradually she suffered a land-change. I wouldn't believe that I could be so mistaken in a person, have always thought I was a wonder at reading character. I hoped that if we had an old-fashioned Thanksgiving dinner together — I hadn't told her that we were not going to a gay place, my mistake — shows what an incurable nineteenth century romantic I am — the girl I had imagined her to be might return. She didn't, so, that's that."

He laid money on the table. "Sorry, I forgot it. The dinner was perfect. My secretary, Jane Cryder, selected your answer to my advertisement from among fifty others. None of my friends are old-fashioned enough — perhaps New England enough — to serve the kind of dinner I remembered. I wanted to spend the day on the Cape. I craved a whiff of the country in which I was born, wanted to come back to it, if only for a day, with a fresh appreciation of what it had meant to me as a boy. Miss Cryder selected your reply because she loved your name, Pamela Leigh. Isn't that like a woman's reasoning? I will admit that in this case it was intuition. Suppose I talk with your father about those bills while you are having your dinner?"

"Will you? The hounding creditors are such

a nightmare." The eagerness departed from her eyes and voice. "But, we have no money with which to pay a lawyer."

"I haven't earned a fee yet. After all, you don't know anything about me. Why should you trust me? That's merely a rhetorical question. I hope you will. Here is my card. Put a Bertillon expert on my fingerprints, if you wish."

Pamela looked down at the bit of pasteboard in her hand, up at the gray eyes watching her.

"I trust you without the expert."

"Thank you."

Gaunt Mehitable Betts with a plate in each hand kicked open the swing door. The parrot broke into a wheezy chuckle. "Look who's here!" he croaked sardonically.

Pamela hastily averted the tirade she knew would follow. The woman and bird were ancient enemies.

"Hitty, will you show Mr. Mallory to Father's room?"

Miss Betts set down the plates with a bang. "Sure I'll show him up. Like's not he'll show him down, quick, but he looks as if he could stand it."

Her father had not shown Scott Mallory down, Pamela rejoiced, as an half hour later she arranged the table silver in the drawer of the maple lowboy. She could hear the rumble of voices overhead. Terrence poked his red head into the room.

"The plot germs came back all right, didn't they? Saw the roadster beating it this way just as I was shooting through the village. Mr. Mallory'll lose his train if he doesn't get a hustle on. Just asked me to take him to the station. I'll say that the girl had nerve to go off in his sporty roadster. He gave Hitty and me each a fat tip. I returned mine. Hurt like the dickens to let it go but I wouldn't take money from him when he has offered to help Father. But Hitty — boy! When she realized what she had in her hand — Miss Betts lugged out pail and brush, flopped to her knees and began scrubbing the kitchen floor. Listen to her hymn of praise." From the other side of the door rose a rough voice hoarse from disuse.

"'Praise God from whom all blessings flow

   Praise Him all creatures here below

   Praise Him above ye —'" the song cracked and rattled into a gurgle.

   "Poor Hitty. Life hasn't handed her many tips. You'd better remind Mr. Mallory of the time."

   Eyes on the shifting color values of sea and shore Pamela stood at the window. A far off white sail flashed against the dusky horizon like a bit of mother-of-pearl. Beyond the orchard stretched a forest of scrub oaks and stunted pines through which at intervals white birches gleamed like swaying ghosts. Rose tints in the blueness of the sky deepened to claret. What a day! Scott Mallory appearing like a modern dragon-slayer at the exact dramatic moment. The relief, the inexpressible relief of knowing that there was someone of whom she could ask advice. Should she allow him to help when she couldn't pay him? The same old obstacle bobbed up to confront her at every step. Money! Money! Money! She turned as Mallory entered. Terrence hovered impatiently in the background.

"Your father has authorized me to represent him. I have a list of his securities — somewhat of a misnomer — and debts. I hope to pull enough out of the lot to settle up, stop this nightmare, as you call it. If a creditor appears or phones refer him to me."

"We haven't any money to pay —"

"Don't think of that. Let me help." On a breath of laughter he suggested, "I'll collect my bill in chowders. How's that?"

"Ready to go now, Scott?" From the hall threshold Hilda Crane asked the question. Her pleading violet eyes seemed too big for her small face, her painted mouth too red. "Did you think I had run away? I wouldn't leave you. Been poking round the antique shops in the village waiting for you to finish your important business." Her voice was honeyed.

Her tone, her pouting lips, her provocative eyes, set off little fiery pinwheels in Pamela's mind. Giving an imitation of the charming girl of the steamer, was she?

Scott Mallory's voice was as grim as his lips. "My business is finished, Hilda. You have ruined this day, and by rights you should be sent home by train, but, when I start out on a party with a girl I see it through. Go on."

She hesitated.

"Goo'-bye! Goo'-bye!" croaked the red and green parrot testily.

Terrence camouflaged a chuckle in a racking cough. "Sorry! Have these attacks occasionally." He patted his sister's arm before he left the room. His song drifted back.

"'The fool frog sank in the swashing tank
  As the farmer bumped to town.
But the smart frog flew like a tug-boat screw,
  And he swore he'd not go down.'"

Pamela choked back a nervous giggle as she sensed his reminder to her. Hilda flung her a furious glance before she sauntered into the hall.

Mallory caught Pamela's hands in his. "I'm coming back — tomorrow. Dinner for two."

Aware that Miss Crane was observing them, Pamela explained gaily: "Second-day party, we call it on the Cape. Like warmed-over turkey?"

"Mad about it."

"Then come. There are dozens of questions I want to ask you about Father's business."

He spread the burned fingers gently on his palm, looked down into her gallantly smiling eyes.

"Sweet child!" He cleared his voice. "When I have answered them I have one or two to ask you."

"Scott!"

"Coming Hilda."

Chapter III

WITH a growl like the distant rumble of thunder the Belgian police dog in his smart breast strap sprang at his double standing near the curb of the sidewalk before the post-office in the village. The challenged one laid back his ears, snarled, bared his teeth invitingly. Pamela Leigh's dark eyes dilated with concern even as she caught the challenger by the collar, tried to drag him back.

"Stop it, Babe!"

"Drop him! Good God, drop him!" shouted a man who was leaping down the steps of the brick building three at a time. The girl had a confused sense of brown hair, blazing eyes, brown skin, curiously blanched, a mustache like a third eyebrow, impeccable sports clothes, the faint, far drone of a plane beating like a rhythmic pulse in the air, before she tightened her hold. She twisted the leather collar, choked the aggressor back upon his haunches. The man snatched at the tail of the other Belgian, yanked him away. He deftly caught the dog's collar, face ashen, demanded:

"Don't you know better than to mix up in a scrap

like this?" He turned at a shout behind him,
glared at the man in an army coat belted with a rope
who was running toward them. "This dog yours,
Eddie Pike? Grab him. What the devil do you
mean by letting a fighter like this loose?"

The breathless, unshaven man, with a mouth designed on codfish lines, caught his charge by an up-
right ear, glanced apologetically at the girl who still
clutched the collar of the challenger.

"Sorry, Miss Pamela." He scowled at his ac-
cuser. "Why shouldn't I let him loose? 'Twant
him started the trouble. There ain't no law 'gainst
exercising dogs here, are there? Come along,
Bozo."

He snapped on a leash. With a rumble and a
savage glare in the direction of his adversary Bozo
obediently started off at his keeper's heels.

Now that the late unpleasantness was over
Pamela's knees wobbled treacherously, her heart
pounded deafeningly. Under pretense of adjusting
the Babe's breast-strap she dropped to the steps.
A vision of the picture the contending factions had
presented set her a-quiver with nervous laughter.
The man protested with a hint of arrogance:

"What's the joke? Can't see the comedy in
taking a chance on getting chewed to pulp."

Pamela made a valiant effort at control, explained
in a voice still shredded with mirth: "When you
grabbed that horrid dog's tail — I thought — I
thought even as I choked the Babe — sup-suppose it

sh-should come off? After that your technique was su-superb." The sentence ended in a spasmodic gurgle.

"Pull yourself together. I don't wonder you were frightened. You'll have hysterics if you don't watch your step."

"I never had hysterics in my life." Indignation brought Pamela to her feet. She met his concerned eyes defiantly, even as she admitted to herself that she had been frightened, she never had been in the ring at a dog-fight before.

"Beg pardon for yelling at you when I butted in on the little party, but your recklessness frightened me stiff."

"But not dumb."

He laughed. She liked his laugh.

"I'm sorry. May I get your mail?"

She looked from him to the dog who had dropped to the sidewalk, whose throat rumbled as with a retreating thunder-shower.

"If you will. The Babe is as popular in the post-office as an ice-storm in an orange-grove. The R.F.D. man collects from the box at our gate in the early morning as he passes. Delivers at noon. We come for the afternoon mail. Box 52. I'm Pamela Leigh." Did he look startled as he turned away or was it merely her imagination?

She sank to the steps. The vicious line-up of the two dogs had left her limp as a de-sawdusted doll. Catch her bringing the Babe to the village again.

Babe! Anything but. Soon after that memorable Thanksgiving dinner for two, Scott Mallory had asked them to board the dog. He had tried to keep him in his apartment, much to the detriment of the furniture which he had a playful habit of chewing, and the indignation of neighboring tenants. Who was the man who had come to her rescue? A native son home for the week-end? He was about twenty-eight. Nothing so young in males had crossed her path since she had come in June to live in Grandmother Leigh's house.

Perfect afternoon. Lavender-winged gulls soared and dove above the sand dunes which were patched with the shadows of drifting snowy clouds. The out-going tide pitilessly exposed their sea-weedy, tin-can strewn gums; trailed fringes of white foam as it ebbed in curling amber-green waves. Beyond stretched an indigo sea, amethystine where it met the horizon. The sun dropped behind the highest dune, splashed the sky above with lovely color. Pamela felt its beauty like a tangible thing. Crimson, lemon, green, orange, fluffs of mauve, scarfs of rose. Lavish splendor! The afterglow tinted the roofs of the sedate old houses which bordered the main street, gilded the black bands on their white chimneys, transformed windows into molten sheets of brass and copper. Columns of smoke from wood fires spiraled and spread. The air was soft, salty, with an indefinable hint of spring. Pamela filled her lungs with it. This wasn't much like a February afternoon in New York City. One couldn't go about coatless in a green jersey frock there, at this time of year.

She watched the villagers trickling out of the post-office. She knew them all. One couldn't live in an old house which one had inherited in a Cape Cod town without being the object of speculation, the cynosure of every eye when one appeared in public, especially when every living inhabitant above ground — and perhaps some under — knew of the creditors who had hovered like vultures to collect the bills which her father and his wife had lavishly contracted before the crash.

Had hovered! Since the day Scott Mallory had offered to help straighten out the mess, she had not heard from one. Had he in some miraculous way managed to quiet them? Whatever had happened it was a respite for her. She no longer suffered the nausea of apprehension and humiliation when she answered door or telephone bell.

The man who had barged into the dog fight approached with a handful of white envelopes and newspapers.

"Looks as if you would be submerged in a greeting-card blizzard."

She dropped the mail into a basket woven of gay colors. "Thanks lots. Tomorrow will be my birthday. Everyone I ever knew has sent a greeting this year. I suspect that as they posted them my friends sighed.

"'Poor Pam! Marooned on Cape Cod.' Come Babe."

The dog rose leisurely, stretched one hind leg after another, yawned, wagged his tail.

"Mind if I walk with you? Our house is at the foot of the hill. I am Philip Carr."

Philip Carr! Son of Grandmother Leigh's legal adviser with whom her father had quarreled furiously! Quarreled because the lawyer had urgently advised him to carry out his mother's expressed wish, that he settle a sum of money on each of his children. Had the senior Carr had a premonition of what was to happen, had he lacked faith in Harold Leigh's judgment? Whichever it was, it was a pity he hadn't won out.

Philip Carr, about whom the townspeople conjectured, romanced, gossiped and whispered not too kindly! Several years before, his father had restored the house of his paternal great-grandfather for use a few months of the year. "Spoiled, terrible spoiled and a born lady-killer," Hitty Betts had described the son. He seemed more like a grown-up boy out of tune with the world, whose brown eyes sparked defiance, whose full red lips below the slight mustache curved in a suggestion of contempt. In spite of what she had heard in disparagement, she liked him.

"Well? Does my request require so much wrinkled-brow consideration? Say no, if you don't care for what you've heard about me. Our neighbors here are a sturdy little band of knockers.

They've told you probably that I spend most of my time about theatres. I do. Not because I'm crazy about actors as people, but because I want to design stage-settings. You may feel that we have not been properly introduced. Have I made a social blunder? Perhaps I should not have spoken to you until a third party had shouted above the growls and barks of the contending factions: 'Miss Leigh, allow me to present Mr. Carr.'"

She ignored the bitterness of his voice. "Introduced! Don't be silly! I have no aversion to theatres — I'm mad about them — or actors" — "except one actress," she added under her breath.

She saw the color steal to his hair, caught the instant's unsteadiness of his boyish mouth. Evidently he had been hurt. Nothing in the world was more cruel than small-town gossip. Often she had seen Mehitable Betts clamp her lips, before she opened them to preface a bit of scandal with:

"Folks is sayin' — "

Philip Carr shifted step to suit hers. "How long have you had that scrapper?"

"He isn't a scrapper. Usually he is beautifully mannered. He's just temperamental like some humans. You can't be expected to like every dog you meet, can you, Babe?" She patted the head of the Belgian who was walking sedately beside her. "He doubtless had an attack of indigestion and took it out on someone else — as do the majority of his sex."

"Not a high opinion of mortal man, have you?"

"You have guessed it. We are taking care of the Babe — we, means Terrence, my brother, and me — for our legal adviser." The last phrase induced a sense of financial solidity.

They approached a big Colonial house in a setting of spruce hedges. Pamela caught a glimpse of an old-fashioned garden in the rear tucked in for the winter. She approved enthusiastically:

"You have the loveliest home in the village. We are all so glad to have it open again."

"All right to have it open if you are not expected to live in it. Father and Mother hurried home from Europe to be sure the cold frames were started so that plants for the garden would go in early. So they say. I suspect that he is pawing the ground in his eagerness to get back into court. He says that he is through with legal battling, but he never will be so long as he finds a case which interests him. It's in his blood. Did you meet my people before they went across?"

"No. I haven't seen your father since he and my father clashed over the settlement of Grandmother Leigh's estate."

"Montague and Capulet stuff?" His smile was boyish. "That wouldn't make any difference to Mother if she liked you and she will. How did anything so vivid as you get caught in this Cape Cod tidepool? This is my third visit since the house was opened. I can't stand it more than twenty-four hours at a time."

Pamela remembered Hitty Betts' comment on the son and heir of the town's plutocrats. "Folks is sayin', that Phil Carr will bring the gray hair of his parents in sorrow to the grave. He goes with a fast lot of young folks, movie and theatre crowd mostly."

Of course, the natives would think him on the moral toboggan slide if his ideas of propriety differed from theirs. Their views on matters theatrical were strictly seventeenth century, Puritan. She met his friendliness with a swift explanation of her presence in the "tidepool." Added gayly:

"Seeing more immediate returns from cooking than from writing I turned Grandmother Leigh's old home into the Silver Moon Chowder House. Silver Moon because of the roses with mother-of-pearl petals and golden hearts which climb over the walls in June. Making money feeding people is stodgily pre-Lindbergh, isn't it? Since that epoch-making flight, girls are going in for all sorts of aviation angles, radio announcing, business management, banking, posing for commercial photographs, anything which isn't tarred with domesticity. I had to make money at home."

"It's sporting of you. I know your place. Used to go there with Father. While he conferred with your grandmother, the farmer's wife filled me up with milk and cookies in her cottage. Do you make the Silver Moon pay serving only chowders?"

"The point is well taken. As I'm not an Alice Foote McDougal yet, while I'm building up the business I give patrons what they ask for. Someone phoned for a reservation for six tomorrow and ordered young pig. Ever seen a young pig ready for roasting? Rear view it looks so like a plump fair-skinned baby that I salted it with my tears, figuratively speaking. I will sidestep and make Mehitable Betts put it into the oven." She was aware of his cynical regard.

"You don't impress me as being tender-hearted. There is a frozen quality in your voice which makes me a little afraid of you."

"Ever had your feet so cold at a football game that you wished they would hurry up and get numb so they would stop hurting? I am hoping that my heart will freeze so that it will stop feeling. Being a house-owner seems to be just one repair after another. Terry reported this morning that the roof of the farmer's cottage — which you remember — was leaking like a sieve. I wish the building would consume itself before the taxes consume it." She went on lightly: "Forget the sobbie. Don't think that I dislike my business venture — perhaps adventure; I love contact with people, even if I do hate having them wandering all over the house and patronizing, ' Nice little place!' Feeding them is just one problem after another."

"Are you the cook?"

"I am. At this stage of the enterprise I can't afford to have even one guest find anything wrong."

"You don't care a little bit about yourself, do you?"

" Crazy about Pamela Leigh," she attested gaily.
"Oh, there's your mother! I met her once years
ago but she probably does not remember me."

A woman in a smart gray gown was waiting at
the gate. Her hair was surprisingly white in contrast to her youthful skin. Her eyes were as brown,
as eager as her son's. She held out her hand.

" Miss Leigh, I am so glad to see you again. I
have been wondering how soon I might run up to
call. I wanted Phil to meet you but apparently he
has accomplished that pleasure without my help.
Won't you come in for tea ? "

Had the son wirelessed that suggestion to his
mother ? "Thank you, but I must hurry home.
We have a full day tomorrow. Has Terry brought
the eggs you ordered ? When I left he was in the
poultry house mumbling incantations over the hens.
With that utter disregard of the timely so characteristic of the species, they have gone on strike just
as you have opened your house."

"You don't mean that you run a poultry farm as
well as the Silver Moon ? "

" The poultry is my brother's enterprise, Mr.
Carr. I wouldn't go so far as to say that he runs it.
At present it is running him — ragged. However,
as we have adopted for our coat of arms two green
frogs, a milkpail rampant, with Kick Frog! Kick!
illumined on a silver field, we should worry."

The blaze of admiration in his eyes brought warm
color to her face. The drone of a plane overhead

almost drowned his boyish wheedle. " Mother, ask
the little girl if your little boy may play with her."

Mrs. Carr regarded him with smiling adoration.
" Phil's unprecedented shyness takes my breath.
May he call? I should be happy to have you
friends."

" I would love to have him come after business
hours, but you are witness to my warning, I am dull
company at the end of the day."

" I'll risk that. Do you good to go for an airing in
my roadster. I'm a safe non-skid driver warranted
steady at the wheel. Here comes the omnipresent
Milly! Wouldn't you know it? The fairies who
presided at that girl's advent into this old world
scrimped on her chin and spread themselves on her
bump of curiosity. How can you stand her snooping, Mother? "

" Because she is an excellent waitress, prefers to
remain near her brother, and while she spends every
cent she can get on clothes she hasn't the city urge.
What is it, Milly? "

The girl in a pink linen frock with dainty white
collar and cuffs and apron, who had run down the
path, was slightly breathless. Her pale blue eyes
were interrogation points as they shifted from face
to face, her mouth was a trifle pinched, her light
hair waved close to her head, her skin suggested the
tint and texture of a magnolia blossom. If she had
a trifle more chin and a suggestion of soul in her
make-up, she would be beautiful, Pamela decided.

She took an instant dislike to her. Untrustworthy. Philip Carr was right. She had prying eyes.

"Mr. Phil! Long distance call."

"Must be my client." He chuckled. "Why are our offices crowded?"

Mrs. Carr's eyes were starry. "Phil! Have you a client? Did you get the theatre contract?"

Her son reddened, laughed. "Mother! Why reveal the humiliating fact that this is my first?" He pointed his question by a glance at the maid who with jaw slightly dropped was staring at him. "See you tonight, Miss Leigh," he called back as he started for the house.

"M's Carr, please may I go down to the field to see the airplane? I've never seen one close," pleaded Milly Pike.

"Run along, but be here in ample time to serve dinner."

The girl raced away. The street, which had seemed under the spell of an afternoon siesta, suddenly came alive. Men and women boiled out of houses to hurry in the direction of the field.

Pamela's fingers tightened on the Babe's leash. "I'd better get back to the Silver Moon. There were no reservations for the afternoon so I left Hitty Betts in charge while I ran away for an hour. She won't be able to resist the lure of that plane."

Mrs. Carr's eyes were luminous. "My dear, you will never know until you have a son of your own how glad I am that Phil met you. It was tactless of me to betray the fact that he has not been overworked. He took up architecture against his father's wishes — my husband wanted him to be a lawyer — and studied abroad. Now he has opened an office in New York. Too much leisure is a menace to any man. I don't like the young people with whom he has associated since he came from Europe, their idea of twentieth century liberation seems to be to acquire habits which shackle them with steel. Not but what they are decent enough," she hastened to assure loyally, " but they don't bring out the best in Philip. You will." With which declaration of faith she turned away.

Chapter IV

◆

PAMELA absentmindedly returned greetings of villagers as they passed on their way to the store.
Terrence, buoyant with the zest of living, his auburn
hair glinting red-gold in the late sunlight, dashed
by with a basket.

" Got to deliver these — eggs — going to see the
plane," he shouted as he passed.

Her thoughts returned to her meeting with Philip
Carr. Had she been too friendly? After but five
minutes' acquaintance she had practically told him
the story of her life. Would she ever learn to be
reserved with strangers? If she liked a person at
all she was too ready to credit him or her with all
the virtues. She must have inherited her Virginia
mother's friendliness along with Grandmother
Leigh's New England conscience.

What would young Carr's father think of their
friendship? He had been Grandmother Leigh's adviser for years. Her husband had willed half of
his large estate to his son, Harold, half in trust to
his wife, the income to be hers, at her death the
principal to revert to their son. He had given no

thought to protecting the interests of his grand-
children. Immersed in important legal battles as
Carr was, he had found time to attend to his elderly
client's business.

Her faith and dependence upon the advice of her
attorney, the fact that she had appointed him sole
executor of her estate, had maddened her son. He
had been insultingly antagonistic to Phineas Carr's
suggestion that he settle even a small amount of
money on his children. That he would provide for
them generously had been his mother's hope and
prayer. The lawyer had steadfastly continued his
duties until the estate was settled. He had turned
it over to the heir with a few vitriolic comments
which had sent Harold Leigh home white-lipped.
The remembrance of her father's version of the
interview had kept Pamela from consulting her
grandmother's old friend when she needed advice.
What would he think when he discovered that his
son was friendly with the daughter of the man whom
he must heartily dislike!

Mehitable Betts met her on the threshold, a shawl
flung over her thin drab hair, was drawn severely
down across her high temples.

"Land's sake, Pamela, what you thinking 'bout
so hard? Look's though you'd been to a funeral.
Thought you'd never come. I just got to see that
plane. Everything's ready for tomorrow, so I won't
come back. You don't need me. 'Most forgot to
tell you, while you were out a girl phoned and asked

if Mr. Mallory had reservations here tomorrow. I wa'n't born yesterday. So I told her I didn't know and I wouldn't tell her if I did. The way girls nowadays follow up the boys beats me. Milly Pike, who works down at M's Carr's — Carrs are the only folks in town who keep two hired girls — says that the minute Phil arrives for a week-end, the telephone begins to ring. Must keep her busy trying to find out who's calling. Never have seen anyone beat that girl for curiosity. She finds out things and then she tells anyone who'll listen to her. Fortunate Phil Carr doesn't come much or she'd never get her work done."

" He is at home now. I met him."

" Is he? The village will hear all about it from Milly Pike. He and his father don't jibe. The boy was set on being an architect — always drawing houses in his school-books — they say he planned all the decorating inside when the old house was done over — but the Judge — that's what folks call a lawyer round here — tried to badger him into the law. Didn't succeed. Driving a square peg into a round hole isn't being done so much as it used to be. Phineas Carr thinks his wife is spoiling the boy. I guess she is, too. She'd get the moon for him if he cried for it. M's Carr's a quiet appearing woman but when once she sets her lips there isn't no use trying to budge her. She's rich in her own right which condition helps a female to be independent more'n all the amendments you can cram into the

Constitution. I'd better start if I'm going to see that plane."

Pamela's eyes followed her as she hurried away. She did need her. She had planned to have her prepare supper and wash the dishes while she took things easy in preparation for a strenuous day to-morrow. No use trying to stop her. Hitty considered the service she rendered in the light of a favor. She had to handle her with gloves, nice, soft plushy gloves. Who had phoned to inquire about Scott Mallory? Hilda Crane? Her name had not been mentioned between them since Thanksgiving day. He had come to the Inn in the village almost every week-end since. He had held business conferences with her father, had carried her off for drives in his roadster. Week-ends were more than week-ends at the Silver Moon. Fridays and Saturdays were a steady procession of meals. Sunday evenings he took her out for supper and a long drive before he went back to the city.

He had old-fashioned ideas about being at his office early Monday morning. Grandmother Leigh would have liked that, he would have been decidedly "our kind of folks." She had had a theory that one morning hour was worth three of the afternoon for accomplishment. She would have liked everything about him, his tolerance of the opinions of others; his sympathetic understanding which was almost divination; the standards he steadily maintained for his own conduct; his unaffected courtesy;

his eyes, most especially his eyes; his smile which warmed one's heart; his good looks and his clothes. Grandmother Leigh had liked men. Once she had said: "You'll never know how drab life can be, Pam, till you live in a house with only women, with no men coming home at night."

As Pamela entered the living room of the old house the burning logs in the fireplace sputtered a welcome. The flickering flames accentuated the sheen of the pine paneling, brought out copper tones in rug, damask hangings, chair and couch coverings. They sent shadows flitting over the bookshelves like ghostly fingers searching for an old time favorite among the volumes, lighted little flares in the Spanish topaz on the neck of the Lady Claire in the portrait above the mantel. From the radio in her father's room came the high, shimmering chords of a violin.

The Babe flung himself to the hearth rug with a boisterous sigh. Pamela opened the white envelopes in her basket. Birthday greetings. She would be twenty-five tomorrow. Dear of her friends to remember her in the rush of their busy lives. College and newspaper days seemed a million or two light years away. She had been on her toes with the zest of living, had laughed away any approach to sentiment; time enough for that when she had made good in her profession. Not for a moment had she expected continuous smooth sailing, exemption from problems and disappointments. She had tried to acquire a fulfillment-may-be-waiting-round-the-next-curve philosophy which would steady her through swift water, she had meant to take the breakers of life on the surf-board of gay courage. Now that each day was a hectic struggle to evade the reaching claw of debt she found it increasingly difficult to practice her creed. The birthday cards were responsible for her depression. Each greeting had set a tiny fibre of memory vibrating. Philip Carr's suggestion that she was caught in a Cape Cod tidepool hadn't helped. Caught! She was tied hand and foot. She couldn't marry. She must take care of her father. What man would shoulder that burden? She wouldn't permit it if one wanted to. Was self-sacrifice always so tragically lacking in allure?

The greeting cards fell in a white drift as she sprang to her feet. "What's the big idea sitting here stiff with fear of the future?" she demanded of the looking-glass girl who frowned at her. "Didn't Scott Mallory lift a crushing load from your shoulders when he took over the liquidation of your father's affairs? Isn't the business of the Silver Moon growing? Can't you be patient?"

The mirrored eyes which gazed steadily back were the velvety richness of black pansies as Pamela answered her own question.

"I hate being patient. I want to get behind and push. Grandmother Leigh used to say:

"'Never pray for patience, Pamela, pray for courage to keep on keeping on, to march straight up to the firing line.' I must crash through the barriers which lack of money conjures in front of me whichever way I turn." She wrinkled her nose at her reflection. " You won't do much crashing if you waste time thinking about your troubles, woman."

She ripped the wrapping from a newspaper and glanced at the headlines. Scott Mallory's picture! What had he done? The printed caption marched in eye-filling type across the head of a column.

SCOTT MALLORY WINS $1,500,000
SUIT AGAINST SOUTH AMERICAN
DEALERS. MASTERLY PREPARA-
TION AND CONDUCT OF CASE HAS
SET PARTY LEADERS A–TIPTOE.
GUBERNATORIAL MATERIAL?

Scott had won! Pamela rejoiced for him. Gubernatorial material! Would he become a politician? He would be an ideal candidate for any office. Fearless, unshakable in his principles but — what would become of his law practice? Hilda Crane would regret now — the thought dragged a comet-like tail of light through her mind. A possible governor! First Lady of the State! Would she let him go? Never. Evidently she had telephoned as soon as she had seen the paper.

Her father's bell! Pamela flung her soft green hat to the couch and ran up the stairs to his room. He was at the window in a wing chair looking at the crimson sky above the sand dunes through which one brilliant star was twinkling. An open letter lay on his shawl-covered knees. A letter from his wife? What was she after now?

" Want me, Father? "

His eyes were dull and clouded as they met hers. He looked as a man might who had received a stunning blow. Pamela had an instant of inexplicable panic.

" I — I've had a letter from Cecile."

She dropped into a low chair beside him. Something in his tone took the stiffness from her knees. She tried to keep her sense of apprehension from showing in her voice.

" How is she getting on? Still in the same show? "

He cleared his throat. " She has had to leave. She is in New York. She isn't very well. She writes that she needs money for hospital care."

Pamela clasped her hands hard to steady them, stared unseeingly at the stain on the wall whose outline suggested a cat done in the modernist manner. Why should the fact that young Mrs. Leigh had to go to an hospital shake her? Surely it was not affection. She cordially detested the woman if she was her father's wife. She tried to answer sympathetically, laid her hand over his, cold and supine on his knee.

" Don't worry, Father. Perhaps she thinks that you have money which you are holding out on her?

She would better page Mr. Mallory and learn the
truth. She has a mother and sister to help her.
She has been acting for eight months. Hasn't she
saved anything? "

Harold Leigh stared out at the purpling sand
dunes. " She's due for an operation, a very delicate
operation on her foot. She has had a wonderful
chance in a revue offered her, she thinks it will make
her reputation. She hasn't signed up yet because
she can't walk."

The world crashed about Pamela's ears. A vision
of white-clothed surgeons, starched nurses, bare,
but expensive hospital rooms, burgeoned. Curious
that she didn't feel a prick of sympathy for the patient. Was she contracting hardening of the emotions? Through the turmoil of her senses she heard
her own voice mocking:

" Another redskin bit the dust."

" What do you mean by that? Are you quite de-
void of sympathy? " Anger accentuated the hook
of Harold Leigh's nose.

" I'm sorry. I went goofy with surprise, perhaps
a touch of despair, that's all." Pamela's mind
cleared to practicalities. " Where is the money
coming from to pay the bills? Have you thought
that out? "

" Mallory has my securities. He will have to
realize on those."

" Securities! Mostly insecurities. It will take
those and more to settle your debts — one third
yours and two thirds Cecile's."

" The money must go to her instead. I will talk
with him. She wants it within forty-eight hours."

Pamela regarded him through narrowed eyes.
Within forty-eight hours! A fast worker, Cecile.
Why hadn't she told him before? She must have
known that the operation was hovering in the offing. Did he still love the woman? Could he after
her desertion of him at the moment of his illness?
She had married him for his money; when that had
taken wing she had hastily departed. Apparently
he had not missed her, but perhaps humiliation,
heartache, were at the bottom of his irritation. She
must be more tender with him, but — where, where
was the cash coming from to meet this expense?

" If we can't get money from the securities, you
must raise some on this house, Pamela. It is free
and clear."

" Mortgage Grandmother Leigh's home to pay
Cecile's expenses? Have you forgotten that all
my jewels went to settle the hotel and doctor's bills
which you two contracted? Mortgage this house?
How do you think we would meet the interest? All
Terry and I can do now is to squeeze out taxes and
insurance." She rose in perturbation. Her father
looked up at her with shrewd eyes.

" You've always been jealous of Cecile. She
knew it. Used to say that you would separate us if
you could."

" Be fair, Father. I've not been so jealous of her
as she has been of me. You know that she was
speechless with rage when she discovered that Grand-

mother's jewels came to me, not to you, for your wife."

"You're right, Pamela. I — I would have done more for you and Terry if — what's the use looking back! The money must be procured for Cecile somehow."

"How much?"

He looked at the letter. "She says that she ought to have a thousand dollars, but she will try to get along with eight hundred if she can come here to convalesce. She will be unable to walk for two months."

"Eight hundred!" Pamela giggled. Caught her breath in a sob. Good grief, was she cracking-up? She set her teeth in her lips to steady them. "What price operations! It is time for your supper. Better not think of the money any more tonight or you won't sleep."

She patted his hand, smoothed his hair before she turned on the light on the table beside him. She ran down the stairs. Hands clenched, she stood in the middle of the fire-lighted living room. Eight hundred dollars! Mortgage the place! Never. Of course, Cecile would have to come to the Silver Moon until she could use her foot. That would save a few hundreds. The Ancient Mariner with the albatross hung round his neck had nothing on Pamela Leigh. Would any man want to marry her? "Marry me, marry my family." She was not enchanting enough to swing that.

"Hi! Pam! I'm sunk!" Terrence dashed into

the room. "What do you think's happened now?
The duck eggs in the incubator have exploded!
Laugh that off!" He patted the head of the dog,
who sensing excitement, sprang to his feet. "Keep
your breast-strap on, Babe. This isn't your funeral."

"Terry! Those expensive eggs! What have
you done wrong?"

"Starting in the poultry business, I guess."

Pamela sank to the couch, dropped her head in
her two hands. Her laughter was punctuated with
tearing gulps of emotion. Terrence shook her
shoulder.

"Cut that out! You'll be having hysterics.
Everything's going to be all right! What's so
funny about the duck eggs?"

"It isn't the eggs, Terry. It's — it's — life — so
tangled, so confused — and Cecile. Her foot is to
be operated on, and — and you and I must produce
the money for it!"

Terrence went beet-red. "Honest, Pam?"

His sister nodded. "Father just told me. Cecile
wants a thousand dollars. She will try to get along
with eight hundred if she can come here until she
can walk again."

Terrence dropped to the corner of the table desk.
"Eight hundred *dollars* for an operation on her
foot! They ought to take off a leg for that. Sure
it's only eight hundred? Might just as well have
asked for eight thousand. Someone's knocking!"

"Answer, Terry. If it is a patron for the Silver

Moon, say that it is closed for the evening. I just couldn't serve anyone tonight."

She listened as Terrence opened the door.

"I wasn't expected until tomorrow, but I have won my case! Couldn't stay in the city another minute. The Cape road tempted me — and — here I am. Where is your sister?"

Scott Mallory! Almost before he had finished speaking he was in the room. He looked from her to Terrence.

"What is the matter? Something gone wrong with the Silver Moon?"

Pamela shook her head. Terrence answered.

"Nothing — much. A prospective addition to the family, that's all."

Mallory's face went white. He caught the girl's hands in a grip which hurt. "Does that mean that you are to be married, Pam?"

She wrenched herself free. All the bitterness of the last months welled to the surface, the futility of plans for herself, the sense of a crushing load to carry, her father's self-absorption, and lately — the deep and insistent demand of her heart for love.

"I married! I hate men! I wouldn't marry an angel from heaven were he to lay his halo at my feet." With which pronunciamento she departed for the kitchen.

Chapter V

PAMELA'S anger cooled as she commenced preparations for supper in the green and white kitchen. Why had she allowed her temper to blow-up? Her cheeks burned. Xanthippe! Scott Mallory's assumption that she was engaged had been unbearable when she knew that a husband was the last thing on earth she was likely to acquire — or want. She had not said a congratulatory word about his legal victory. After that outburst he would put her in the class with Hilda Crane. So much the better. He would stop coming.

She turned the faucet with a force which sprayed hot water over the front of her green jersey frock. What a mess! Served her right for letting her temper get the better of her. She fastened an enveloping apron about her neck. If she didn't watch her step she would get as drab and crabbed as Hitty Betts. That thought didn't help either. Scott Mallory pushed open the swing door.

"Terry has told me about it, Pam. He will look after your father while you come out for supper with me."

Pamela's spirits soared like a captive balloon let loose. She had not realized before how deadly tired she was of preparing meals. Nevertheless, she hugged her chains.

"Can't. Too much to do."

"That's bunk and you know it. Everything is ready for tomorrow, isn't it? Be honest."

"Yes — but — "

His fingers against the back of her neck as he unbuttoned the apron sent a quiver feathering along her veins. He had charm, he had tact, he had distinction, but she sensed steel under his easy friendliness. He would be a difficult person to combat.

"No 'but' in this party. Get your coat and hat. You said that you wouldn't have a minute to celebrate on your birthday, we'll break loose tonight." As she hesitated, he added, "You and I ought to talk over this demand of young Mrs. Leigh's before I discuss it with your father. We are likely to be interrupted here."

She shed the apron. "You are right. I begin to suspect that you are always right. I'll go. Don't think that I am not thrilled by your legal victory, I am. Read of it in the paper just before you came. Thought of telephoning you, then Father's news crashed in. Congratulations — Governor Mallory!"

Color stole under his bronzed skin. "Now I know what paper you read. The man who wrote that stuff will get fired, if I'm not mistaken. No politics in mine, thank you."

"I had supposed that the practice of law was the world's best stepping-stone to politics."

"It is, but my ambition doesn't point that way. I'll put all there is in me into my profession and then, 'Beyond the Alps lies Italy!' Ever hear of the Supreme Court of the United States?"

"You mean that you want to be——"

He reddened darkly. "I don't mean anything. Forget it! The decision of that case in favor of my client has gone straight to my head. Just because I know how Christian felt in Pilgrim's Progress when the burden loosed from his shoulders, I'm talking like a wild man. I've got to celebrate —with you. Come on!" He caught her by the shoulders.

"Just a minute! You wouldn't have me go hatless, would you? I——" She answered the ring of the telephone.

"The Silver Moon. . . . Here. . . . Yes, I know you did, Mr. Carr, but you mustn't lose that client. . . . Next week Sunday? Supper with your mother? I should love it. . . . The farmer's cottage? . . . Move it to the shore! *I* suggested the idea! I never have thought of it. . . . An income from it! Four thousand dollars will remodel it? Sounds as visionary as a rocket to the moon. . . . Sunday week at six? . . . Thanks lots. Good-bye."

Pamela hung up the receiver. Her eyes felt like over-developed stars.

"That was Philip Carr."

"So I gathered. Who is he and where did you meet him?"

"He and I refereed a dog-fight this afternoon. He had said he would call tonight. He phoned that he had to get back to New York. In the excitement of Father's news and your victory I had forgotten him. What do you think he suggested?"

"Something stupendous. You look as if you were ready to hit the ceiling. What was it?"

"He proposed that we move the farmer's cottage to the shore. I had told him that it was being consumed by repairs. That gave him the idea, he says, to make a few additions and rent it. It would be a marvelous location. He will draw the plans. Hitty says that he's a born architect." The light of enthusiasm waned in her voice and eyes. "It sounds wonderful, but as bristling with impossibilities as a trip to Mars. Up bobs the same old Jack-in-the-Box, Money! Money! Money! He is sure that it can be done for four thousand dollars. I wonder what Philip's father will say when he discovers that his son is advising a Leigh."

"What's wrong with advising the Leighs? I'm doing it."

Pamela paid an instant's tribute to his smile. "Nothing generally. Only his father, Phineas Carr, was Grandmother Leigh's —"

"Phineas Carr! Carnation Carr! Always wears a white pink. His florist had orders to forward them to him wherever he was trying a case.

If the flower was late in arriving he would fidget and wait until it came. He's a colossus in his profession. He the Leigh attorney! Did I butt in on *him* when I offered to straighten out your father's affairs?"

"No! No! Don't look so aghast. Father had quarreled with him. He has not seen him since the estate was settled."

"I feel better. Do you like this Carr boy?"

The curt question sent the color to Pamela's hair. Indignant with herself, inexplicably angry with Scott Mallory, she answered flippantly.

"Mad about him. I know now what Hitty Betts meant when she said he was a born lady-killer. What a profile lost to the cinema! What an answer to a director's prayer! Speaking of irresistible males, reminds me, a girl called on the phone this afternoon, inquired if you were expected here over the week-end. Someone to congratulate you on your success, doubtless."

"Doubtless. What did you tell her?"

"Don't scowl. I didn't talk with her. Hitty, who keeps a keen, if glum, watch over the love-life of our patrons, told her that she didn't know and wouldn't tell her if she did, and sourly reminded me, 'I wasn't born yesterday!'"

"I owe Miss Betts a season's talkie money for that. I will let that 'love-life' thrust, pass — for the present. Let's go. We'll celebrate first. Not a word about business until we start for home. Then we will talk things over. Your outlook will be different after a change of scene and something to eat."

He had been right, Pamela admitted, as tucked into the roadster beside him she looked up at the stars which spread like an intricate pattern of gold lace over the dusky blueness of the heavens. The air was cool and clear, soft as transparent velvet against her face. They had driven miles for a delicious supper. Now they were homeward bound. She nestled back with a contented sigh. If only she could go on and on. Dreading to go home was getting to be a habit. It wasn't the work which mattered, it was the conflict.

She shook herself mentally. If this was the effect of breaking loose from care she would better keep everlastingly on the treadmill. Better get back to realities at once by tackling the Cecile proposition. If she had learned nothing else in these last perplexing months she had learned that the sooner one faced a problem the sooner one got it behind one. She sat straight. Her determination was reflected in her tone.

"Mr. Mallory."

"My friends call me Scott."

"In spite of the fact that it dates my bringing-up, I wouldn't dare be that familiar with so august a personage as my legal adviser." She could see his eyes narrow, the muscles of his jaw tighten.

"Glad you are properly impressed with my authority. You will get a lot of it from now on. Just what did your father tell you about his wife, this afternoon?"

Pamela repeated the conversation. He listened without comment. That was one of Scott Mallory's comfortable traits, he never interrupted. As she talked, the roadster slid smoothly forward over the shining black asphalt bordered on one side by shrubs and scrub-oaks, on the other by sea-drenched sand over which a white scalloped tide advanced and retreated for all the world like a dainty lady trailing her laces back and forward in the measures of a dance. The car swerved sharply to avoid a pair of emeralds in the road.

"Lights must have mesmerized that cat." Mallory slowed the pace to a crawl. "When did Mrs. Leigh leave your father?"

"The first of June. The date is seared into my memory, as well as the picture of the Silver Moon roses which were rioting all over the old house the day we brought Father down."

"And this is the middle of February. How long has he known that she had serious trouble with her foot?"

"If he knew before he received that letter, the stage has lost a star; he seemed stunned by surprise. When she left us stranded in New York she went directly to Hollywood. We haven't seen her since. She was in musical comedy when Father met her. I suppose she thought him a millionaire, though to be just, he can be charming when he likes, and he really didn't look more than forty. Mother left him a fair fortune and he inherited from his father. Grandmother Leigh had the income from a trust fund which passed to him unconditionally at her death. She told me before she died that she had tried to save a little for me, with which to carry on this place, but, she loved beautiful things and traveling—she and I were abroad together for a year—so there were only a few hundred dollars.

"Mother, who was an F.F. of Virginia, died when Terry was a little boy. We made our home with Grandmother Leigh, summers. She gave us an emotional, an intellectual outlook, a sense of confidence and stability, which we never would have acquired at the schools we attended. As a little girl, I adored my father. One tender word or look from him now and I fling my heart at his feet. He must have had a sizable income. He never took his children into his confidence as to the amount. Mother left Terrence and me each fifty thousand dollars, the income to be used for our education, the principal to be paid when we were twenty-five. It was in Father's hands, was swept away in the financial cloudburst. Hope you enjoy biography."

"I do. Yours. And you will be twenty-five to-morrow. Tough luck. If your father had no business what was his interest? He must have had something."

"He traveled a lot. He had only one hobby—that I know of—collecting stamps."

"Stamps!"

"Why so explosive?"

"Nothing. I was interested because like every other boy in the world I collected stamps for a while; it's the healthy, normal interest of the human male to collect something. My book is kicking round somewhere now. Did his wife know of his hobby?"

"I can't believe that she didn't know everything about him before she married him although when he told Terry and me that he was to be married — we had one day's notice of the coming event — he asked us not to mention his stamp complex to Cecile. He said:

"'She thinks collecting — anything but jewels — a symptom of senility. I shall sell the few specimens I have at once, anyway.'

"I supposed that he had done so and was surprised when he produced a book of them after we came here. Terry and I hailed it with delight. It has kept him more or less interested. I suspect that he amuses himself trading duplicates. He sends and receives letters from a stamp concern."

"He does! Interesting but it doesn't get us anywhere. To return to a subject of more importance — he suggested that you mortgage your property to pay his wife's bills?"

"Yes. Scott, do you think I ought to do it?" Not until his eyes met hers did she realize that she had scrapped formality.

"No. Make no move without talking it over with me first, promise."

"I promise, though it makes me feel that I'm a spineless leaner."

"If women would lean a little more before they walk blindly into a fool complication, they wouldn't have to be derricked out."

"Haven't an overwhelming respect for the female of the species, have you?"

"Not for the average when it comes to her judgment on legal matters. Men aren't so much better. Remember, my job is to untangle complications which need not have been tied into a hard knot if advice had been asked before, instead of after the blunder. It is like pulling teeth to get the whole truth out of people. That client is a menace who, before trial, wilfully or in ignorance withholds facts from his lawyer which are brought out in cross-examination. It is like advancing through sharp-shooters' sector. You never know where the next crack will come from. Tell me something of Mrs. Leigh. Try to be impartial. I know that you don't like her, but, has she any qualities which you do admire?"

"One. Her ability to think quickly. She is a sophisticate. I would be willing to wager the Lowe-stoft bowl that two minutes after Father had come to her rescue in the road, she had determined to marry him. Within twenty-four hours after she learned of his financial crash, realized his physical collapse, she was off on her own with every bit of cash available. Now she demands money within forty-eight hours. She has a hair-trigger mind and she dislikes and distrusts me. Our spirits buckled on their armor the first time our eyes met."

"She is in New York?"

"Yes. Her mother and sister live there."

"Is she pretty?"

"Beautiful. Blonde, with provocative eyes — when animated. When in repose they are sullen, broody, always made me think of a darkening sky before a tempest. Her frocks are ultra chic, but she herself isn't, if you get what I mean. Rather mussy. She never looks quite smart."

"Does she use her married name on the stage?"

"Neither there nor anywhere else. Father sends his letters to Miss Cecile Mortimer — that was her maiden name. When I inadvertently picked up an envelope he had so addressed, he explained elaborately that she had more chances professionally if she were known as Miss. I can't make him out. Part of the time I think him numb from the shock of the loss of his fortune and his wife. At other times when I enter his room I surprise a swift look of cunning in his eyes. I have the curious feeling that he is concealing something. Yet, what would he have to conceal? He hasn't been in business for years, can't be complications of that sort. I wonder what he will say to Philip Carr's real estate proposition. Coming from that source he will probably turn his thumbs down hard."

"That summer-cottage idea is good. I think you'd better do it."

"Where would I get the money, Scott?"

"I know someone from whom you could borrow a building loan."

"Not you!"

"Don't be so shocked. Not I. It would mean putting up a part of your property as security."

"Suppose I have to borrow on that for Cecile."

"You will not borrow on it for Cecile. Get that straight, Pamela."

"I wish I might feel as sure as you sound. Once I would have forged ahead, had the farmer's cottage moved before you could say 'Hands up!' Now, I stop to consider the risk. That is what this last year has done to me. The nightmare of those pursuing creditors lingers in the offing like a thick fog threatening to roll up and envelop me again the moment I depart from my pay-as-I-go policy."

"This is a different proposition. The element of risk is inseparable from any business enterprise, but there is such a thing as open-eyed risks. If one never embarked on a project for fear it might turn out a failure, one never would get far. Have you a plan of your land?"

"Yes, a blueprint. In the safe in my room. Grandmother had the plan made. She was born with business sense, she wasn't one of the average whose intelligence you scorn."

"Something tells me that you resent my conclusions. Let me have the blueprint tonight. I will go over the land tomorrow, then we'll get down to cases. I'm sold on the idea of making over that cottage. If it is to be done it should be started at once. No bookings for Sunday?"

"No. I am hanging on by the teeth but I have managed so far to resist the lure of profitable patrons on that day. Grandmother was a pillar of the church. I can't give money so I play the organ. Trying to live up to her standards is the least I can do to show my appreciation of what she did for me. Besides, if I didn't go to church, Terry wouldn't."

"Isn't there something in the Bible about the Faithful Steward? To return to real estate. Trust me enough not to commit yourself to Carr about moving the cottage until you hear from me?"

"Would that be fair when it was his suggestion and we think we may put it through?"

"We will make that up to him later. There are reasons why the fact that you are considering borrowing should not leak out until the title has been looked up and the mortgage is nailed."

"Oh, you lawyers! Always laying a smoke-screen of caution. You think that Father would oppose it. He would. Anything which Terry or I might suggest."

He concentrated upon passing a line of trucks which were chugging along like prehistoric monsters. When once more the road stretched clear and shining and black ahead he said gravely:

"Perhaps we should be more charitable to your father. Irritability is often the last resort of the defeated. His wife's desertion must have cut deep."

"I realize that, Scott—though there are moments when I wonder if it was not a relief. Every morning I wake with the determination to be patient, tender with him, tenderness is so different from kindness, but by noon my endurance is worn to a frazzle. What right has one person to take the joy out of life for everyone else in the house? He is not the only member of the family who has been disappointed."

"Do you hate your life here so much?"

"I don't hate it at all, but, Philip Carr was right when he said I was caught in a tidepool."

"Darn Philip Carr!"

The soft, succinct exclamation was death to conversation. Withdrawn and silent, Mallory brought his roadster to a stop at the door of the old Leigh homestead, followed Pamela into the living room. From the radio above came the sound of strings and wood instruments in the music of Beethoven's Pastoral Symphony. It served as a faintly harmonious background for the charm and light and color of the old room.

Terrence looked up from a book on the table desk. His red hair, shot through and through with gold in the lamplight, had been furrowed by his fingers till it stood on end. His fine eyes so like Pamela's were black from concentration, his handsome face was flushed. He stretched long arms, clasped his hands behind his head, balanced his chair on its hindlegs at a breath-snatching angle.

"Miss Crane phoned you, Mr. Scott."

"Here?"

"Yep. Said your office told her you could be reached at the village Inn. Nothing doing there so she tried the Silver Moon. She wants you to call her house tonight. Important. She said to tell you that Belle was in difficulties again. Suppose you know who Belle is? Sounds like a horse or cow to me."

"Belle is her sister. A rich woman who spends her income before she gets it and is everlastingly being sued by creditors."

"God have mercy on her soul," sympathized Pamela fervently.

Mallory laughed. "Don't pity her. She brings it all on herself."

Terrence scooped up his school books, yawned prodigiously. "And so to bed. Everything's locked up, Pam, but the front door and Father. He pulled his usual line about being neglected, but, he managed to eat a square meal."

"Thanks lots for looking after him, Terry. I am all rested and refreshed for the big day tomorrow."

"I'll say you are; I could light a cigarette at your eyes, they shine so. Good-night, Mr. Scott. Good-night, Pam." His whistle, musical, muted, drifted back from the stairs.

Mallory laid his hands on Pamela's shoulders. "Take off your coat." She slipped out of the soft camel's hair garment. As she curled up in a corner of the couch she asked:

"Isn't it time now to advise me what to do about the eight hundred dollars for Cecile?"

He backed up to the fire. "I will talk with your father about that tomorrow morning."

"He may be furious that I have told you."

"Why? He has retained me as his attorney. As I intimated before, the client who withholds information from his legal adviser is just naturally looking for trouble. Will you get the plan of the land?" She started for the door. "Just a minute. Think you can find the address of the stamp firm with which your father corresponds?"

She paused on the threshold. "I believe you have contracted a touch of stamp fever, from hearing about his small collection. I've heard that it is as contagious as any of the other children's diseases, the longer and harder the search for a treasure the more acute the attack. Look out, little boy, or you will be having measles next."

She smiled to herself. Somehow she couldn't imagine Scott Mallory being interested in stamps; he would be more likely to collect books, or fine prints. She hummed as she snapped on the electricity in the room which had been her grandmother's and now was hers. For some inexplicable reason she felt absurdly light-hearted and young. Getting out of the rut of daily living had done the trick. She must beware of mental staleness. From now on she would try to slip away from the Silver Moon more often. Better to have fewer patrons and keep her viewpoint normal.

Even her room took on fresh charm. The four-poster with its snowy canopy and valance, the hooked rugs with their impossible roses and less possible fruits, the white Staffordshire dogs on the mantel with their red ears and tails, had occupied the same places as far back as she could remember.

The little safe against the wall had been a more recent acquisition. On her knees before it Pamela twisted the knob till the door swung open. As she pulled out the plan for the land an envelope fell to the floor. She didn't remember putting it in. She looked at the name in the upper left-hand corner.

"Brown of Boston."

That was all. It was addressed to her father. He had asked the combination of the safe explaining that he had an important paper he wanted to keep there.

Brown of Boston. What was that curious sound? Someone choking? She looked up. Her father was braced against the door-case. His face was ashen. In his lounge robe he looked gaunt and abnormally tall. His lips trembled, his voice shook as he demanded:

"What are you doing with my papers?"

Chapter VI

◆

PAMELA regarded him with honest incredulity. "Your papers! I came for the plan of the land and this envelope fell out." She remembered Scott Mallory's warning to say nothing about the cottage proposition. "If I am to borrow money on the place I must have something to show the extent of the property."

She sensed his relief. "That's all right. Saw you with the envelope in your hand, thought you might be — might be watching my correspondence. I will take that letter."

Still on her knees Pamela handed it to him. "If it is important enough to put in the safe once, shouldn't it be kept there? However, that is your business." She closed the door and rose.

"Where are you taking that plan?"

"Downstairs to Mr. Mallory."

"How long has he been here? Why didn't he talk with me?"

"He is to be at the Inn until Sunday night. He said he would see you tomorrow."

"Did you tell him about Cecile?"

"Of course. I must have someone to advise me."

"What did he say?"

"About raising money? He asked to see the plan."

"Hum! Well, he should have conferred with me." Harold Leigh shuffled toward his room, the heels of his worn slippers flapping. His daughter watched him out of sight. He had been brought to the Cape in an ambulance in June. For months he had not left his room. Now he was walking about. He must be much stronger. However, nothing made him quite so furious as to be told that he looked better.

Mallory stamped out his cigarette as Pamela entered the living room, pulled a wing chair nearer the fire, now a bed of red coals stabbed through and through with flashes of flame. The Babe flopped a languid tail in greeting before he relapsed into noisy slumber.

"Sit here." As the girl sank into the comfortable depths he pushed a stool under her feet. "That better? Did I break it?" he demanded in consternation as it shed a foot.

"No. It isn't a break. It's a habit." She leaned back and looked at him with solemn eyes. "I adore my old furniture, Scott, but it is always going maimed. When I achieve my best-seller I will live in an apartment — I am sold on the penthouse idea — furnished in the contemporary manner — *Salon des Artistes Décorateurs* — lots of color, simple lines, sharp contrasts of dark and light. Perhaps a black mirror-top table in the dining room to repeat the gleam of silver and the sparkle of glass. A silver wall, egg-shell lacquer, somewhere.—That's my dream."

"And mine is to own a summer home on Cape Cod. A house with a black-banded white chimney, a picket fence and an old-fashioned garden." His voice, which had sent little curleyques spiraling along Pamela's arteries, was back to normal as he asked: "Where were we when the casualty occurred? I remember. Did you get that plan?"

He settled himself in the Hong Kong wicker chair which had been brought from the Orient in one of great-grandfather Leigh's ships. Pamela held out the roll of blueprint. He thrust it into his pocket.

"I will examine that later. I heard you talking with your father. Hope that you didn't bother him with my request for the name of the stamp concern."

"I forgot it. When I opened the safe, an envelope addressed to him with 'Brown of Boston' in one corner — just that, nothing more — fell out. While I held it, speculating about a person who could be of sufficient importance to print his name like that, he appeared. I felt that he suspected me of undue interest in his correspondence, though he didn't accuse me of it. He cooled down when I told him that I was there for the plan."

"Did you tell him why I wanted it?"

"Hadn't you warned me not breathe a word of the remodeled cottage proposition? Would I dare disobey my legal adviser?"

"Good child. 'Brown of Boston.' Seems to me

I've heard that combination before. I won't keep you up any longer. I will see your father in the morning. I'll be here at nine o'clock tomorrow evening to take you for a drive."

"We are to have a tremendous day. I shall probably be so tired that I'll go to sleep with my head against your shoulder."

He bent over her. "All right with me. Ever think how temptingly sweet you are, Pam?" The roughness of his voice startled her. He straightened abruptly. "Don't get up. Good-night."

Pamela sat curled in the big chair long after he had gone, eyes on the dying fire, his disturbing voice echoing through her consciousness, the feel of his hands still warm upon her shoulders. She heard Terrence close his door and bang open his window. The house stilled. A board squeaked in the stairs as if a light foot had pressed it. The coppery tints in the room gleamed in the soft light. The Hong Kong chair creaked as if relaxing strained muscles after holding a man's weight. A dried vine tapped eerily at the window. Pamela jumped to her feet. What price air-castles! The Babe whined and twitched in his sleep. She tenderly pulled his ears.

"Wake up, old boy. Dreaming of that dog you almost knocked out today?" Today! Was it only this afternoon that she and Philip Carr had separated the fighting dogs? In her concern over Cecile's demand she had completely forgotten the poor little rich boy until he telephoned. She would be willing to wager that he wasn't bad at all, village gossip spread like the downy contents of a pillow flung on the air. No one ever took time to chase the feathers and put them back. Had she been wise to accept the invitation for supper before she knew whether the head of the house would welcome or resent her presence? Perhaps Phineas Carr would forget that she was her father's child and remember only that she was his old client's dearly loved granddaughter. She would adore seeing the inside of his home. She had heard that it was a treasure-house of priceless antiques.

There would be nothing more charming than the portrait of the Lady Claire. She looked up at the picture above the mantel flanked by carved Sheraton candlesticks with tall tapers. Chestnut hair piled high on a haughty head, eyes the velvety brown of pansies, magolia tinted shoulders and throat, their delicacy accentuated by a necklace of Spanish topaz set in medallions of intricately carved gold. Long matching earrings hung from the shell-like ears, bracelets girdled the arm, a massive ring was on the patrician hand which held a soft yellow rose at the point of the low-cut brown bodice.

Pamela sighed enviously. She could picture herself in that set of topaz. She would be twenty-five tomorrow! The birthday upon which she would have received the legacy from her mother, had there been any legacy left to receive. Twenty-five! A quarter of a century!

She set the brass screen before the smoldering

fire, snapped out the lights. From the threshold she looked back at the dear, familiar room. Through the interstices in the plant window she could see the lawn. Snowing! Flakes as big as half dollars were drifting down casually. And she had thought that spring had come. Just as she had thought her anxiety about the debts was over when Scott Mallory had offered to stand between. Now, along came this demand for money from Cecile.

Suppose Cecile were bluffing? Pamela was brushing her hair before the triple mirror on her chintz-hung dressing table when the thought came to her. Suppose the second Mrs. Leigh were trying to get money for a different project? It had been done. The face reflected went quite white. Had Scott thought of that? She reached for the telephone. An extension set in her room was the one luxury she allowed herself, it saved countless minutes and miles of steps. She would pass her suspicion, more of a hope, on to him at once. Her hand dropped to her lap. No. He might at this very moment be talking to Miss Crane. He was attorney for her sister. How old was the irresponsible Belle? Did he still care for the soulless Hilda? He never mentioned her. He had gone darkly red at the little gibe about his love-life; there had been a biding-my-time glint in his eyes, but he had let it pass.

"Ever think how temptingly sweet you are, Pam?" She must forget the shaken question. He had probably said the same thing to other girls. Hadn't he brought Hilda Crane to the Silver Moon for a Thanksgiving dinner for two? A man didn't do that sort of thing unless he was quite mad about a girl. What possible difference could it make to her whom Scott Mallory loved or did not love? She must not let herself care for him. It would be tragically easy. Hadn't she a father to support? Suppose Cecile were telling the truth and had to be cared for at the Silver Moon to save money?

She brought the brush down on the waves of her already satiny hair with a force which started tears of pain. She admonished the girl in the mirror.

"That's crossing a bridge before you come to it, my dear."

A breeze blew in cold and clear as she raised the window softly that she might not disturb her father. What a night. A light snow covered fields, powdered trees. Moonlight tranformed the sand dunes into silver domes. Fair tomorrow. How still the world was. Not a creature stirring — not a creature — but a long purple shadow at the entrance of the drive by the mail box. Curious, she never had noticed that before. It was walking! Coming up the path stealthily. A burglar after the old silver?

Unmindful of the frosty wind fluttering the delicate pink crêpe of her pajamas, she knelt by the window. How slowly the person came. Kept stopping as if for breath. Was he shrouded in a shawl? Now he was at the steps. Would she better call Terry? Was that the front door opening? Excite ment tightened her throat. She stole to the threshold of her room. Listened. The old house quivered with cautious sounds, its aged joints creaked. Someone coming up the stairs! Coming heavily, with labored breathing. The hall was kept dimly lighted in case the invalid rang in the night. Whoever it was was making a clumsy attempt at caution. The banister groaned as if a heavy weight had lunged against it. Each stair squeaked a protest. Almost at the top! Pamela opened her door an inch wider. Peered out. Closed it soundlessly. Her father!

She leaned against the wall, breathless from surprise. He had been to the mail-box. Why the secrecy? The R.F.D. man picked up the mail as he went by at six o'clock in the morning. Had he sent a letter? To Cecile? Of course. To assure her that the money for hospital expenses would be forthcoming? Perhaps this was not his first surreptitious midnight trip. Perhaps Tinker, the postman, left letters for him. As boys, the two had fished the surrounding ponds together. She remembered Hitty Betts' comment, "Folks is sayin' he'd be a sight better if you didn't coddle him."

Ooch! It was cold. Shivering, she snapped off the light. "I'll investigate in the morning before Tinker comes," she told herself as she snuggled down under the bedclothes. "I wouldn't care about Father's mail ordinarily but when mortgaging this house is at stake it is time someone knew what was going on."

Tinker had come and gone when she awoke. She had an instant of self-castigation for oversleeping before the day's activities swept her into their vortex. When Scott Mallory came at nine in the evening she demurred against going out in the roadster.

"I am all in. I should be a dumb companion. Now that the rush is over, my mind feels as cramped as a stowaway in an airplane."

"Come for an hour, Pam. It will rest you to get away from the house and your problems."

At the word "problems" the memory of her father's midnight pilgrimage shot to the surface. "I had forgotten. I'll go. I have something curious to tell you."

For the first half hour she drifted in a Nirvana of relaxation. Mallory drove slowly. A dusky amethyst veil, vague as her own thoughts, blurred the horizon. Little white clouds chased one another across the deep Ionian-blue sky like a flock of woolly sheep. From a field came the distant clank of a cow bell, the drowsy purl of running water on its leisurely way to the sea. Lights on the highway blinked like nocturnal owls caught in a glare of searchlight. A line of red, Cyclopean eyes was dimming into the salty gloom of the night. Pair after pair of green yellow orbs approached, "whooshed" by and were gone. Rested, refreshed, she straightened in the seat.

"Anything the matter with my shoulder?"

She looked up, startled out of her preoccupation. Mallory was smiling. She remembered.

" Nothing doing in shoulders tonight. You were right about coming out. It has rested me. I am all made over. I have much to tell you."

" Shoot."

To the accompaniment of the soft purr of the engine she told him of her father's trip to the mailbox. " I didn't know that he had been downstairs for months. It gives me a plot for a story, MIDNIGHT MAIL MYSTERY."

" You miss your writing, don't you? "

" Frightfully — when I have time."

" Cheer'o! All of these problems and disappointments are providing material for later work. You can put more emotional color into the portrayal of an episode, deepen it and broaden it, if you have experienced its meaning even to a slight degree. Cold comfort but it is true. To return to your father. You can think of no one to whom he would write surreptitiously except his wife? "

" No one. But why surreptitiously to her? I never have commented on his letters."

" Has she ever before proposed coming back to him here? "

" Only once that I know of. He read me part of a letter in which she wrote that she was not well, that the doctor said that she should be where she could relax and be waited on for a month or two."

" What answer did you make? "

" What answer could I make but one? She had left us high and dry when Terry and I didn't know

which way to turn. We had just started the Silver
Moon enterprise. It took every moment and every
cent we could scrape together to keep things going.
Waited on! Had I thought that Father really
wanted her here I would have managed to take her
in somehow, but, he didn't. He said she would tire
him. I told him to tell her that she must find some
other place in which to rest. She has a mother and
sister."

" Did he?"

"I suppose so, he never mentioned the subject
again. Oh, I didn't leave it all to him. I wrote and
told her what I thought of her desertion, told her I
wouldn't have her in my house, that I was sure he
would be happier, get well faster without her."

" Good Heavens! "

Pamela stared up at the man at the wheel. His
profile looked cameo clear in the dusk.

" What did you say? "

" Did I say anything? Did you keep a copy of
that letter? "

" A copy? I didn't even keep it in the house a
minute after it was written for fear I wouldn't send
it. I am apt to compose a red-hot masterpiece, think
it over until my fury has cooled, then tear it up.
I meant that to go while it sizzled." A troubled note
crept into her voice. " Perhaps had she come this
foot trouble wouldn't have developed. But — but
— I don't believe there is anything the matter with
her! I believe it is a touch for money. I almost

phoned you last night when that blinding suspicion flashed into my mind."

" Why didn't you? "

"I thought probably you were telephoning Miss Crane."

She met his direct gray eyes, eyes that saw much, much beneath the surface of things she was sure. Had the miracle of mind-reading come to pass? Did he know what she was thinking, know that she was wishing that a polite, gentlemanly typhoon would catch up Hilda Crane and swirl her into matrimony?

" We'd better talk over the Cecile and cottage business now," he announced with a curtness which confirmed Pamela in her suspicion that he was a mind-reader. " I shall not be here next week-end."

"Not coming!" She was hotly aware that the words wailed.

" Why should I? You will be at the Carrs', won't you? "

" But only for supper, Sunday. Did you talk with Father about the money for Cecile? "

" Yes. I will hold off the creditors and give her some of the cash from the securities I've sold — if she is telling the truth."

" Then you doubt her too? "

His smile almost drew her head to his shoulder. " In the language of Hitty Betts, ' I wasn't born yesterday.' "

Chapter VII

———◆———

PAMELA squeezed a few drops from the almost juiceless half of a lemon on the fluted layers of the plump oyster in the half-shell. She shut her eyes in gastronomic ecstasy as the cool, salty morsel, not without some difficulty slid down her throat.

" That was luscious, Cap'n Crockett."

The small eyes in the short man's face which was weather seasoned to the color and consistency of the dark boards of the walls of the shack behind him, twinkled in their setting of fine lines. " Kinder reckon that one was big enough for you. You're always sayin' the bigger the better, Miss Pam-ee-lia."

" If it had been one millionth of an inch larger or fatter or juicier it wouldn't have slipped down."

" Have another? "

Pamela looked from the rough shell into which he was about to thrust a short dull blade, to the pile with purplish eyes dotting their mother-of-pearl linings, on the board before her. She shook her head, and wiped her hands on the handkerchief she pulled from the pocket of the green jacket of her sports suit.

"I'd love it but I have had ten now. Why is it oysters never taste so good as they do here?"

Cap'n Iry Crockett dried his brawny, hairy-backed hands on his blue denim apron. "'Cause they're right out of the water. How many you takin' in bulk today?"

"A bushel."

"Guess trade's hummin'."

He lifted a rake, its iron tines curved in a semi-circle, from a hook on the wall, caught up a burlap bag. Pamela followed him into a dusky compartment, sat on a box while he scooped oysters from dark depths. The place smelled of brine and sea-weed.

"Yes. Business is growing. Not long now before I stop serving oysters. Why don't people eat them in the months without an r, Cap'n Iry?"

He shook a rake full of rough shells into the burlap bag which Pamela held open. "They spawn in May and June round these parts — they're right prolific — an' they're not so good eatin'. There, guess that's a bushel. Sure 'twill be enough? Beats all how you know how much of things to lay in."

"I don't, always, but most of our patrons order ahead, then after school Terry can hop into the old fliv and get shell fish in a few minutes. It isn't as if I served meats and steaks."

Back in the outer room he tied up the bag. Pamela paid him. "I'll lug this to the car for you."

She followed him from the floating shack, across

the swinging bridge that rose and fell with a tide which reflected the clear blue of the sky, to the sandy road. He lifted the dripping bag into the shabby flivver.

" Those ought to last you for a while. They tell me the Inn's fillin' up early this spring."

" I am glad of that, it will mean a hungry horde for the Silver Moon. People like a change of eats even if the table is good." The sunlight struck a metal disc partially concealed by the strap of his overalls. "What's the decoration, Cap'n Iry? Been made the High Ruler of something or other? If you have, make the Town Fathers give you a decent road here."

He touched the badge with a gnarled brown. finger. "That? That means I'm deputy sheriff."

A flash-back of the man in a yellow truck waiting to seize her antique furniture set Pamela's heart thumping uncomfortably before she remembered that the creditor-haunted days were over, thanks to Scott Mallory. They were unless he had had to take money due on bills to send to Cecile. She was aware of Cap'n Crockett's thoughtful regard. He must wonder why she was sitting staring at the wheel. She started the car, nodded to him.

" Thanks, Cap'n Iry. See you soon. Bye-bye! "

The Inn truck passed laden with trunks, a score of them, sets of smart luggage, smooth tweed hat-boxes and suitcases. The season was beginning early. That meant business for the Silver Moon.

She must engage someone to wait on table. It was getting to be more than Terry could do alone. Perhaps one or two of the Academy boys would be glad to earn extra money. She liked to deal with boys better than with girls. She drew a long breath of the salty air. Glorious day.

Highty, the postmaster, lumbered down the steps as she neared the brick office. He waved a letter. She drew up to the curb.

" Special delivery for you, Miss Pamela. Guess whoever sent it didn't stop to think that you live more'n a mile from the post-office. I was hoping some of your folks or neighbors would be going by to take it up to the house."

His second chin quivered; his small eyes, sunk in pouches, twitched nervously. His spotted waistcoat, which never had been even a collateral of his baggy trousers, displayed an imposing array of fountain pens. He looked at the letter before he lingeringly relinquished it.

" Never've seen that writing before in your mail."

Pamela tucked the envelope into her pocket. Neither had she. She started the car. Above the protesting groan of the engine she suggested:

" Better not try to follow my mail, Mr. Highty. I'm always getting letters in regard to reservations."

His chin quivered over a flagged question, his mouth hung open, he blinked furiously as after a preparatory lurch or two the car started. Pamela had a curious feeling that the letter in her pocket was not from a prospective client. It broadcast magnetic currents. In sudden determination she turned down the rough lane which led to the shore, her shore. She had heard nothing more from Scott Mallory about raising the money with which to move and make over the farmer's cottage; neither had she heard from Philip Carr. Why should she? She was to have supper at his mother's house Sunday night. He would tell her his plan then. Much more satisfactory to talk it over than to write.

She stopped the flivver. Her spirit quickened to the beauty of the sparkling water, only a degree bluer than the cloudless sky above. Gulls sunned themselves on the silver dunes, which were beginning to show tufts of coarse grass; two marsh hawks sailed above them. Far off on the horizon floated a faint haze of smoke which meant a steamship Europe bound. A great cloud, gilt-edged, sailed along like a proud ship. Cranberry bogs showed faintly green. This shore was an ideal location for summer cottages.

She pulled the letter from her pocket, frowned over the post-mark. New York. Couldn't be from Scott, he lived in Boston. A man's writing. Perhaps it was from Philip Carr. Club stationery. She tore open the envelope and looked at the signature. Scott Mallory! What was he doing in New York and why write to her? She pulled off her close hat, settled back in the seat. The salty breeze ruffled her hair as she read.

NEW YORK CITY

DEAR PAM —

You were right in your suspicion. The operation yarn was a hold-up for money. I wasn't satisfied myself so came over here at once to investigate. Invited a man named Latimer who was in my class in college, and is now making a name for himself on the stage, to dine with me at the Club. Thought he might know your stepmother and I would get a line on her from him. Over smokes I asked him if he had met a girl in his profession named Cecile Mortimer. He said:

" Curious you should ask that. She's all but engaged for a show in which I'm cast. Never've seen her but hear that she's one of those pink and blonde perils — and some little plunger in the market. I am asked to meet her tonight."

It wasn't difficult to extract an invitation to go along. It was to be a party, I discovered, where half the guests were unknown to the hostess and were likely to remain so. I went. I met Cecile Mortimer, "the second Mrs. Leigh." She is beautiful. I recognized what you meant about her clothes. Her gown was smart but crushed. We danced together several times. Each time I waited for her to stop because of a troublesome foot. Not so much as a fraction of a flinch. It was a noisy party, an exceedingly wet party. Young ex-marrieds, ex-marrieds not so young. Wild women, lit ladies by the giggling score; swashbuckling gents, even if they were arrayed in the latest word in dinner clothes, they were swashbucklers just the same. She grew talkative but made no mention of her past. I asked her no questions — I had found out the one thing I wanted to know — neither of her two feet required surgical attention — had they, she couldn't have danced so incessantly. I don't drink. Perhaps because of that I sensed her suspicion. Her animation waned. Her eyes smoldered, "sullen, broody." There was a tempest brewing, I felt it in the air. When Latimer swayed up and suggested — you see, I'm giving you all the sordid details — " Want a divorce or two put through, Miss Mortimer? Now's your chance, darling. One of the brightest lights of the Massachusetts Bar is at the present moment eating out of your hand."

" Massachusetts Bar! "

Her repetition was a whisper. I remembered what you had said about her hair-trigger mind. She sprang to her feet, caught Latimer's arm, repeated:

" Massachusetts Bar? "

" Sure. Boston. You know Boston. The place where the censors come from. That's good — "

Cecile Mortimer was not interested in his wise-cracks. Her face blanched, her eyes narrowed to pin-points. She said under her breath:

" How could I have been such a fool." She caught Latimer's arm. " I had begun to suspect that your friend didn't belong at this party. You are an actor as well as a lawyer, Mr. Mallory; you are showing just the right amount of incredulity — you're good, but not good enough."

She walked away. I left without saying good-night to the hostess whom I had not met. That was an hour ago. Ever since, Latimer's words, " and some little plunger in the market," have been milling round in my mind. Where does the money come from with which she plays the stock market? I am writing to you at once that one burden may be speedily lifted from your shoulders — no money will be needed for an operation — would that I could dispose of others so easily. I have written you in detail first because I want you to know all that happens, second because it seems to bring me near you, as if I were talking to you. Better say nothing of all this to your father. I will be down on Saturday. Have secured the loan on your land. We can push ahead on the cottage. Will be off again before your party at the Carrs'.

Sincerely,
SCOTT MALLORY.

"Sincerely." Pamela made a little face at the word. New England granite. As an antidote she re-read — "It seems to bring me near you, as if I were talking to you." That had some warmth.

She admonished herself sharply. Ungrateful person, sitting here criticizing Scott when she should be giving loud thanks that there was no need of raising eight hundred dollars. How had Cecile dared! She must think the Leigh family an easy mark. Why not? Hadn't they allowed her to walk away with everything cashable at the time of her husband's breakdown? Where was she getting money to invest? How like her to jump to the conclusion that Scott Mallory was shadowing her to make certain that her claim was valid.

It wasn't, glory be! What would she try next? Perhaps even now she was preparing another coup. How could she think that there was money to be had from the Leighs? The raw grinding of gears as she started the flivver was an outlet for Pamela's emotions. She was still pondering the question as she drove up to the kitchen door.

Mehitable Betts hurried out, thinner, gaunter, drabber than ever. "Get the oysters, Pam? Seem's though the whole world's gone crazy 'bout your oyster chowder. Three parties, four each, phoned for supper tonight." She picked up the still dripping burlap as if it were a five cent bag of popcorn and carried it into the kitchen. Mentally cal-

culating a problem in liquid measure, Pamela
followed.

"Three fours — twelve — fourteen —"

"For the land's sake, what you mumbling 'bout?"
Miss Betts emptied the oysters into a pan, perched
on a green enamel stool, jerked her spectacles in
place, inserted a dull blade into a tightly clamped
shell, with unbelievable economy of motion.

Pamela studied the reservation pad with wrinkled-
brow intentness. "I don't recognize any of these
names, Hitty."

"They said they were new, told who the folks
was who'd recommended them, but I couldn't be
bothered taking that down. My, isn't it warm for
this time of year? Folks is sayin' that the rooms
are taken at the Inn from now till clear through
October."

A shadow fell across her busy hands. She looked
up. "Eddie Pike, what you stealing up like that
for? Might's well kill a body as scare her to death."

The loose jointed man in a rope-belted army over-
coat, with barnyard mud on his boots, a stubby
young beard sprouting from his round face, surveyed her with big, vacant, light blue eyes. In the
drive an aged white horse hitched to a top-buggy
drooped in harness. He drawled:

"Terry asked me to come up an' kill them chickens fer him. I couldn't come tomorrer 'cause I
have to pump water for Kelley-the-miser. He's apt
to take a bath round the end of the week."

Pamela consulted the reservation pad. "The squabs for Saturday. Six. All right, Eddie, come out to the poultry house and I will show you where to find them."

Pike rubbed his hand up and down his unshaven cheek. The sound resembled nothing so much as an able-bodied young buzz-saw in operation. His loose mouth twitched.

"Squabs! You mean pigeons? I couldn't kill a dove, Miss Pamela."

Knife in one hand, oyster shell in the other, Mehitable Betts stared at him. "Eddie Pike! How long since you've got so sensitive? You trap and hunt and fish all the year round, open season or not open season, and now you—"

"They are chickens, not pigeons, Eddie." Pamela stemmed the caustic torrent of words. "Squabs is a term applied to small chickens. Come on."

He shuffled along beside her, a burlap bag in his hand. She led the way to the poultry house. Long rows of buildings with tidy yards only a few of them inhabited, were enclosed by a galvanized wire fence. A great white Leghorn rooster, wattles and comb like coral carvings, flew at the netting in a vain attempt to attack. Pike shrank away.

"Gee, that fella's a fighter."

"Yes. He's a terror, he flies at anyone who comes near him. Terry has named him the White Hope. Here are the chickens to be dressed." As a

dozen or more plump, small, yellow feathered cock-
erels flew and fluttered in the coop in the expectation
of food, she added hastily, "Don't take them out
till I get into the house. I — I — hate this part of
the poultry business."

She was conscious of his grinning regard as she
dashed away. She slammed the kitchen door to shut
out the sound of frightened chirping and wildly
flapping wings. "That's that!" she sighed in relief.

Mehitable Betts sniffed. "Open that door again,
Pam. Room smells like a barnyard. Folks is sayin'
Eddie Pike sleeps with the old white horse. 'Tisn't
hard to believe. That's better. What do you know
about his being so sensitive about dressing pigeons?
Pity he isn't more tender-hearted some other ways."

"He is fond of his sister, isn't he?"

"If you call it being fond to suspect every man
who looks at Milly Pike of wanting to run off with
her and lead her astray. He's got a twist that way.
There's your father's bell. I'd like a dollar for
every time he jingles it. I wouldn't have to work
much longer."

Pamela answered the impatient summons. Her
father was in the big chair by the window, eyes on
the cloudless blue sky and the shimmering sand
dunes. There was a book on his knees, the stamp-
laden table had been pushed aside. He looked up
as his daughter entered. His face seemed rounder,
his eyes clearer, his voice stronger than it had been
since he came to the Cape.

"When is Mallory coming again?"

"Saturday."

"Has he sent Cecile the money?"

"If he has, he hasn't told me."

"I don't like him, he's — he's so unflinching."

"Father!" Pamela disciplined her indignant voice, said more calmly: "After all he has done to help you! How ungrateful. Had he not been unflinching we might be sitting on packing boxes instead of on choice old maple chairs. We haven't paid him a cent for the time he has given to our pesky problems."

"He offered to help, didn't he?"

"And did it."

He stared out of the window again. Color crept under his waxen skin. He cleared his throat. The cords on his forehead stood out.

"I didn't wait for him to send the money to Cecile. I got it for her myself."

Pamela's world whirled, steadied. He had sent Cecile money! She had lied to get it. Where had it come from? Was that the explanation of his midnight trip to the mail-box? She tried to keep her voice steady.

"I thought that Mr. Mallory had charge of all your securities?"

"I realized on an antique a — friend held for me. I — you have done so much — I wouldn't let you mortgage your property for us."

Pamela blinked furiously to keep back a sudden,

unexpected rush of tears. He did care a little for her! What a child she still was about her father!

"Cecile wrote that if I didn't send the money she would come here. We couldn't have that. I told her that you had convinced me that she and I never could be happy together again."

"Father! I never have advised you about your wife!"

"I had to say something to prevent her coming. We don't want her, do we? My nerves wouldn't stand the excitement of having her around."

His nerves! Indignation dried even Pamela's long, drenched lashes. "Don't worry, she won't come now that she has the eight hundred. You might have saved your precious antique. Cecile fooled you. That operation story was a try-out for money."

The knuckles of his hands strained white as he clutched the arms of his chair.

"How do you know?" The question was sharply incredulous.

"A friend saw her at a party in New York. She danced and danced and danced. She wouldn't do that, would she, if she were slated for the hospital?"

Harold Leigh's face was colorless. His eyes were wide with fury, his voice hoarse.

"Fooled me, did she! I'll make her pay for that, even if she is a woman who never pays for anything, but just digs, digs, *digs!*" His chin quivered like a hurt child's. "My mint block! My mint block!" The last word was a wail.

Chapter VIII

SCOTT MALLORY laid a paper on the desk in the living room. Pamela smiled radiantly.

"I am so glad you came. You said you would not be here this week."

His face and eyes were as noncommittal as his voice. "Wanted to get this loan through. I stood over the title-examiner with a club — figuratively speaking — to be sure he pushed ahead. Work should be started on the cottage at once or it won't be ready to rent this season. That would mean a loss to you. Read the mortgage before you sign."

Under the light of the lamp Pamela dutifully scanned the printed words.

"Perhaps sometime I will understand legal terms. This seems a muddle of whereas and whereupon and grantor and grantee to me. However, the gist of it is that I am placing a mortgage for four thousand dollars on thirty acres of shore land. Who is this trusting person who is willing to plunge to that extent?"

"A friend of mine. We could have borrowed from a bank but I wouldn't take a chance at the news of the loan leaking out until the deal was consummated. Hurried it up on that account. Sign here — and here."

He laid a note on the mortgage. She wrote her name on both. He witnessed her signatures and stamped the document with his Notary's seal.

"I understand that this leaves the house, the cranberry bogs and the rest of the land clear. Am I right, Scott?"

"Correct. Here is your cheque. The first six months' interest has been deducted. By the time the next comes due the cottage should be finished, rented, and an advance payment made. When you get a tenant I'll draw the lease and make sure it is water-tight."

"It won't be your fault if I am not an efficient business woman." Pamela looked at the pink slip of paper. "What shall I do with it? Deposit it with the money I keep for current expenses?"

"Better not. Better open an account in a Boston bank."

She tapped the desk with the end of her pen as she looked up at the man looming above her.

"Scott, of what are you afraid?"

"What do you mean, 'afraid'?"

"Don't fence. You are afraid that Cecile will try to get that money, aren't you? How could she? Why should she?"

"If it once occurred to her as a lucrative possibility, she might attempt it. You never know what the power of suggestion, combined with the tendency of the human mind to see and believe what it wants to see and believe, can accomplish."

"I still can't see why she should try to get money from me. Have you paid her any?"

"No. I wrote why."

"Father sent her some."

"Where did he get it?"

"Don't shoot questions at me like that and please sit down."

"Come over here on the couch." He caught her hand, seated himself beside her. Spread her fingers on his palm. She doubled them up.

"Inky, aren't they? I despair of ever domesticating a fountain-pen. Just as I think I have one well-trained it leaks."

He laughed. "I'll send you one that won't. I'll put a spell on it so that it always will write to me the things I want to hear. Tell me what has happened since I have been away."

The fire snapped accompaniment as she repeated the conversation with her father. "When he said that he wouldn't let me mortgage this property for Cecile and himself, my incurable romanticism vaulted to the saddle, I — I almost hugged him, I was so touched by his consideration. Luckily I remembered in time that he hates demonstration. Later, when he said that his 'nerves' wouldn't stand having his wife about, I flung the truth at him, told him that she had been lying to get money. I thought for an instant her deception had killed him. He looked ghastly, then furious, then threatened to make her pay, crumpled and wailed:

"'My mint block! My mint block!'

"That meant nothing to me. Do you suppose he owned a rare block print — if there is such a thing? Had he said mint-bed, it would have been within the scope of my practical ken. There is a marvelous patch in Grandmother Leigh's herb-garden, you can smell it a mile away — almost."

"What a good little sport you are, Pam. Your sense of humor will buoy you in the roughest water." Head back, Mallory blew smoke rings at the ceiling, repeated thoughtfully, "'My mint block!' I wonder if he has more treasures up his sleeve."

"If he has it seems frightfully unfair that Terry and I should be worried to a frazzle trying to make both ends meet. It isn't the work I mind, but it is this everlasting counting pennies. A dime assumes the proportions of a gold piece when I consider parting with it. Shall I get so niggardly that I shall forget how to spend?"

He laid his finger lightly between her brows. "That pucker is adorable, but don't worry about forgetting how to spend. The knack will return, you'll be surprised. I can't bear to see you working so hard. Who the dickens is that?" Pamela waved him aside when he would have answered the telephone.

"Probably someone to make a reservation." She

spoke into the transmitter. "Silver Moon. . . . Right here. . . . Mr. Carr! . . . Of course I am coming tomorrow. All excited about it. . . . You have. . . . I'm crazy to see it . . . I have the money! My legal adviser approves. . . . You will! Marvelous. . . . No, don't come for me. Terry will drive me over. . . . Of course, you may bring me home. Good-bye."

Pamela returned to the couch. Her eyes shone, her cheeks were pink from excitement.

"That was my poor little rich boy. He has a cardboard model of the cottage as it will look made over. I am having supper at the Carrs' tomorrow night."

Arm on the mantel Mallory met her eyes. "I have not forgotten."

"Why so solemn? You don't disapprove of a little change of scene for me, do you?"

"No. I would pack your days full of pleasure if you would let me."

Pamela swallowed her heart which had soared to her throat at the emotion in his voice. She steeled herself to say practically:

"You are doing something for me all the time, Scott."

He took a step toward her. Put his hands hard in his pockets. "I am going back to town tonight. Can't you come to the city one day next week? You really ought to deposit the cheque, and open an account personally."

"To town! I haven't been away from this house for a day since I came here in June. It sounds heavenly. It would have to be Thursday. I could get everything planned ahead for the week-end. I am sure of Hitty Betts that day and Terry has a light schedule. He would be here. I could buy the new machines."

"What machines?"

"A big tricolator and an electric ice-cream freezer. We have been making coffee, four cups at a time, and freezing ice-cream in small lots. We have saved money enough to get big ones."

"All right, Thursday. Come to my office first. I will take you to the bank, then we'll have luncheon and go to a show. It will be a talkie, no real theatre on that afternoon. Couldn't make it Wednesday, could you?"

"I couldn't. Taking Thursday is a risk and we will cut out the matinée. I should lose the last train down."

"Forget the train. I'll drive you home. Don't say 'no.' Good-night."

He was gone before she could answer. Was he afraid that she might change her mind about going to Boston? She was not so heroic. Now that she had had a vision of what a day in the city would mean she would grab the pleasure though the heavens fell. Lucky she had the excuse of the purchase of the tricolator and freezer as a sop to fling to her New England conscience.

A sense of anticipation glowed in her heart during

church the next morning. It was difficult to keep her mind on the service, keep from visualizing shops and crowded streets and luncheon with Scott. The downpour of rain dimmed her vivid imagination not at all.

At home as she changed her green crêpe to a simple print in which to prepare dinner, she frowned at the sleeve. Thin on the elbow? What would she do for clothes when her present supply gave out? She and Terrence had planned to put every cent they didn't need for living into equipment.

She was still pondering the question as she fastened her belt at the window. A dingy day. From horizon to horizon the sky was spongy with formless clouds. A pair of drenched birds snuggled close in a bend of the eaves, kept up a monotonous, Cheep! Cheep! Water rivuleted down the shingles, dripped in a platinum fringe from the roof, settled in pools which looked like fragments of a shattered mirror on the sodden lawn which showed a tinge of green in its russet. Little mists hung above the hollows. Village chimneys were darker blurs against the drab sky, the church spire was of no more importance than the cupola of the little red schoolhouse. Rain, like a gauze curtain, turned all color to a neutral gray. The smell of the sea stole into the room. An open car chugged up the drive. Cap'n Ivy Crockett's! Why was he coming? She hadn't ordered oysters. Who was with him? Someone in yellow oilskins.

She stared incredulously as the sou'wester blew

back from a blonde head. Cecile? Her father's wife! Here!

Pamela flew down the stairs. The Babe, roused from a doze in front of the living room fire, joined her as she opened the door, his hair bristling. He dashed to the porch, stopped for an instant to regard the oilskin figure picking its way from stepping-stone to stepping-stone, then, with a growl, charged.

The woman screamed as he snapped at her yellow slicker, tore at it. For a stunned instant Pamela felt turned to stone. Cecile here! Why? Had she come for more money?

"Pamela! Pamela! How dare you set him on me!"

The scream unlocked the girl's muscles and tongue.

"Babe! Babe!" She had the dog by the collar. With all her might twisted it. A growl gurgled in his throat as she dragged him back.

"Run for the house, quick, Cecile! Run!" she gasped.

The woman took a step forward, sank to the ground, panted through livid lips:

"I knew you hated me! You've turned your father against me! You'll pay for this! What beastly luck that my attorney isn't with me!"

"Cap'n Crockett! Come! Help!" Pamela called as the dog almost pulled her arms from their sockets in his attempt to reach the yellow slickered figure.

The Captain in his black rubber coat, which glistened with rain, puffed up.

"What in tarnation's that pup raising such a row about? Ain't he notional!"

"Never mind! Never mind! Help her into the house. Quick! I can't hold him much longer. Come along, Babe! Come!"

Spanking, pulling, pushing, Pamela dragged the infuriated dog toward the barn. Devoutly she prayed that the collar would not give way under the strain, fervently she hoped that Cecile was safely in the house, she didn't dare turn to look. Why, of all days in the year had one of the Academy teachers selected this one to invite Terrence to dinner? The barn at last!

At the girl's tempestuous entrance a Jersey cow stopped chewing her cud to gaze with ruminative eyes; an old horse neighed a welcome; a hen flew down from the loft and with a frenzied cackle scurried into the rain; a mouse which had been feasting on chaff scuttled into its hole. She pushed the dog into a box stall, slammed and fastened the door. White, breathless, shaken, she leaned against it outside. She shut her eyes tight to keep back tears of relief, set her teeth into her lips to steady their nervous twitching, clenched her hands to control her shaking body.

Cap'n Crockett poked his head into the barn. "The lady's all right, Miss Pam-ee-lia. She wasn't so hurt as she seemed when she tumbled to the ground. Ain't surprised she was frightened. Thought when you an' that pup burst out of the house you was settin' him on her. Guess she'll wish she hadn't pestered me to death to bring her."

With an effort Pamela steadied her voice. "Where did you pick her up, Cap'n Iry?"

"She was in a mighty han'some sedan stuck near the oyster shack. A real natty man come to my door and asked if I would take a lady up to the Leigh place.

"'But I haven't got nothin' but an open fliv,' says I. 'Just cruise along nor'-east, an' glimpse up toward the hill an' you'll see the house, find it yourself,' I told him. 'My car's stuck. Haven't you a slicker you can lend her?' says he. 'She's my client, she's got to get there. I'll have this thing tinkered an' you can bring her back to the Inn.'

"I didn't want to do it but he pestered me so I fetched the slicker and sou'wester an' brought her along. She was pleasant-speakin'. Asked me a lot about you an' the old Leigh place. I gave your family a great setting out, Miss Pam-ee-lia. Told her that the Leighs had been the first family here since the place was settled, that they was awful proud of their record, never'd been a breath of scandal or a charge of dishonest dealin' against one of them in all the years they'd lived here. I forgot for a minute your father owed a lot of money folks couldn't collect. Guess I bragged some. Told her your grandma left you most a peck of di'monds, that she'd refused a fortune for her land. I wasn't goin' to let her think 'cause you run one of those new fangled eatin'-places that you wasn't just as good as any city folks as might come here. She seemed terrible interested. Said she thought that this might be a pretty place when the sun shone, she might like to spend the summer here, she hadn't been very well.''

Consternation slashed a zig-zag course through Pamela's mind. Evidently the "real natty man" was Cecile's attorney. They had been on their way to the Silver Moon. Why? In all good faith Cap'n Iry had set forth the value of the Leigh property. His reference to the "peck of diamonds" must have been a flick on the raw; Cecile had been wild to have them. Would she take advantage of the information? Try to get more money? Hadn't Scott said that it might occur to her as a lucrative possibility?

Pamela was aware of the oysterman's dropped jaw as she flashed past him. She dashed into the house. Stopped at the living room door. No one there. No sound but the snap of the fire. Voices in her father's room! His bell. Why should she answer it? Why should she be dragged into a row? The bell again, an irritated protracted ring. With a little grimace of distaste she slowly mounted the stairs.

Cecile, the color high in her fair skin, her green eyes sullen, her small rouged mouth unbecomingly twisted, turned as Pamela entered the room.

"I told Harold that you set the dog on me. He

laughed. Was it his plan as well as yours to keep me out?"

Pamela looked at her father standing behind the arm-chair, his hands gripping its back. He raised warning brows. What did he mean by that wireless? Her anger flared as she looked at the woman who had married him and deserted him at the first sign of adversity. She struggled to keep her voice coolly amused.

"Don't be an idiot, Cecile. Of course I didn't set the dog on you. Think I'm looking for more trouble? Just why are you here?"

"Why am I here! My attorney brought me."

"Where is he?" Harold Leigh's waxen face lost the bit of color it had acquired from the surprise of his wife's arrival.

"His car is stuck in your beastly, wet Cape Cod sand. We missed the main road and landed at an oyster shack. I came to demand an allowance from you, Harold."

"An allowance! That is almost funny, Cecile. You know that I have nothing left."

"Then where did that money come from you sent me?"

He set a little back-fire. "You lied to get it, lied about the operation, didn't you?"

Cecile blazed. "So, that lawyer was sent by you! I knew it!"

"Lawyer?" The surprise in her father's voice closed Pamela's lips. She had been about to defend

him. He had not known that Scott Mallory went
to New York to check up on Cecile. He may have
suspected who the "friend" was who had reported
back, but he had asked no questions. She would
better say nothing.

"You're good, but not good enough, Harold.
It didn't take me long to realize that your Mr. Mallory was there to shadow me. He was as out of
place in that party as Galahad in a speakeasy. As
for the lie — as you call it — nothing hackneyed
about that. I might have claimed that an appendix
was clamoring for removal, or high blood pressure.
The foot operation was much more original." Her
flippant voice hardened. "I was advised to make
the test. I knew that you and your daughter had
money cached somewhere. I suspected that you
would sacrifice your last treasure rather than have
me here for a few weeks. Now I know it."

Pamela noticed in her father's eyes the furtive
look which had puzzled her before. "My last
treasure! I have nothing left except a few lame
ducks I picked up in the stock market."

"I'm not so sure. If you did not send Mallory —"

"Send Mallory! Would I have sent you that
money had I doubted your word? The Leigh
women don't lie, Cecile."

"Oh, don't they! *You* and your family! I was
glad of the excuse to break away when you were ill.
It wasn't all lack of money. I was fed-up with your

talk of what your ancestors had done. You! You sitting back and spending what they had made and never trying to make more. *You*, one of those millions of the living who are already dead! You don't know the first letter of the word ambition!"

Her voice lashed. Harold Leigh winced. Pamela's love for him flamed as a gray coal blazes into red light when blown upon. She tucked her hand under his arm, comforted as she had when a little girl:

"Never mind, Dad, never mind!"

His clammy fingers clutched hers as he answered his wife. "Didn't try to make more! My God, when I did try what happened?"

"You crashed, you being *you*. I suspect now that you didn't crash. I know that you and your daughter have money. I shan't sue for a divorce, I should cut myself off from inheriting my share of your property. I don't want to marry again, not a chance. I have been advised that I am entitled to an allowance. I came to talk with you amicably. As usual Pamela steps between us. I suspect that the loss of fortune was your way of getting rid of me, Harold. I —"

"Would I give up the work I love, come here and run a chowder house if we had anything?" Pamela interrupted stormily. "You are crazy!"

Cecile recovered her voice with the convulsive swallow of one whose determination to riot and revel in an orgy of tirade had been blocked suddenly.

" Really! Before you came upstairs your father had confirmed what he had already written, that you had persuaded him that I was not necessary in his life. The old man who brought me here told me that the Leighs had been the first family since the place was settled, that they were 'awful proud,' never had had a breath of scandal. I'll show them! I will start proceedings for an allowance, but before that—" With a nice sense of theatric values she paused on the threshold to hurl her bomb— "I will drag you into court, Miss Leigh!"

She was out of the room before the smoke of battle had cleared sufficiently for Pamela to sense the threat. Drag her into court? Why? She would make her tell before she left.

She flew down the stairs. The yellow slicker was crackling out of the front doorway. She followed. Stopped on the porch. Philip Carr was smiling at Cecile as he shook hands.

"Hulloa! Thought you hated the country. What are you doing here?"

She shrugged. "Merely calling upon my husband."

His surprise was funny if one could see anything funny in this outrageous situation, Pamela thought. He demanded:

"Do you mean that you are Harold Leigh's wife? The wife who deserted him? I didn't even know that you had been married."

Cecile's lips whitened and tightened. "That

needn't make any difference in our — friendship, need it?"

Carr put his hands hard into his pockets. "Sorry, but it will. Miss Leigh is my friend and — my client. I don't care for the way you ditched her and your husband when they were in trouble. A poor sport! I've heard about it from my father. That's that."

He spoke to Pamela standing rigid on the top step. "I came to confirm measurements of the cottage. I'll get them now. See you tonight."

Cecile followed him with her eyes. Said acidly: "In love with you, isn't he? You have a fatal charm, haven't you? I pulled every wire I could to meet Philip Carr. He is backing a revue, and now he has turned me down for you. Believe me, you'll need his friendship before I get through! *Au revoir!*"

Pamela tried to protest, but her throat contracted, shut off her voice. She watched her stepmother as she picked her way along the wet stepping-stones. Retort after scathing retort flamed in her mind. Why hadn't she thought of them in time to hurl them at Cecile. Why hadn't she told her that she had met Philip Carr but once before? A lot of help, these after-the-fight flashes of invective. She watched Cap'n Crockett's shabby flivver chug down the drive to the accompaniment of a lugubrious horn, till it was but a drab blotch in a gray curtain of rain.

Her father's bell rang as she entered the house. Darn! Her conception of Hades was a place where one would be sentenced to forever answer the imperative tinkle of a bell, she told herself, as she went slowly up the stairs, reluctance in every step. When she reached his room he was leaning back in his chair, his brows wrinkled thoughtfully.

"Has she gone?" His voice was agitated.

"Yes."

"Even in that slicker she was beautiful, wasn't she? I had forgotten. I've been living in a haze." He brushed his hand across his eyes.

Pamela regarded him incredulously. How could he see anything lovely in a woman who had slashed at him as had Cecile? Should she tell him that his wife was trying for a revue which Philip Carr was backing? Better not. The name of Carr was anathema to him. She hadn't told him of the plan to move the cottage yet. Besides, Cecile might be lying. She disagreed passionately:

"Beautiful! Not to me. Cecile won't seem so to you when she begins proceedings for an allowance."

He picked up a newspaper. "What can she get? I have no money. Mallory will stand between and handle the matter for me."

"You wouldn't ask him to do more for nothing?"

"Why not? Lawyers, like doctors, do a certain amount of work for which they are not paid. You'd better get in touch with him, better tell him of Cecile's threat to you before you worry about me." He looked up from his paper to add significantly:

"You own this place. You have more to lose than I have."

Chapter IX

PAMELA caught a reassuring glimpse of her amber-
frocked self in the great gold-framed mirror in the
hall of the Carr house. Her hair was still black.
After the fright the Babe had given her this morning it ought to be streaked with white. Suppose the
dog had bitten Cecile! But, he hadn't. What a
coincidence that she should have been trying for an
engagement in the revue in which Philip Carr was
interested. But it wasn't coincidence. She had admitted that she had pulled every possible wire to
meet him. A maze of crossing life-lines; would
it ever straighten out? For what cause would the
second Mrs. Leigh hale her stepdaughter into court?
But, of course, that had been merely an angry
threat. Suppose she did? More annoyance for
Scott Mallory on her account? Never. Why had
she let him step into her life that first day? Let
him? How could she help it? His smile and eyes
had gone so straight and deep into her heart, his
voice had been so steadying, his mouth so clean, his
eyes so clear, and she had been so hungry for a nice
man to talk to. Suppose Cecile did sue her? What

could she get? Forget it! Wasn't this a party? She would much better spend thought on the brand of greeting she would receive from her senior host. She met Philip Carr's eyes in the mirror. Laughed.

"Not too bad."

"Look swell to me. By the way, better not mention the fact that I know your stepmother. I'll explain why later," he added in a low voice before he led the way through the hall.

Pamela paused on a threshold. What a room! The walls were of cypress to a height of six feet, warmly brown, paneled like an ancient vessel's cabin. Behind glass panels reposed the most comprehensive, rare collection of books on ships and shipping to be found in the country, she had heard. The plaster above was tinted blue, the blue of the sky on a windy day at sea. Ship models on the shelves which topped the book-cases were arranged with a nice attention to artistic and chronological relativity. There were ships of wood, metal, bone, ivory, glass. There were ships with bellying sails, ships with guns, ships rich with decoration. There were man-o'-war models, whaling models, models of Chinese and Japanese junks, of Spanish and Dutch ships, of Greek coasting vessels, of Viking galleons. There were models of ships which had helped make American history. There was the clipper ship *Flying Cloud*, nearby, the packet *Massachusetts*. Ships pendant from the ceiling held cunningly concealed bulbs in their hulks the light from which shone softly down through glass bottoms. A tall Willard clock in the corner, topped by three brass balls which reflected the firelight, showed on its face a scudding barque about to dip below the horizon.

After the involuntary pause Pamela stepped forward to greet her hostess whose delicacy might have materialized from a fan of the Louis the Fourteenth period. Her gown was a blend of violet and flesh color, the latter no more delicate than her rose-petal skin. Her hair, white and soft as the silk of a Scotch thistle, was arranged to show the charming contour of her head. Her eyes were lovely, but, for all her apparent sweetness her mouth had a stubborn line when in repose. The value of her string of pearls would have reinstated a deposed ruler in the king business, supposing, of course, his subjects wished him reinstated. Her hand clung to the girl's.

"This marvelous room stampeded my manners, Mrs. Carr. I'm sorry!"

"You will win my husband's heart if you like his ships, Miss Leigh. Phin!"

There was a note of appeal in her voice. Was she afraid of him, Pamela wondered. She had met women before who handled their soul-mates as if they were high explosives. Must be wearing to live with a man of whom one was afraid. The tall one looking into the fire turned. Since the settlement of her grandmother's estate she had seen Phineas Carr in the distance only, his long arms, swinging as he strode, giving the effect of a walking-beam. Her eyes met his. Her heart broke into a quickstep. She had a flashing premonition that this man would ineradicably change her future. That silly plot-construction stuff again! She would better get it out of her system, it dramatized even the most commonplace events of life for her. There was power in his black eyes, inflexibility in his stern mouth. His thick hair, streaked black, white and gray, had the lustre of smoked pearl. His arm seemed abnormally long as he extended his hand.

"Glad to see you here, Miss Leigh. I admired your grandmother. She was a wonderful woman. Hope you have inherited her grit and her sunshiny philosophy. It was always, 'Fair tomorrow', with her. Hers was not a shallow optimism but a deep and abiding faith in the ultimate victory of the dragon-slayer."

His gruff voice was kind, his smile whimsical. He was not holding her responsible for her father's sins of omission or commission — whichever they were. Thank heaven! Pamela sensed the relaxation of his wife and son. What had they expected? Was he a martinet? The villagers spoke of him with mingled awe and affection. "A hard man but a just one, the Judge."

If the dining room was an example of Philip Carr's taste she was all for it, she told herself, as he drew out a chair for her at the beautifully appointed table. It was in dark and light burgundy shades with dark rose and light rose, vivid thrusts of gold, mauve and tender green. Rose brocade on the seats of the mellow wood chairs; rose brocade at the windows, across one of which were shelves holding up pink Opaline against the light; vases; bottles; curious flagons with touches of gilt in their rims. A rich burgundy carpet covered the floor. Mirrors on opposite sides of the room amplified the proportions, gave back the rose and burgundy tints, gave back also the pale amber of her gown which was like a shaft of sunlight. The house had an up-to-the-minute atmosphere. She loved it.

She was conscious of tension throughout the delicious supper——a compote of fruit, sea-food newburg on crisps of toast which made her wish she might keep on eating forever——a hot-house tomato salad, ice-cool, to accompany it——fluffy rolls and fresh unsalted butter——a baked Alaska which was a perfect thing of its kind——served by pink-frocked Milly Pike.

Mrs. Carr and her son kept the conversation-puck within bounds. Perfect teamwork between them. Was it because of the presence of the maid with her over-developed bump of curiosity or were they afraid of an outburst from the stern, silent man at the head of the table? It was abundantly evident by the way he looked at his wife that he adored her; it was equally apparent that he disliked——no, that wasn't the word——distrusted Philip. Once when discussion evidently neared thin ice, the mother swept it to safety again. Pamela caught a sardonic gleam in the senior Carr's eyes. He was aware of her tactics, indubitably.

It was a relief after supper to escape to Philip's work-room. He swept a pile of drawings from a small drafting-table and placed a chair in front of it.

"Sit here, Miss Leigh." He ran his fingers through his hair. "Gosh! This place is a mess. It isn't Mother's fault, really, I turn the key on it when I go away."

The room was large and exceedingly dusty. Tall rolls of paper, cardboard and tracing-cloth there were, a corner full; portfolios, a fat and bulging collection; paints, crayons, brushes, squares, triangles, scales, by the battered score; a desk crowded with ruling pens and inks in bewildering variety. On the wall, drawings in frames, plans thumbtacked; bits from colorful gardens; a drypoint or two; the fragment of a peristyle; gateways; antique façades; a water-color of marvelous Taj-Mahal. A guitar lay on the window-seat.

Pamela's eyes returned from their voyage of observation. "I believe that you really work — or — is this clutter for artistic effect?"

He took her seriously. "Of course I work. I'm doing some stage settings for a revue. To nail the chance I had to help back the show. That's how I ran into your — Cecile Mortimer. Mother knows what I'm doing — Mother always understands — but we don't want Father to hear of it until I've made good. He wouldn't see it at all. Get me? That's the reason I warned you in the hall. This is my play-room. I fool with plans when I come home. I've worked like a dog this last week in New York that I might have something to show you."

From an alcove he dragged a large table on wheels. On an expanse of green paper, to simulate a lawn, was a cardboard model of the farmer's cottage. Dormers had been let into the roof, a porch faced a shellac shore sprinkled with sand, which edged a scrap of brilliantly blue painted sea. Pamela regarded it incredulously.

"How could you copy the cottage so perfectly?"

Philip Carr perched on the arm of her chair. His eyes were boyishly eager. "I told you that often I feasted on milk and cookies in the farmer's house. Besides my memory of it I had a photograph of your grandmother's place to work from. It belongs to Father but I lugged it off to New York and — there we are! This noon — after leaving you and your stepmother — hope I didn't mess things up more — I confirmed the measurements. Like it? A man I know gave me pointers on a development scheme. See those marks? They indicate where more houses will stand if we make good on this. I'm out to make your real estate a going concern. We'll keep the cottages of the same type as the Leigh house. The severely straight lines cost less to build. Big central chimney in exact centre of roof, windows placed directly above each other, entrance door in centre.

No porches on old houses but I have added one. See the garage? Looks like a woodshed. Notice the pitch of the roof? Slightly less than a right angle. That, and no visible foundation give the squatty look."

"It is perfect. I hate to be little Miss Kill-joy, but won't remodelling cost more than four thousand dollars? There it is again. Money! Money!"

"It won't cost that. The model is made to scale of ¼ inch to the foot. If you okay it I will go on with specifications. We ought to get at it. You will have the time of your life selecting wall-papers. Got any furniture you are not using?"

"The attic is full of it."

"Bully! This will be the house of the month when we get through. Come in, Mother. What do you think of the development scheme? Houses going here and here and —"

"*After* we have rented the first cottage," Pamela interpolated gaily. She slipped her arm within Mrs. Carr's. "See the windows just like those at the Silver Moon, the black band on the chimney?"

"That band stood for loyalty to the King, in the old days. You have been wise to keep the lines simple," Mrs. Carr approved. "Sandy-the-carpenter can make those alterations and additions without supervision."

"I shan't leave it entirely to him. I mean to be here every week-end to boss the job, Mother."

"Really?" Her face was pathetic in its radiance.

The light of happiness waned. "Then you must be more diplomatic with your father. Try, *try* to agree with him at least one time in ten."

"I'll do my best for your sake, Mother, but nothing I say or think seems right to him. We are everlastingly arguing. He is so infernally suspicious of me. I'll bet that when he hears that I suggested moving the farmer's cottage he'll think I have a personal rake-off up my sleeve. Just because stuffy court rooms are the breath of life to him, he can't bear it that I prefer to work on houses and stage-sets. I'm sorry, Pamela — don't mind if I scrap formality, do you — to rattle the family skeleton in your hearing."

Mrs. Carr defended, "There isn't a family skeleton, only — only Philip's father is so much older than he that he fails in sympathetic understanding. The moment a subject comes up they take opposite sides. They have many traits alike; oh, yes, you have, Philip, that is the trouble." She abruptly changed the subject. "Have you planned the inside of the cottage?"

Young Carr flung down his pencil. "Not yet. What say if we go nail Sandy-the-carpenter, Pamela? He won't mind talking business on the Sabbath day. When we get back to the Silver Moon I'll take another look at the cottage."

Pamela sensed his mother's wince at his curt answer to her query. It was as if he had slammed a door in her face. Did it pay to lavish love and care on a child? Even the best of them were brutal at times.

"Coming?" inquired Philip from the threshold.

Pamela spoke to her hostess. "Thank you for a delightful evening. It has been perfect in this perfect house. May I say goodnight to Mr. Carr?"

What inexplicable urge had prompted the request, she asked herself, as she noticed the glance between mother and son. Why hadn't she let sleeping dogs lie? Mrs. Carr acquiesced smoothly:

"Of course. We will find him in the Ship Room."

The tall man rose as they entered. Courtly manner; no wonder Grandmother Leigh had liked and trusted him, Pamela thought, as she laid her hand in his. Again she felt the premonition that somewhere behind the curtain of the future he would cross her life-line and change the pattern. Uncanny feeling. She tried to shake it off as she said lightly:

"Sometime I will show you my one lone ship. It is bottled."

"I know that ship, Miss Pamela, it is a museum piece. I know every treasure in your grandmother's house. There is nothing finer in the country than the old maple she left you. I hear that you are talking of making over the farmer's cottage."

How had he heard? Pamela knew from the startled glances exchanged by mother and son that the information had not come from them. Milly! Had she overheard Phil at the telephone? She acknowledged quickly:

"It is more than talk. I shall do it. Philip has the model ready."

She was aware of the challenging earnestness of her voice, for all the world as if she were pleading a cause. Phineas Carr warned curtly:

"Don't rely too much on Philip. He is more artistic than practical."

Pamela refuted indignantly: "Not practical! I think him most pratical. Hasn't he figured out a way to increase our income, at least to take care of taxes and repairs? Turning the farmer's cottage from a liability to an asset is my idea of constructive planning."

"If — he sees it through," Phineas Carr amended drily.

"Believe me, I'll see this proposition through." Philip's voice was hoarse with anger. "Going to fool you this time. Come on, Miss Pamela Leigh."

Outside the air was cool and clear, scented with the fresh smell of wet earth. Pamela drew a long breath. What a night after the storm! Stars blinked through hazy patches of cloud; one low-hung, brilliant, was setting in the west. All day the world had been overcast. Now it was gleaming into beauty. Was life like that? While apparently it was befogged with problems, were happiness and good fortune just waiting their chance to break through the gloom?

Philip Carr yanked the roadster into gear. There was light enough for Pamela to see his angry eyes, his sneering lips. Evidently his father's words still rankled. His resentment boiled over.

"You heard him! Never gives me credit. Just because I hate law, he thinks I can't do anything. I'll show him a thing or two on this cottage."

"He didn't really mean it, Phil. Why don't you tell him about the stage settings, and the revue?"

"If he can't trust me he doesn't deserve to know. I'm his son and Mother's; that ought to count for something."

"Some day you'll make a grand crack at fame and then he will be so proud of you that he will bore his cronies to death talking about his wonderful boy. Meanwhile, cheer'o! Fair tomorrow!"

Not until the words were spoken did Pamela realize that she had adopted her grandmother's " sunshiny philosophy."

Chapter X

PAMELA leaned her head against the high back of
her chair in the Pullman and closed her eyes. Only
eight o'clock in the morning and she was dead tired.
It was the first time she had sat down since she had
risen before the crack of dawn that she might leave
everything arranged for Hitty Betts and Terrence
to carry on. Was a day off worth the exertion?
Yesterday had been hectic. Through her absorption,
at intervals, had pricked Phineas Carr's caustic
comment:

"Don't rely too much upon him. He is more
artistic than practical." Then his doubting, "If he
sees it through."

Had the indictment been merely an older person's
impatience with an obviously spoiled boy or was
there truth behind it? She liked Philip Carr.
Would he lose interest in the project he had started
once she was committed to it? Was life disappointment all along the line? Maybe everyone was
unstable inside, maybe everyone rebelled against
carrying through to the finish when a newer project
beckoned alluringly. Would she herself go on with

the Silver Moon Chowder House if old-man Necessity did not wriggle his automatic between her shoulders to keep her stepping forward? She would not. She would abandon it so quickly that a chance oyster left in stock would gape open in surprise.

Her eyes were on the confused blur flying past outside. The wheels ground an accompaniment, as her thoughts and time trooped on. Even if Philip Carr lost interest in the cottage she could carry it through. She had the money. Last night Sandy-the-carpenter had been eager to begin moving it. Scott would help. She would not tell him of Cecile's visit, of the Babe's attack on the second Mrs. Leigh, of her threat to hail her stepdaughter into court, of Philip Carr's acquaintance with her — most certainly not that. He was carrying enough of their perplexities now. Scott! The thought of him warmed her. That didn't get her anywhere. If numerous telephone calls were an indication he was still stepping out with Hilda Crane or her extravagant sister. Was Pamela Leigh a dog in the manger? That was what he could call a rhetorical question. She was.

The city! Already she could hear the main roar punctuated by crashes and bangs and an ear-splitting siren. She adjusted her hat, removed any possible speck of dust with her powder pad. Even before the train stopped, her mood was quickstepping to the stir and stimulation about her, so different from the unchanging sameness of the country. She smiled at the reflection in the mirror of her compact. That girl tired? Her eyes were brilliant, her color high. She was on the very top of the world. She could have done without that absurd dimple at one corner of her mouth which her smile routed from ambush. It was too childish for the business woman she had become. She would go directly to Scott Mallory's office, get the banking business behind her. Once her credit was established, she would cash the cheque she had brought to spend on electrical equipment for the Silver Moon.

The elevator shot to the fourteenth floor with a speed which gave her the sense of having somehow, somewhere lost connection with her breath.

"Far's we go," announced the boy. He cocked his head in its rakishly tipped, gorgeously braided hat toward a door down the corridor. "Mallory & Carter."

She gave her name to another boy at a switch-board. Her old tweed suit, garnished with the neck-piece she had had fashioned from Grandmother Leigh's Russian sables, had looked sufficiently smart in the mirror in her own room but one glance at the modish, obviously, girl-on-her-own, who opened a door marked "Mr. Mallory," made her hotly aware that fashion had broken into a forward run since she had retired to the country. Miss Cryder? She recognized her at once as the perfect office secretary of the talkies. Her head with its ruddy waves might recently have left the expert hands of a hairdresser;

her brown frock was smartly simple with collar and cuffs of incredible fineness; hosiery and shoes were the last word in shade and model; her hands were perfect with almond-shaped nails which gleamed like gems. Pamela was also aware that her arrival had interested the occupants of the outer office. It seemed to have paralyzed their fingers if one could accept the sudden cessation of the click of type-writers as a sign. Miss Cryder smiled.

"Mr. Mallory will see you at once, Miss Leigh."

As Pamela entered the book-lined office Scott Mallory stepped from behind a desk on which she noticed one perfect rose in a slender crystal vase. He seemed a curiously different person from the man with whom she had motored, upon whose shoulder — figuratively speaking — she had sobbed out — again figuratively — her troubles. He appeared as impersonal as the Chief Justice of the Supreme Court. Not that she ever had seen that dignitary while earning his daily bread, but as enthroned in authority as she imagined him to be. In short, he was a stranger. As Miss Cryder closed the door from the outside she had the sense of being abandoned on an unfriendly doorstep without the fictional locket of identification about her neck.

Mallory held out his hand. The sense of remoteness vanished. He picked up his hat.

"We will attend to the banking business first and then —" He answered the telephone in response to a buzz. As Pamela waited through a conversation in which recurred the words "hearing"—"brief"—"printer"—"away for the day," she looked out over roofs alive with strutting, preening pigeons, crossed with aerials like gigantic cobwebs, fluttering with flags; looked down into innumerable sunless canyons where taxis scooted, busses lumbered like dinosaurs. Haze dimmed the outlines of towering skyscrapers, of ships and tugs in the distant harbor. It was like a huge Claude Monet canvas. The hum of the city rose. From far away came the muffled beat of a drum.

"Ready."

As beside Scott Mallory she crossed the outer office under fire of a battery of eyes, she felt as childishly self-conscious as she had her first day at school. Down in the crowded elevator, along the street they went, neither of them speaking. As they waited at a corner for the traffice light to change to red and yellow, Pamela looked up at her companion surreptitiously. He was looking down at her. He laughed boyishly. Caught her elbow as she started to cross.

"Not yet! As a pedestrian's caution so shall her days be. That is the first time you have seen me this morning. You have looked through me before. You froze me stiff back there in the office."

Pamela's voice reflected the lightening of her spirit.

"Your obvious importance and the sartorial perfectness of your secretary struck me dumb."

"You look like a million yourself. Come on."

Nice of him to say it but she was increasingly conscious of the contrast between her costume and the last-minute frocks and suits — cheap though many of them were — worn by the women and girls hurrying past.

With the completion of their business in the marble and mahogany fastnesses of the bank the last tinge of Scott Mallory's professional absorption vanished.

"That's that! Now we'll celebrate! Let's plan before we leave here. You want to get that electrical stuff, don't you? Mind if I go with you? Luncheon, talkie — there's a super-production in town — dinner somewhere we can dance and then home."

His voice, his enthusiasm almost swept Pamela into the vortex of his plan. The sight of a woman with every accessory keyed to her chic costume, steadied her. Dinner and dance in her present clothes! Never! Then she would stay at home forever. When would she get money to buy new ones? Every cent she made for a year or two must go into equipment for the Silver Moon. A tide of rebellion swept her. Why should it? She had a purse full of money now. Why spend it for electrical gadgets? Why not on herself? Terry would say, "Sure, Pam! Go to it! You've earned it."

"Well? We have just this one day to spend together — at present. Where shall we begin?"

Heart-quickening impatience in Scott Mallory's voice, the least glint of the pursuing male in his gray eyes. A wave of recklessness left Pamela high and dry on a rock of determination. She would live this one day to the full — no matter if when the clock struck twelve she had to cut all thought of romance from her life for years. The Cinderella motif. Cinderella had had a godmother who changed her calico to satin and pearls. Pamela Leigh had a god-mother — of sorts — in her purse. She glanced at the marble and gilt clock on the marble and gilt wall.

"I will meet you at one-thirty."

"Not until one-thirty! It's a lifetime to wait."

"You are an eloquent advocate, aren't you? I have things to do — heaps and heaps of them. Tell me where to meet you for luncheon. After that my life is in your hands."

Sparks of laughter in his eyes flamed to fire. "Do you mean that?"

"With — reservations. Don't notice what I say. I'm a wild woman when I get to the city."

He hailed a taxi. Wheedled: "Sure I can't help? I left word at the office that I would not be back today."

"Very sure."

He stood on the curb, hat in hand, looking after her as the cab started. A taxi! The first step on her downward course in extravagance. Undoubtedly she would bring up with a smash — not literally, she hoped — but the going promised to be smooth and swift.

With mounting excitement she looked from the window. The city again! It was heady. Automobiles running the gamut of the scale from unbelievable shabbiness to amazing luxury, crawled up and down the broad street in response to a Cyclopian eye. Shop windows flaunted their riches. Garishness and charm. Elaboration and costly simplicity. Here a choice rug from the Orient; there a painting of tranquillity and beauty; a canvas blazing with color; a bronze depicting man and horse vital with primitive emotions. Jewels dazzled and tempted. Flowers lured by their color and fragrance. There were frocks in all the tints of the spectrum; there were florid hangings; there was furniture from palaces across the sea. A band! "Stars and Stripes Forever!" Marching men! The steady rhythm of feet on the sun-patched pavement. Flags! A bugle! The boom, boom, boom of drums. Pamela sat back with a little bounce of sheer exuberance. The city! The adorable city! She had been starved for it.

Mallory was waiting when she reached the green and gold foyer of the restaurant at thirty-five minutes after one a little breathless. He looked straight at her without a sign of recognition, before he turned to glare at a wall clock, to impatiently confirm its story by a glance at his watch. Why should he know her? Hadn't she spent the morning and most of the electrical equipment money in an attempt to look as little as possible like the girl who had entered his office? To save precious time she had confided to a shopping expert what she wanted, what she had to spend and the brief time in which she had to spend it. The capable about-forty woman, had appraised the Russian sable at a glance, had purred enthusiasm. The result was the hat of the week, with a sparkling clip the twin of one which glittered on her antelope bag, a chic short-sleeved black velvet frock with a coat for street and luncheon, cream chamois gloves, a string of synthetic pearls. Pamela — remembering the real gems she had sacrificed — flinched at those, but submitted — they were ravishingly becoming — and crowning extravagances, a pair of long gloves for evening and adorable shoes, smartly modern, fashionably impractical. She had spent the time while alterations were being made, in the beauty shop. She had emerged with a modish wave in her hair, a touch of perfume under one ear and a glaze on her nails like opaline glass.

"I'm here!"

Mallory wheeled. Regarded her incredulously. "What have you done to yourself? You look taller."

"High heels. Don't you like me taller?" She threw just the right amount of wistfulness into voice and eyes. Truly the decent to Avernus was as swift as it purported to be — and more heady.

Scott Mallory laughed. "Changed your line with your clothes, haven't you. Come."

To the accompaniment of the quick, stimulating syncopation of an orchestra, the major domo conducted them through a table-bordered lane with the air of one leading a legion into battle. Mallory responded to the greetings of a gay group. A smartly clad girl removed a cigarette from her lips with jeweled fingers. Hilda Crane! Pamela held her head a little higher. No chance of developing an inferiority complex in her present costume. This moment paid for all it had cost in money, all it would cost in labor.

"Scott!" Miss Crane cooed. Her eyes deep violet pools of amazement as she glanced at his companion. "Well, of all people! The cook!"

Mallory's eyes glowed like black coals as he took the seat opposite Pamela at a small table. A snowy Isle of the Blest. Not too wide for low voices to carry across nor hands to touch. Not too near the music. Not too deeply shaded by a synthetic palm. An old waiter, wise-eyed. Violets — a fragrant bunch with a gardenia heart. Candles, pink-shaded. Silver. Crystal. Roseate seclusion. A table in a thousand. A companion not inexperienced along the flowery paths of sentiment? Had he done all this for Hilda Crane, Pamela wondered as she lifted the lovely blossoms. She interrupted the order he was giving.

"Please! Not so much. Why spend our precious afternoon eating."

He revised the order. The major domo handed the slip to a minion. The minion scuttled away. Scott Mallory leaned forward.

"I'm sorry. You seem always to be the victim of the rotten manners of my one-time friend. Let's forget her." A laugh cleared his eyes and voice of annoyance. "Did you travel up from the Cape with a wardrobe trunk concealed about your person?"

"'The feel of Paris.' Like them?"

"The clothes? Mad about them."

She was conscious of a guilty accession of color. "These are not clothes. The frock and hat are a mammoth coffee tricolater. The electric ice-cream freezer—plus a few much needed kitchen utensils—completes the ensemble." His laugh brought her eyes to his.

"And it was only a short time ago you were wondering if you would forget how to spend money!"

"Ladies must dress. Then you are not shocked?"

"Shocked! My dear girl, I am inexpressibly relieved to find you so human. I had begun to fear that you were all saint and sacrifice."

"Me! There is something grammatically wrong with that exclamation, but we'll let it pass. All saint! That's funny. I was tempted and I fell. Crashed, is a better word. Besides what you see, I have a slinky frock the color of the gorgeous breast of an oriole for evening. I am sitting on the lid of my conscience at this very moment. Oh, I shall repent and pay and pay and pay—unfortunately Terry will too—when I struggle with inadequate equipment in the green and white kitchen. Let's forget my brainstorm."

"Just a minute. Breath-taking as you are now,

you will never look lovelier than in the white apron
and cap. You looked so young and troubled, yet
your eyes were so valiant that Thanksgiving day that
when I said good-bye, I felt as if I were heartlessly
abandoning an adorable child who was struggling
against fear."

"I remember that you called me, ' child.' "

"Not plain, 'child.' "

She leaned toward him. "Honestly now, how
could you call me ' plain child' ? "

His laugh was one of the nicest of the many nice
things about him, Pamela decided, his teeth were so
perfect.

"If a demure little Quaker had suddenly gone
tap-dancer I couldn't be more surprised. I didn't
know you had it in you."

"Dual personality. I told you that I shed my
work-day line with my linen frock. Hope you are
not disappointed."

"Disappointed? — Gorgeous! "

Her heart caught and plunged on. For a party
which was to be kept gaily impersonal that "Gorgeous" had been too deep, his eyes too ardent. Did
Cinderella suffer a warning ache at her heart, a,
"You know this can't keep on," reminder through
the gaiety and splendor of the royal ball and the
Prince's devotion? Silly to cloud the present when
she had recklessly mortgaged the future for this one
day. Did Scott suspect what she was thinking? His
eyes were tenderly amused as they met hers.

"Don't let a wraith from the past or the future

flit across our party, Pam. You won't be troubled by
a word you don't want to hear from this minute till
I leave you at the Silver Moon. Think I don't realize what I have to live down? That Thanksgiving
dinner for one thing. Think I didn't know when
you looked at the violets that you wondered if I had
given violets to Hilda — never, she preferred orchids. I've got to prove to you that I am naturally
a one-woman worshiper — when I find the right
woman. Get the idea? I know better than to
crowd my luck. It is luck to have you to myself for
a few hours. How are things going at the Silver
Moon?"

His casual question restored the equilibrium his
impassioned voice had undermined.

"Wonderfully. Each week sees an increase in
revenue. I had my staff up at daybreak this morning
to help me off. Hitty wished to be remembered to
Mr. Mallory, Terry sent his best, and the Babe his
love."

"Thanks. Makes me feel as if I had a family
which cared. I come of poor but honest parents —
wonderful parents." His voice had deepened, the
muscles of his mouth twitched as if he were master-
ing emotion. "I worked for my education, you
know. I am quite alone now."

She hadn't known. Not until this moment had she
realized how little he had told her about himself.
She was forever referring to her family. She grew
uncomfortably hot as she remembered Cecile's
scathing:

"You and your family—I was bored to death by your talk of what your ancestors had done."

Live and learn. Did one keep on blundering all through life? It seemed as if one ought to be wiser than she was at twenty-five. She watched the super-prosperous appearing men, the chic and sophisticated women who chatted and smoked and tasted at the flower bedecked tables to the accompaniment of violin and harp. They appeared care free and gay. Were they preoccupied with problems, perplexities, perhaps tragedies, behind their smiling masks?

"Come back!" Scott Mallory's laughing reminder interrupted her reflections.

"I'm sorry."

"Don't be sorry about anything today. Glad the Babe remembered to send me his love. He and I were great pals when we shared bachelor quarters."

"You must miss him. Why did you send him to us?"

"With all sorts of patrons driving up to the Silver Moon, thought you needed a dog while Terrence was at school. Feel safer about you, with the Babe there. He wouldn't stand for nonsense."

He would not indeed if his attack on Cecile were a criterion. What would Scott say if he knew of it? He wasn't to know of it; that was that. He was to know nothing of what had happened during the second Mrs. Leigh's visitation. Pamela thrust the heckling memory of it into the background as Mallory continued:

"The city is no place for a dog. The Babe was born near the sea. I bought him of a fisherman who had raised him from a little pup. The man's weather-bleached eyes were full of tears when he parted with him. He had to let him go because his son, who also was a fisherman, had abused the Babe until the dog showed his teeth whenever he came near. It wasn't safe to have him around."

From luncheon to a super-talkie, on to a portrait show. Conversation, real conversation about things which mattered. They two seemed never to lack interesting subjects for discussion. Long silences. Laughter. She told him of the plan for the cottage, touched lightly on Philip Carr's interest. Dinner and dancing.

She never had danced with him before. She had a sense of security as his arm went about her with disturbing possessiveness. The music was throbby, muted. The leader sang softly:

"'Should I reveal exactly how I feel
Should I confess I love you—'"

Scott Mallory's arm tightened. Pamela fought an impulse to lay her cheek against his—other couples were doing it—and stiffened. Instantly he loosened his hold.

"Happy?" he whispered.

She lifted her face. "Top of the world!"

The musicians crooned, saxophones wailed, violins soared and sighed. The dancers swayed, making, breaking colorful patterns. Everyone caught the contagion of the music. Everyone hummed:

"'Should I reveal exactly how I feel
Should I confess I love you.'"

In an intermission, above the babel of voices, a steeple clock ponderously told off the hour. Pamela smiled across the small candle-lighted table, sighed regretfully.

"We must go."

"So early? Is your fairy godmother lying in wait to snitch those swanky clothes at the stroke of midnight?"

Even as Scott Mallory protested, he held her coat, settled her sable scarf across her shoulders. His lingering touch sent a thrill feathering through her veins. Curious that the Cinderella motif should be in his mind as well.

"The Silver Moon is my fairy godmother. It watches out that I punch the time-clock when there is a full day ahead."

He signaled to the waiter. Pamela tried to appear sophisticatedly indifferent to the denomination of the greenback he laid on the tray and waved away. It seemed to her perturbed fancy that he had paid out a fortune since she had joined him for luncheon.

Money had Aladdin's Lamp beaten at its own game of magic, she reflected, as Mallory's shining roadster purred to the curb. Tucking in of rug. Touching of hat. Mumbled "Thank you, sir!" The slam of a door. They were off through streets twinkling with lights. A golden dome gleamed against an indigo sky for an instant and was gone. A beam from an air-beacon silvered roofs and leafless trees. In a pale tower a red eye flamed and faded. The river road. A line of lights hung like a glittering girdle where a bridge spanned water, kicked-up to white caps by a salty east wind. Buildings but vague outlines, their lighted windows — like the hundred eyes of Argus, fabled watch-dog of the gods — peered unwinkingly into the night. Moonlight glorified the unglorious, silvered factories and spires with lavish impartiality. The stars seemed nearer and brighter than the lights which gemmed the water-fronts and distant hills.

Glamorous night. Pamela drew a long sigh of content. Mallory bent to tuck the soft rug, which matched perfectly in color the morocco upholstery, more securely about her feet.

"Warm enough? Too much breeze?"

"It's heavenly."

"Happy?"

"Too contented to talk."

"Don't try. We have a long ride ahead. Better get a nap."

"Sleep! That last coffee was so strong it curled my eyelashes up tight. I shall be little bright-eyes for the rest of the night."

The road beckoned alluringly. A broad beautiful road, blanched by moonlight, jeweled with incandescents. Red lights warned. Green lights like cabochon emeralds beckoned. Spurts of conversation. Long, companion-conscious stretches of silence. Gay, amusing give and take of badinage. Far off the sound of a baying dog. Stars trembling on the obsidian surface of a lonely little pond. Houses with lighted windows. Scraps of gossamer mists in the hollows like fairy linen spread out to dry. A solitary horseman. Houses with no lights at all. Luminous shadows. Sooty shadows. A village like a toy town in the moonlight. Mallory slowed the roadster.

"See that white church and the dove-gray parsonage beside it: I helped put through a run-away marriage there before I went to South America, never have forgotten the place."

"Why the elopement? Cruel parents?"

"No. No one objected. The couple had planned a smash of a wedding. Both got nervous about it so slipped away by themselves. Have often wondered since if the wife ever regretted giving up the splurge."

"I doubt it. A large wedding is a terrific strain on a girl's disposition. The last time I was maid of honor, the bride — who really was sweet and lovely — had been lunched and dined, fitted and showered, till she was on edge. The emotional strain of the wedding was the last straw. She went to nervous pieces after the ceremony and snapped at her new husband. He was hurt to the soul. In a moment she was sobbing in his arms. He was dear, but — I've often wondered if the rapture with which he had looked at her at the altar ever again reached the same high peak."

"Would you be satisfied with a small wedding?"

Pamela remembered her father. "I shall be — satisfied not to have any — for some years — to come."

Mallory laughed. "You are half dead with sleep aren't you. It is cruel to keep you talking."

The roadster picked up, and like a racer demonstrating speed, shot forward.

Plans, thoughts keen as rapiers, thrust their way into Pamela's content. Fluffs of haze dulled them as clouds scooting across the moon toned its brilliance to a dream-like quality. A song hummed over and over, "Should I reveal exactly how I feel." Fragments of stories she had written, characters she never had conceived, kept breaking in on her train of thought, just as when tired after a full day at the Silver Moon, she would lose her place in her prayers and begin over, lose it, and begin again. Perhaps if she closed her eyes — heavenly not to have to hold her head up. She was snuggled in the corner of the big couch at home. She could feel the copper-toned damask against her cheek. And she had thought that she was motoring. She hadn't been to Boston. Spending the equipment money was a nightmare. Queer things, dreams. One could laugh and cry in them. Happy things sometimes. She could smell violets.

Light. Morning so soon. "Pam, dear!" Terry calling her? Not Terry. He would shout "Hi there!" She lifted heavy lids. Gazed straight up into a man's eyes. Their expression shocked her wide awake. She looked about her. The roadster had stopped. The porch light of the Silver Moon had wakened her!

"Have I slept all the way from Boston?" she asked contritely.

There was a husky break in Mallory's laugh. Was he surreptitiously flexing an arm as he stepped from the car? Had she slept against his shoulder?

"Not all the way. For the last fifty miles, that's all. Come on. Watch your step!" He caught her as she stumbled. "Sleepy child. You are not awake yet."

"I am, wide awake. My heart is as light as a balloon, a gay balloon. I feel as if the tide of fortune had turned. I know that there's a grand and glorious bit of good luck about to round the corner. That's what a day off has done for me."

The door was flung open. Every red hair of Terrence's head seemed on end as he waved a paper.

"Thought you'd never come! Boy! I'm glad you're here, Mr. Scott!"

"What's the matter, Terry?" Pamela caught his arm.

"Go slow, Terrence. You are frightening your sister. What has happened?"

"Father?" The word caught in Pamela's throat.

Terrence shook off her clutching fingers.

"Father! Nothing so simple. It's a summons! Cap'n Iry Crockett served it today! Cecile has attached this property for thirty thousand dollars!"

Chapter XI

PAMELA raced to her room to answer the telephone. More privacy there. Scott had told her last night that he would call her as soon as he found out why Cecile had attached the property. The summons had merely stated the fact. That summons! Its content was burned into her brain forever. If she closed her eyes she saw in great letters:

COMMONWEALTH OF MASSACHUSETTS
To Pamela Leigh

WE Command you that you appear at our Superior Court —

She must put the thing out of her mind! Her heart pounded as she held the receiver to her ear. "The Silver Moon. Pamela Leigh speaking. . . . Scott! What was it? . . . For alienation of Father's affection! Good grief! What can she do? . . . She can? . . . Oh, no, I won't worry. What's a paltry thirty thousand dollar suit in my young life? . . . I'm not laughing, I'm not hysterical. . . . No! *No!* Don't leave your work again this week! . . . I know you will, but I won't let you. Good-bye!"

She hung up the receiver on his eager, "Pam, listen!" Hands clasped hard on her knees she stared at the sand dunes steeping in the sunshine. Scott had called the New York lawyer, who had brought the suit, on long distance. He had explained that Mrs. Harold Leigh, known on the stage as Cecile Mortimer, was suing her stepdaughter for alienation of her husband's affection. Of course Cecile had thought that up the day she had come to the Silver Moon. Hadn't she departed on the threat:

"I will start proceedings for an allowance, but —before that, I will drag you into court, Miss Leigh!"

Scott had said, "Don't worry. I will look after it for you." And she had refused passionately, "I won't let you."

She wouldn't. Even in the instant of his communication of the facts something within her had protested against his aid. He had done enough for them in attending to her father's tangled affairs. It had troubled him last night to leave her with the summons unexplained, but he had been due in court this morning. She would not be a ball and chain hitched to him. To whom could she turn? Scott must have anticipated some such mix-up. When she had accused:

"You are afraid Cecile will try to get that money.

aren't you?" he had answered: "If it occurred to her as a lucrative possibility, she might."

Cecile had tried it. Was she counting on an easy settlement? Settle! Pamela Leigh settle! She wouldn't if she could. She would make Cecile prove that she had come between husband and wife. She shrugged. Bombast. Commendable but inane. How could she make her prove it without a lawyer and how could she retain a lawyer without money? Her father's bell. He must be told. What would be his reaction?

Harold Leigh frowned as she entered his room. Sunshine patched his green lounging robe with gilt, lay warmly on the stamp strewn table by the side of his chair. He demanded petulantly:

"What has happened? Something going on, I know. Terrence was jumpy when he brought up my breakfast. There isn't a tinge of color in your face. I heard you at the telephone. What is it?" He rapped an irritating tattoo on the table. It set the tiny, colorful squares of paper a-twitter like autumn leaves doing a double-shuffle in a sudden breeze.

Pamela crossed to the window. Eyes on the placid sea and cloudless sky she flung over her shoulder:

"Cecile has attached this property for thirty thousand dollars."

"Good God! What for?"

"She is suing me for alienating your affection." She wheeled to face him. "It's a joke, isn't it?"

"What do you mean —'joke'?"

"This alienation suit. You don't want her here, do you? You are mighty glad to get rid of her, aren't you? You know that I never have said a word to influence you. You will have a chance to testify to that in court."

"In court! I am not able to appear in a court room."

"Not to help me? Thirty thousand dollars for Cecile if she wins the case. Perhaps, though, you don't care. Perhaps you have a few more antiques you can turn into money with which to pay the verdict."

"What do you mean?" His voice caught in his throat. He pulled at the collar of his soft shirt before he went on: "I have no money. Mallory will handle the matter for us, of course."

"He will not! He won't let us pay him for the time he has already given our affairs."

"That is nothing. I've told you before that lawyers, like doctors, expect to do a certain amount of work for which they are not paid. Look at Phineas Carr! He is one of the biggest men in his profession. Think he never helped anyone out?"

Phineas Carr! It was the first time her father had mentioned his name since Grandmother Leigh's estate had been settled. Would Mr. Carr help her? What effect would that daring thought-contact have on her life? Tangle it more or help unsnarl it? There she was again thinking in plot terms. Suppose he consented to appear for her? She couldn't pay him. Yes, she could. The old maple. He was a lover of antiques. He had said there was nothing finer than the furniture her grandmother had left her. Forgetful of her father she started for the door. His fretful voice halted her at the threshold.

"You needn't take it so hard asking Mallory to help. He butted in on my affairs. I didn't ask him."

Shame scorched Pamela like a flame. Why didn't the hot tears behind her eyeballs come out and relieve the smart? She opened her lips to protest. Where did a voice go when it left one's throat, she wondered frantically. With an inarticulate murmur she fled.

Her heart and mind were still stinging from her father's caustic comment when she poked her head into the kitchen.

"I am going to the village, Hitty. I won't be long. I will do the marketing." She stopped in the living room to snatch the summons from her desk. She ran to the barn and backed out the sedan. Lucky Grandmother Leigh had left something besides the old flivver. She didn't dare stop a moment for fear she would lose her courage.

"Don't wobble!" she admonished herself sternly as she rapped on the front door of the Carr house. The sight of the rare brass knocker halted her stampeding courage. Phineas Carr was mad about antiques. Hadn't he said there was nothing finer than her old maple? Wasn't she giving him a chance to earn it?

She caught a glimpse of her slim, vivid self as she passed the gilt-framed mirror in the hall. She had forgotten a hat. The breeze had ruffled her hair, little dark curls twisted about her ears. She had caught up a yellow cardigan as she ran through the hall. Color instinct. It matched her linen frock.

She followed Milly Pike, whose eyes were round with surprise, to the open door of a room, the walls of which were covered with a curious old sporting paper, all dull browns and reds, with queer little bob-tailed rabbits and beefy hunters with over-developed muscles and under-developed raiment and wicked guns. Was there a swift gleam of apprehension in Phineas Carr's keen glance as he dropped the rod he had been examining and rose to greet her, or was it her hectic imagination? Without a preliminary word she laid the summons on the broad table littered with a sportsman's paraphernalia.

"Please read that and tell me what I ought to do."

He glanced through its contents. This time she was sure of the relief in voice and eyes.

"Sit down, Miss Pamela, and tell me what has happened. You needn't wait, Milly," he spoke sharply to the maid who lingered at the door.

Swiftly, breathlessly, Pamela told of finding the summons when she returned from Boston the evening before, of Cecile's suit for alienation. Phineas Carr looked at the paper.

"You didn't see this until midnight. It does not state what the attachment is for. How did you find out?"

"Mr. Mallory got in touch with Cecile's New

York lawyer — he said his name is Horace Hale —
and phoned me this morning."

"Mallory of Mallory and Carter? The young
man who has had the vision to specialize in South
American law?"

"I don't know about the specialization but he is
the Mallory of that firm."

"I have been watching him. Fine old Cape family. His father died when he was a boy. His
mother, brought up in luxury, took in sewing to keep
the home going. The lad worked his way through
high school, through college — majoring in lan-
guages. The war came. He went to Plattsburg.
Was sent across as First Lieutenant, came home as
Captain. Probably saved most of his pay for he
pushed through law school." Pamela remembered
Scott's, "poor but honest parents — wonderful
parents."

She said eagerly: "He must be brilliant to interest you in his career."

Phineas Carr brought his hand down with a
thump. "Interested! I'm envious as the devil. I
have a son, younger to be sure, but with as good a
mind if he would use it. He fooled through college,
lost his crew letter because his marks were low, now
he wants to plan houses. I admire the man, who,
without foolishly sacrificing health, has ambition to
push ahead of the herd and stay there." He drew
his hand across his eyes as if trying to brush away
an annoying memory.

"You don't trust your son enough." Pamela caught her breath at her own daring. Phineas Carr's brows almost obscured his eyes.

"I don't? Perhaps you're right, perhaps you're right, Miss Pamela. I've been thinking over his plan for getting an income out of the farmer's cottage. That is constructive. Wouldn't believe he had it in him."

"That's the trouble. You don't believe in him. He would do much better if you did. The knowledge that someone believes in one keeps one trying to make good."

He smiled. "Philip has an earnest champion in you, Miss Pamela. That is to his credit. When you came in I thought you had come to report that he had let you down on the cottage."

"You didn't really think I would come to complain of your son, did you? I came for advice."

"Forgive me, my dear." He tapped the summons with a long finger. "If you already have a lawyer why come to me with this?"

Pamela denied breathlessly: "I haven't retained him—isn't that the legal term—on this case, really I haven't. Scott Mallory has spent hours and hours on our affairs—of course you have heard of Father's debts—he won't let us pay him. Now along comes this abominable accusation. I am aching with shame about it. He will think me a girl with a sheriff forever at her heels—The Girl and the Sheriff—there's a title! I won't let him do it!

I can't pay him. I know that Father was insulting to you, but — but Grandmother Leigh adored you and I thought that if you would take the case — you might accept the old maple in payment." Her voice sounded humiliatingly beseeching in her own ears.

Phineas Carr drummed lightly on his desk. A ghost of a smile haunted his stern lips. " Mm. The old maple is a temptation. Were you and your father's wife friends before she left him? "

" I rarely saw her. But even if we weren't, what an absurd move for her to make. I would think that the case would be thrown out of court. There is no sense, no reason in it," Pamela declared passionately.

" There is rarely sense or reason behind an alienation suit; it's generally hysteria, or greed, or jealousy. You have only to follow the newspapers, my dear, to find that there are litigants — and lawyers — so sure that in that bright lexicon which Fate has reserved for the daring contestant there's no such word as fail that they will try anything. From what you have told me I deduce that your stepmother has devised a plan by which she may possibly gain money — by which at least she may vent her jealousy and dislike of you."

" Would a respectable lawyer take a case like that? "

" The man who is bringing the suit has little to lose if he is defeated, much to gain if he wins. Several times he has been spectacularly successful. Don't underestimate the advertising value of this suit both to your stepmother — she's an actress, isn't she — and her counsel. It would cost them thousands of dollars to get the same amount of publicity in the usual way. The case has, at least, the element of beauty which comes from extreme simplicity. Jealousy is an old emotion. It goes back to the first domestic triangle, Adam and Eve and Lilith. I don't like Hale, I've run up against him before, but I hand it to him for being keen. You realize, of course, that I cannot appear for you if Mr. Mallory has the slightest claim. You must explain this to him before I can file our answer in court."

She was on her feet, her eyes starry. "'Our answer'! Then you will take it?"

"If it can be ethically arranged."

Ethically arranged. The phrase rotated through Pamela's mind as she did her errands in the village. Her exultation oozed. Had she been horribly unfair to Scott to turn to Mr. Carr? She glanced at her wrist watch. How had she dared take so much of a great man's time? She frowned at the bulbous-eyed storekeeper who left the sugar he was weighing for her, to rush to the street to watch a plane which was circling.

"It's coming down!" he called over his shoulder. The men who had been huddled round the stove shuffled out to see it. Pamela resisted the temptation to join them. She had not yet become accustomed to the marvel of the gigantic birds of the air.

She might as well have gone, she told herself, as she watched the clock tell off the minutes. Five. Ten. Fifteen, before business was resumed and she could depart with her purchases.

Had Hitty deserted to see the plane, she wondered indignantly as she stopped the sedan at the back door and no gaunt figure made an immediate appearance. She lifted a heavy package.

"Let me take that!"

"Scott!"

She dropped the bag. Twenty pounds of sugar spread in a white drift on the ground between them. Surprise, an oppressive sense of guilt, the expression of Scott Mallory's eyes, set fire to her temper which was not of the steadiest these days.

"Now see what you've done! Walking up behind me like that!"

Mallory caught her elbows, lifted her over the sugar, swung her to the threshold of the kitchen.

"Methinks the lady hath a guilty color. Did you suppose I would stay in Boston when you hung up on my half-finished sentence? You don't know me. I chartered a plane and here I am to fight it out with you."

"You flew!"

He followed closely as Pamela backed into the kitchen. "What did you mean, ' I won't let you' ?"

She freed the hands he had caught tightly in his, clenched them behind her to steady their trembling.

"What I said, Scott. You have done enough for

us. I—I—have just re—retained Phineas Carr
to fight this case."

She shut her eyes for a moment to shut out his,
black, with little flames in them, in a white face.
Had she made him furiously angry? She couldn't
help it. This suit of Cecile's was only the last of a
long series of humiliations. She couldn't bear to
have him mixed up in it. This would end their
friendship . Wasn't that what she wanted? Hadn't
she an invalid father to support? Would she drag
him with his temperament into any man's life? Just
because her heart glowed whenever he smiled at her,
was no reason why others would forgive his moods.
Time she faced the fact that Scott Mallory had her
heart-fast, that her whole being responded passionately to his touch, to his voice.

"Carnation Carr! I am your legal adviser.
Carr won't take the case if he knows that. It
would be unprofessional."

She hadn't known that a human voice could be
so cold, that gray eyes could be so black, so inscrutable, that a fine hand could be so like iron on her
arm.

"I told him that I did not want you to appear
for me."

"What sent you to him? I thought he had given
up practising."

"He has, but Phil said—"

"Phil! Phil! So he's at the bottom of this! His
father is rotten with money. His mother has a

chain of power plants working for her. I have only what I earn. He is young and care-free. Already I have lived an ordinary lifetime of work. I am too old for you, of course. You think if his father takes the case you will see more of him!"

He dropped her arm. "You won't! I'll tell Carnation Carr to keep his hands off my business! I'll tell him now!"

Chapter XII

"MAKE the Babe stop wriggling, Terry, while I scrub his legs."

The sun brought out curious red-gold glints in Pamela's black hair, rouged the magnolia tints of her face and arms. A green rubber apron protected the front of her gay, sleeveless print frock as she vigorously applied a brush to the lavishly lathered dog who shivered violently in the galvanized iron tub set on a lawn, freshly, velvety, springily green. Terrence held the Babe's hindlegs down with one hand while with the other he grasped the leather strap about the black and tan neck. His red hair, ablaze in the sunlight, stood on end. His handsome face was crimson and moist from exertion.

"Easy enough to say. 'Make him stop wriggling.' Try it yourself." His indignation worked off in a chuckle. "Looks 's if he'd bust right out crying, doesn't he?"

A soft, salty breeze blew from the shore, picked up the scent of spring from the brown earth and danced on. Between house and barn a clump of white birches, with a vague misty aura of unborn leaves, murmured among themselves. Distant sand dunes gleamed like nuggets of gold in a lapis lazuli sea. Fluffs of feathery clouds, scattered haphazard over a radiant sky, added the last perfect touch, the dreamlike quality of a Daubigny pastoral. From somewhere in infinite space drifted the faint far drone of a plane. From the shore came the thud of hammers on wood, the voices of men. A tipsy bee lighted on the girl's bare arm. She cautiously brushed it off before she tenderly removed the lather from around the dejected Belgian's jaws.

"Cheer'o, Babe! The agony is almost over."

The dog shook himself violently. A monster dab of suds landed in Terrence's eye.

"Boy! That smarts."

Stinging discomfort loosed his hold. The Babe leaped to freedom. He dashed madly across the lawn, shaking himself as he ran, showering suds like foam from a water-wheel. He raced toward gaunt, grey Mehitable Betts coming from the poultry house with a basket.

"Go 'way, you pesky fella!"

Repulsed by her shrill squeak he ran toward Harold Leigh in a wicker chair in a sunny corner of the porch. Pamela scrambled to her feet.

"Why didn't you hold him, Terry? Hitty, who boasts that she 'ain't afraid of any man livin',' is frightened to death of a dog. Lucky she didn't drop those eggs when he charged at her. If he spatters Father there will be a riot."

The green and red parrot, sunning on his gilded perch, mewed like a cat. Mocked stridently:

"Bad boy!"

The dog barked furiously at his tormentor. Harold Leigh put hands to ears. Called fretfully:

"Terrence, make him stop that infernal racket!"

"Come Babe! Come!"

The dog started toward Pamela in answer to her call, noted the galvanized tub. With soapy tail between his soapier legs he streaked for the long, white barn. The girl pulled off the green apron.

"That's that. We won't see him again for a while. His first fisherman master must have sent him into the sea for a swim. The Babe has been perfectly trained in every way except in the little matter of being tubbed."

Terrence furiously blinked a smarting eye. "And giving the glad-paw to stepmothers."

His sister dropped to the warm, fragrant lawn, clasped her hands about her knees. Her eyes were troubled. "And that day I stood as if turned to stone and let him fly at Cecile. When she appeared in Cap'n Iry Crockett's flivver in a fisherman's slicker and sou'wester, I thought for an instant that she was a villager come to sell tickets for something. Suppose — suppose he had bitten her!"

"What started him after her? He's never showed his teeth before nor since."

"Instinct. He knew what she had up her sleeve. Suing me for alienating her husband's affection! Perhaps had I been politic the day she came here I might have staved this off. Father told her brutally that he did not want her. Why sue me? She claims that he wrote her that I had advised him that he was happier without her. I never talked with him on the subject of his wife, but when her lawyer produces in court that red-hot letter I wrote months ago, and Cecile is on the stand with her beautiful face and her moanin'-low voice, adorning her tale with all the trappings which seem to her good theatre, do you think those twelve men will believe anything I say?"

Terrence patted his sister's shoulder. "Kick frog! Kick! Lucky we got the loan for the cottage before she attached the house and the rest of the land."

Pamela sprang to her feet. "Lady luck had nothing to do with that, it was Scott Mallory's foresight. I know now why he pushed through that loan, he anticipated this possibility." She waited for Terrence's return from emptying the tub in the drive before she exulted: "The cottage is finished — except for a few shelves the men are putting up today — and furnished. Philip Carr has attended to everything for me, even selecting papers and fixtures in New York. Never could have done it myself, the Silver Moon has kept me so busy. It is rented too. I'm all excited. Rented by correspondence. If stationery doth proclaim the woman, the widow, Mrs. Isabelle Stevens, is the last word in fashion."

"What brand of widow? Heaven, Hell, or Reno?"

"She referred to her late husband, not her for-

mer. It is a nice distinction. Phil Carr says she is top
socially. A man he knows looked her up for me.
She has plenty of money and is renting for a
much longer season than we expected. I wonder
though——"

"What's on the little mind?"

"The fact that she wouldn't sign a lease. She
protested that her credit never had been questioned.
Phil Carr said, 'Grab her. She's good for it. You
won't pick another six-months' tenant in a blue
moon.' I knew that, so I took her but — sometimes
I wonder what Scott would say. He's such a demon
about having everything signed on the dotted line."

"Knock us for a gool if she did walk out on us
with that interest and the taxes to pay, wouldn't it?"

"Of course she won't walk out on us, Terry.
Let's drop it. I'm sick of the thought of money.
Since that clothes-orgy the day I went to Boston I
squeeze every nickel till the Indian on one side
whoops and the buffalo on the other bucks in protest.
Such extravagance! I've never worn the costume
since."

"You should worry. Got your money's worth
out of it that one day, didn't you?"

As in a flash-back Pamela saw the flower-bedecked
restaurant, saw Hilda Crane looking up at her with
amazed, appraising eyes. A little smile of gratifica-
tion twitched at her lips as she agreed fervently:

"I more than got my money out of it that one day,
Terry. But, just the same, I held my breath when

I hired Hitty Betts by the week, and the two Academy boys to wait on table seemed the last word in extravagance. However, one can't get out of business more than one puts into it, any more than a writer can write any better than he or she is inside. Our clientele has doubled. That's the answer. With Hitty to cook I have more time to superintend the serving. Things are looking up. If only — ooch!"

"Why the groan?"

Pamela laughed unsteadily. "The suit. Every time I think of it I fight and die in spirit. The wicked injustice, the uselessness of it. But, Mr. Carr says that suing for alienation of affection is epidemic this year, that one case spectacularly headlined, suggests to someone else a way to get satisfaction — perhaps — at least to vent spite. Besides that, the publicity is money in the bank for Cecile, even if she loses. He is confident that she can't win unless she bolsters up her case by perjury, that if her witnesses do lie the judge may hold them for conspiracy. A lot of good that would do me. Cap'n Iry Crockett gave Cecile the idea — when, innocently enough, he went lyric on the value of the land, when he told her that the Leighs never had occasioned a ripple of scandal. She thought we would settle rather than have her grievance aired in court — she had her plot. Know the best definition of plot? A problem and its solution."

"Cecile has furnished the problem and then some."

"And the solution is up to me. Philip Carr thought he was helping the day she was here, by championing me. He couldn't have picked a way to mix things more. Ossa on Pelion! That's flung in just so you and I won't forget our classics while digging at poultry-raising and housework, Terry. Of course I can't suggest that to him, he's such a dear. I see red with fizzy green pinwheels when I think of that suit. I, separate Cecile and Father! I wish she would kidnap him and take care of him for a while, she knows how to cook and do house-work, although she wants to forget that as a girl she had it to do. There's a dutiful daughter for you."

The boy laid his hand on her shoulder. "You are dutiful enough. You are too sweet to him. You let him walk over you if he shows a vestige of ap-preciation. Forget it! Carnation Carr will win out."

"I hope so! He is pulling every wire possible to have the case set down for immediate trial. Wants to get it behind us. Cecile's lawyer has hinted — broadly hinted — at settlement. My at-torney won't listen. She cheated about the opera-tion and squeezed money out of Father — it was all right if he had it to give her — the money, not the cheating. Mr. Carr is determined that she shall get none out of me."

Terrence clasped his hands about one knee. "Found out yet where Father got the cash he paid the second Mrs. Leigh?"

"No. When he told me that he had sold the 'antique,' he seemed so appreciative of what you and I had done for him that I just couldn't ask questions."

"Of course you couldn't, I know you. You probably patted his hand and smoothed his hair. I've never tumbled to your reason for turning old Scott down on this court stuff. He's been such a swell guy to us."

Pamela dug viciously at a dandelion which had adventurously stuck its leaves above ground.

"That was the reason. He had done so much for us that I wouldn't let him do any more. We never can pay him."

"How are you going to pay Mr. Carr? They say in the village that one of his fees makes the income tax of a successful business man look like an atom."

"With the old maple."

"Will he take it?"

"He thinks it the finest in the country."

"I'll hand it to you for having nerve to suggest it. If you were going to dispose of the stuff, why not sell it and pay Scott Mallory?"

"You don't understand, Terry! I just couldn't bear to have him know any more about our sordid, debt-logged lives."

Terrence dug his heels into the turf. "Perhaps you're right. I guess he was pretty well fed-up with the Leighs' hard-luck problems. Hasn't been here since the day you spent in Boston, come to think of it, has he?"

What would Terry say if he knew of that stormy interview the day Scott had flown from the city? Pamela corrected hastily:

"I have seen him once. He has been in California and in Mexico. He is the traveling member of the firm, I judge."

"I miss him. He's a great boy." Terrence jumped to his feet. "I'm parking here as if this were a henless world. Gee, I wish it were! If there is any creature on God's earth dumber than a hen, lead me to it!"

"Nothing dumb about that fierce rooster you've dubbed the White Hope. He flew at me as I passed the gate of his yard this morning. I was thankful that there was a wire netting between us."

Terrence grinned. "A dozen like him would repel an advancing army. They'd make good shock troops. He's some bird." He lifted the tub to his shoulder. "Phil Carr showing up today?"

"Tonight. To check up on the cottage, wants to make sure everything is according to contract."

"Check up is good, but not good enough. He hasn't been chasing to the wilds of Cape Cod every week-end because he's all excited about making over the cottage, nor because you've given his father a job, believe it or not. Woman, unless you like him a lot, watch your step." He scowled at her darkly as he quoted the temperamental Mrs. Micawber.

"'All I say is, remember what I say now, and when I say I said so, don't say I didn't.'"

"Terry, you are a hang-over from the nineteenth century! What young person reads Dickens now?"

"I'd rather spend an hour with him than with many of the people I know." He grinned tormentingly. "Think over my tip about Philip Carr. He's a good sport. I like him even if he can't see anything approaching in skirts — young or old, fat or lean — without settling his tie and squaring his shoulders." He shifted the weight of the tub before he asked awkwardly, "You don't suppose he is the reason old Scott has stopped coming, do you?"

"Of course not and I wish you would stop calling Scott Mallory 'Old Scott.' He is only thirty-five."

"Didn't know you were so touchy about his desertion. I'm sorry."

"I'm not touchy, Terry Leigh. I would rather he didn't come. I have no time to spend with him. Doubtless he is running round evenings with Hilda Crane. She is light-weight enough to be mental relaxation for the tiredest attorney at law."

"Meow!"

"It was catty. And I was hateful to you too. You have been such a dear, Terry, about my having spent all that equipment money on myself. Grandmother Leigh used to say, 'I am a jelly fish in paradise with money in my pocket among the shops.' I'm just like her. No sales resistance."

"There you go again, re-morse. Why shouldn't

you spend it? You earned the most of it. You need a change of scene more than anyone I know."

" I won't leave the Silver Moon again. So long as I keep plodding I am all right. Life seems to be just the bursting of one iridescent soap-bubble after another. Nothing but dampish spots left."

Terrence shouted with laughter. " Orphan Annie! You're low, aren't you? "

Pamela flushed. " I'm a poor sport, that's what I am. If the trial of this fiendish case doesn't come along soon I shall begin to scratch and bite. I feel as if we were walking on the thin crust above a volcano which might blow-up at any moment. Cecile is capable of springing anything. Run along and forget your disagreeable sister." She turned to wave and smile at him before she entered the kitchen.

" At this hour watch-out for storms! " she warned herself as she noted the clamped lips of Mehitable Betts who was forcefully wielding the rolling-pin at the porcelain-topped table. The gaunt woman's mouth was an unfailing barometer of the state of her temper. Better to ignore the storm-signal.

Pamela observed chattily as she tied on an apron: "The rhubarb plants are showing pink above ground. Won't be long before we can add your marvelous tarts to our menu. They will make our patrons sit up and take notice."

" Hmp! I guess somebody else'll be making those tarts."

Apparently deaf to the prophecy Pamela hummed as she washed lettuce.

" ' Should I reveal exactly how I feel
      Should I confess I love you — ' "

With the words came the memory of the gaily
lighted restaurant, the feel of Scott's arms about
her. Her heart ached intolerably. She had not
seen him since the day he had stormily announced
that he would warn Phineas Carr to keep his hands
off his business. Mr. Carr had told her casually
that he had talked with Mr. Mallory, that after
some discussion it had been agreed that it would be
better if he — who was so near — were to handle
the suit. Inconsistently she had been fiercely hurt
that Scott had dropped her case so easily.

"Guess you didn't hear me say I might not be
here to make rhubarb tarts."

The sharp voice cut into Pamela's absorption.
The proprietor of the Silver Moon Chowder House
had little time for sentimental regrets — fortu-
nately. What line would she better take? She
would like to tell Hitty Betts to pack up and remove
herself and her temperament from the kitchen. She
couldn't do that. She needed her. She must be
diplomatic. Diplomacy! She was tired of being
tactful with her father, with Hitty, with fussy patrons.

"What is the matter? I thought you liked working at the Silver Moon."

"I like it well enough and I like being with you,
Pamela, but, there can't be but one skipper on a
ship and you're my boss. I won't take orders from

Harold Leigh and he'd better up and learn that or I walk out."

"Orders from Father! What has he been telling you to do?"

The surprise in Pamela's voice was oil upon a troubled sea. Miss Betts calmed down. "I thought you wouldn't approve. While you and Terry were washing the dog he wanted me to leave my work an' walk to the post-office in the village to mail an important letter. Postmaster Highty was sayin' that he has a powerful lot of correspondence for a sick man. Sick! He's well and he don't know it!"

Another surreptitious letter? Was her father in correspondence with Cecile? Was he taking sides with her against his own daughter? He wouldn't do it. She must not harbor that suspicion for an instant. Then what was going on? She felt as if she were living in a dream with a nightmarish mystery drifting wraith-like just beyond reach. She thrust the question into the back of her mind. Her first task was to placate her dour but invaluable handmaiden.

"You were right, Hitty. It takes not-seriously sick persons to make cracker-jack executives, doesn't it? They can't move about themselves but how they can plan activities for others. Every manufacturing plant ought to have its efficiency invalid — with a bell to tinkle. Forget it. You know that I don't want you to do a thing beyond your strength."

Mehitable sniffed. "I know you don't, Pamela.

You're real thoughtful. And you've got a hard row to hoe. Folks is sayin' that when your case comes to trial the verdict's likely to go against you, spite of the fact that you have one of the smartest lawyers in the country trying for you. Don't see how you ever got him. 'Course everyone knows that Phil Carr's your beau, but everyone knows too that Phineas and your Pa quarreled something terrible. Well's I was sayin', your Pa has been so snifty with friends he knew as a boy that they won't have much pity for him if they get on the jury."

" Why should the jury decide against me because some members of it do not like Father? He isn't being sued. I am."

" I know, but, they think he's hiding behind you, that he got tired of the stage woman and left her in the lurch as soon as he lost his money." She cleared her throat. A sure sign that she was about to hurl a gossip bomb. Pamela unconsciously braced. " Who do you think's arrived at the Inn with a maid, and a trunk full of clothes and a car an' all?"

" Who? "

" That Crane girl. Came last night. Milly Pike saw her and then the whole village knew it. It's her sister that's taken your cottage and she's come ahead to get things started."

" Her sister! Mrs. Isabelle Stevens Hilda Crane's sister!" Through Pamela's memory swept Scott Mallory's comment: " A rich woman who spends her income before she gets it and is everlastingly being sued by creditors." She had rented the cottage to a woman like that without a lease! Hilda Crane in a cottage at their very door. Oh, what a snarl, what a confounded snarl!

Pamela carefully examined each crisp green leaf before she dropped it into the cheesecloth bag. If only she could talk the situation over with Scott. That was the one thing she couldn't do. His eyes had had the most curious effect the few times she had been with him before their clash over the handling of the alienation suit. It was as if they held her, while she struggled, powerless to escape. Why look at her like that if he didn't care enough about her to come to see her? Was he that type? Afraid of being caught in the snare of matrimony? Quite ready to philander where the going was safe? Her sense of justice pinched her sharply. Suppose Scott were to tell her he loved her? She would refuse to listen. She would not permit him to come again. Keeping a home for her father was a full-time contract. She should be glad that he had stopped coming. She must put him out of her life sometime, the sooner the better.

"If you haven't anything to do but stare out of the window, Pamela, you might get the butter balls made. I haven't but one pair of hands. Getting to be an awful lot of work round here."

"I know it, and we really need a waitress, Hitty. The Academy boys do well but they can't come every day." Pamela hated herself for the placating tone. Fear of losing Hitty was undermining her boasted independence. "I will try for a girl in the village. I wish I might find one as perfectly trained as Milly Pike."

"M's Carr taught her, but how she stands her round beats me. Curious! Why you can see that girl's ears stand right out when she's listening. She tells everything she hears, that's the worst of it. Have you heard that M's Carr's sister's sick and she's gone to be with her? Folks is sayin' they don't see how she dared go and leave Phil and his father without being there to step between. They get on about as well as that green and red parrot an' that pesky dog would if they were shut up in a room together. She's been a sort of buffer ever since the boy grew up."

"Perhaps Mr. Carr is too stern." Pamela tilted a lance in Philip's defense as she deftly manipulated unsalted butter.

"Stern! He's a disappointed man." Miss Betts held a pie plate on the palm of one hand while she expertly pared pastry dough with the other. "Thinks a lot of handing on the name. He is a big lawyer, even foreign countries tried to get him to represent them. His health broke from overwork and he restored the old Carr place and settled down a few years ago, that is if you can call being in Europe most of the time settlin' down. He must be a lot better to take your case. Phil came along when he was about forty. He had all sorts of plans and dreams, sure the boy was goin' to be a lawyer. I guess he visioned him Chief Justice of the U.S."

"If Philip's taste was for architecture it would have been a crime to have forced him into law."

"He wasn't forced. Folks is sayin' that— Land's sake! Is Judgment Day a-com—"

Her voice was drowned in the frenzied clatter of an engine, the lugubrious bellow of a horn. She and Pamela crashed as they met in the doorway. A coughing, spitting flivver wheezed into the drive, whirled in a crazy circle and charged at the back porch like an infuriated, if consumptive, bull. It sliced off one side of the trellis before it whipped around and lunged at the woodshed. Eddie Pike gripped the wheel, his sister clung to his arm. His vacuous blue eyes bulged like glassies as he shouted:

"Whoa! Back up! Let go, Milly! You're twisting the steerer!" The chalky-faced girl shrieked as the car described a circle on two wheels and with demoniac intent rushed uproariously for the porch again. Pamela emerged from a trance of amazement.

"Shut off the engine, Eddie! Shut off your engine!"

"Now, whoever let that half-baked idiot get a license!" rasped Mehitable Betts as the flivver veered, gouged up the gravel in an about-face turn and with a backfire which would have been no mean accomplishment for a baby Big Bertha, bucked convulsively and shed its forward wheels. Man and girl catapulted through space where once had been a windshield. "There, he's stopped it."

"Stopped it! I'll say he has." Pamela's voice

was choked with laughter as she ran toward the car. "You are not hurt are you, Milly?" she asked, as the girl, with hat smashed over one eye, crawled from the wreck. Miss Pike cast a murderous glare at her brother as she restored her headgear to its usual coquettish angle.

"'Tisn't Eddie's fault that I'm not. He paid ten dollars for that flivver —"

"And got cheated at that," interrupted Mehitable Betts grimly as she tried to restore the splintered trellis to place. "What you doing riding round in racing cars this time a-day, Milly Pike?"

Milly wrinkled her nose at gaunt Miss Betts' sarcasm before she turned to Pamela.

"I came for the eggs, Miss Leigh. Eddie offered to bring me to save time. It isn't his fault I'm not doing time in a hospital. Is Terrence anywhere around?"

"Terrence!"

With Pamela's echo of the name came the memory of her distrust of the girl, so pretty, so vital, so — cheap.

"I will get the eggs for you, Milly. My brother is at school."

Eddie Pike looked up from the wreck he had been studying to scowl at his sister.

"Don't you go chasing after Terry, Milly. Terry's a fine boy. Shan't stand for you hangin' round him like you've been hangin' round Phil Carr lately."

Chapter XIII

After all, this morning Eddie Pike had not accused Phil Carr of "hanging round" Milly, it was just the reverse, Pamela comforted herself as she curled up in a corner of the couch in the living room. Light from the floor lamp brought out the splashy pattern in the pale green Chinese damask of her frock, illumined the pile of magazines on the stand beside her. She was through work early tonight. She would have three whole hours in which to read.

The fire snapped companionably. The Babe, stretched at length on the hearth-rug, cocked one ear as a vine brushed against the window-pane, like tapping fingers begging for entrance. From the radio upstairs thundered the music of one of the stormier symphonies. Its sweep, its strength, its passion, set Pamela's pulses throbbing like muted drums; made her feel like a small and lonely soul battling a tempest of emotion. She tried to shake off the effect as she absentmindedly turned the pages of a magazine, her eyes on the copper and blue flames. Of course what Philip Carr did was nothing to her, but she liked him. It would be unbearable if he were to

mess up his life for a silly girl like Milly Pike. His
mother was away. Would he be furious were she
to speak to him about it? What business was it of
hers what he did? He was a man grown. He had
been wonderfully helpful about the cottage, sympathetically understanding of her turmoil of mind in
regard to the lawsuit. His father had been right;
he was more artistic than practical. She had made
a mistake when she took his advice about the tenant.
Commonsense should have told her that a woman
who refused to sign a lease would be irresponsible.
What would Scott say? Song sparrows, robins,
redwing blackbirds, meadow larks and purple lin-
nets had appeared since he had been at the Silver
Moon. Last night she had heard a hermit thrush.
The arrival of the birds would have recorded the
passing of the weeks even had she forgotten. Was
he still furiously angry? She had had a few clean-
cut business letters from him, that was all. She had
not answered them; they had not called for a reply.

A car sweeping up the drive? Scott? Of course
not. It would be Phil in his creamy yellow roadster.
He was coming to report on his check-up of the
cottage.

She heard a step on the porch, ran to the front
door and opened it. "How is our talented boy
archi — Scott!"

Mallory stepped by her into the hall. He dropped
coat and hat on the settle. As he waited for her to
precede him into the living-room his face was curiously colorless, his eyes inscrutable. He said lightly:

"Sorry to disappoint you. I take it you expected Carr."

Pamela returned to the couch corner. A safe and sane refuge in time of trouble. The symphony above crashed in a stupendous finale; the music was like fingers pressing hard at her throat. Mallory backed up to the fire. His height and sternness caught at her breath. The deep lines between his nose and the corners of his mouth had not been there before. She struggled for nonchalance as she asked:

"When did you return from your coast to coast trip?"

"Just back."

"Was it successful?" She felt as if she were editing a question and answer column.

"Yes."

Silence, unbridgeable silence, rising, rising like a Chinese wall between them. What did one say, what could one say to a man who had left one furiously angry?

"Did you — you find people stirred up over the political situation?"

"Not especially. The country is still fundamentally sound," Mallory assured curtly.

She had reached the end of that line. What next? Stupid of her to be so dumb. Had he lost interest in her or was his attitude merely a carefully thought-out defense mechanism? Pamela crashed blindly through the wall of reserve.

"Don't be so wooden! Why did you come if you have nothing to say?"

He became absorbed in lighting a cigarette. "I have been asking myself why I came ever since you greeted me at the door, thinking I was Carr."

She caught her lips between her teeth to steady them as memory seared like lightning. Hilda Crane had arrived at the Inn today. Scott was here for the first time in weeks! A coincidence? Not likely. She forced her voice to lightness.

"Phil was to check up on the cottage and report that everything was as per contract before I made the last payment. Our Tenant — Terry and I speak of her with a capital T — moves in tomorrow."

"Really!"

Nothing wooden about him now, his eyes were alight with interest, his smile was heart-warming. Pamela felt as if she had been transported into a patch of sunlight.

"That's great. Who is it?"

"Mrs. Isabelle Stevens."

The muscles of his face hardened, his eyes narrowed. Did Mallory of Mallory & Carter look like that when cross-examining a witness? No wonder he won cases.

"Not Mrs. Isabelle Stevens of New York? Hilda Crane's sister?"

She nodded. His change of expression had done things to her voice.

"Where did you get hold of *her?*"

"She wrote to me. Why do you ask so many questions? Philip Carr had her looked up. She is impeccable socially. Has heaps of money and—a charming sister."

He regarded her steadily. "I suppose young Carr drew your lease or did his father—your present legal adviser—attend to it?"

It had come! She might have known that it would. "I—I—haven't any lease." That break in her voice was equivalent to an admission of guilt, Pamela realized furiously.

"What!"

Mallory caught her by the shoulders, drew her to her feet. He administered a shake, too slight to be actionable, but unmistakably a shake.

"Don't tell me, Pam, that you have let your cottage to that woman without any legal hold on her."

She met his blazing eyes defiantly. "Why do you call her 'that woman'? She has money, she has social standing. You don't for a moment believe that she will back out at the eleventh hour and leave me financially in the lurch, do you?"

"That's just what I believe! Don't get me wrong. She isn't planning to do it now. She is a woman who spends her income a year, sometimes two, ahead; she is always in arrears. She gets by because she is so wealthy that dealers lift the price to pay them for waiting for their money. There are worse but also less exasperating women. You can't afford to let your house to a person like that. You've got to meet your interest."

"Phil said—"

"I don't care what Carr said. We've got to get that woman out of the cottage before the renting season is over or make her pay in advance."

"We!" He was still interested. Pamela caught the lapel of his coat.

"Scott, I'm terribly sorry to have been so unbusinesslike. Way down deep, I knew that I ought to have a lease, but, I was so eager to rent the cottage. The prospect of six months' tenancy went straight to my head — we had figured on three, four at the most — I planned to make a payment on the mortgage."

His eyes smiled warmly into the troubled depths of hers. With gentle fingers he brushed back a strand of her hair which had escaped from the smooth wave to stray over her forehead. He reassured:

"Don't worry. I'll straighten it out."

"Phil said —"

Mallory's eyes hardened. He moved abruptly to the fireplace. "If you mention Carr's name again I'll beat him up for letting you in for this mess. He ought to have known better. Why didn't you consult his father?"

"He is doing enough for me."

"Terribly afraid that someone will help you, aren't you? I —"

Voices on the porch. Whom had Phil brought with him, Pamela had time only to wonder, before the front door swung open.

"Oh, Pam! Here's the sister of the Tenant! Wants to ask you some questions about the cottage.

She is here to get things started. How are you, Mallory? When did you get back?"

"Scott!" Hilda Crane paused effectively on the threshold. Her blonde hair was exquisitely dressed; her reddened lips were parted in an ecstatic smile; her eyes were deeply, darkly purple; a wrap of ivory satin only partially covered an azure frock.

"Scott!" In a little rush she was across the room, both hands clasped about his arm, the sophisticate gone ingenue. "It is wonderful to see you. You were marvelous to come the moment I arrived. Did Miss Cryder give you my message that Belle had taken the Leigh cottage?"

A steel hand closed ruthlessly over Pamela's heart. Had he known when he came tonight that Hilda Crane's sister was her tenant? He was an excellent actor. How she hated men.

"I have not been to the office since my return. Drove straight here from New York. What lured Belle to this Sleepy Hollow? She won't find many card players here."

Miss Crane smoothed his sleeve. He freed his arm and poked the fire. She pouted:

"You don't seem a bit thrilled at my coup, Scott. Belle is planning to have you with us every moment you can spare. In spite of the fact that you have ground the money for some long due bills out of her, she adores you. She will have her cronies coming and going. The doctor recommended a quiet summer and I thought of this place."

"When does she come?"

"Tomorrow. She is motoring from New York. You look worn to the bone. Have you been working terribly hard?"

He put his hand to his face. "I've driven over three hundred and sixty miles today. I'm dusty. I want to see Belle the moment she arrives." He turned to Pamela. "Is your father still up? I would like to talk with him."

"I think so. I will find out."

Pamela was thankful for an excuse to escape from the charged atmosphere. Philip Carr had been patently seething with resentment at Scott Mallory's curt greeting. She herself had been unbearably hurt at Hilda Crane's monopoly of Scott.

Her father, who was reading, frowned at the interruption as she entered the room. "Now, what is it?"

"Mr. Mallory wants to talk with you."

"What is he after?"

"He didn't say. Perhaps to persuade you to produce more antiques."

It was an aimless answer, a shot in the dark, one of those things one flings out when one is in a mental turmoil, for the sake of something to say. Pamela was totally unprepared for its effect. Her father's face turned livid.

"What do you mean, 'more antiques'?"

She shrugged. "Nothing, absolutely nothing. It was a fool remark. Will you see Mr. Mallory?"

"Tell him to come up."

Had Scott heard his loud voice? He was half way up the stairs when she met him. He caught her hand.

"What was he saying to you?"

Before she could answer, Philip Carr appeared at the newel post in the hall below.

"Come on, Pam. The younger set is going to the speakies in the village. We'll leave the old duffers to talk business."

With a muttered imprecation Mallory dropped her hand. He took the stairs two at a time. Pamela lingered.

"You look a hundred per cent better, Mr. Leigh," she heard him say before he closed the door.

"That was a bad start. Father will be furious that anyone considers him physically improved," she thought before she joined Philip Carr. Hilda Crane was standing beside him. She said playfully:

"Go on, you two children. I will wait for Scott to take me home."

Had she waited, Pamela wondered the next morning. When she had returned from the village the house had been quiet, no sound except the weird stirring of an old board or two. There was a scrap of pale blue chiffon on the living room couch. The handkerchief gave out a faint scent of *Nuit de Noel* as she picked it up.

As she prepared grapefruit for breakfast she tried to shut out the picture of the man in front of the fire with the blonde girl clinging to his arm. She would much better consider what she should do about her unreliable tenant. It seemed incredible that a woman of wealth would be unable to pay the comparatively small rent of that cottage. If she didn't —

"What are you exclaiming 'ooch' for at this time in the morning," demanded Terrence from the foot of the stairs. "What's gone wrong now in this vale of tears?"

Should she tell him what Scott had said about the Tenant? Why worry him?

"Did I groan? Must have bubbled up from my subconscious where I park that maddening old alienation suit. Take the grapefruit into the dining room, Terry. I will bring the coffee and muffins."

The green and red parrot executed a clog on his gilded perch as she entered.

"Look who's here!"

Pamela laughed. "Not so much to look at, Mephisto. Who do you think called last night, Terry?"

The youth's eyes met in a sharp frown. "Not Milly Pike?"

"Milly Pike! Of course not. Why did you think of her?"

Terrence's ears were unbecomingly red. "She's been racing up for eggs about every other day. Who came?"

"Miss Crane with Philip Carr. I wonder where they met — somewhere socially of course, he knows people in all the large cities. Ostensibly she came to inquire about details of the cottage — she forgot her questions when she saw Scott Mallory."

" Did he come? When did he get back? "

"Yesterday. Terry, I didn't intend to tell you, but, I've got to talk with some — I — "

" Hold on a minute before you confide the mistakes of your young life. Car coming up the drive." He dashed to the window. " I'm getting so rural I just have to see the pass. It's old Scott in that black and red roadster. Gee, how it shines! "

Why had Scott come this morning, Pamela wondered, as she saw him step from his car. He had the best taste in clothes of any man she knew. His gray suit, with a blue shirt and tie were immensely becoming. Last night he had seemed travel-fagged and worn. This morning his face was unlined, his skin was as fresh as a boy's. His eyes and mouth flashed into a smile as he saw Terrence at the window. The youth had the door open before he reached it.

" Come in, Mr. Scott. We're at breakfast. Join us? It's great to have you back."

Mallory flung his arm about Terrence's shoulder as they entered the room together. His eyes as they met Pamela's had the no-surrender glint she had come to know and dread. " Unflinching," was the word her father had used.

" I have breakfasted, thanks. Pam, I have some documents for you to sign."

" Documents! "

Terrence looked from one to the other. "Like me to do a fade-out, Mr. Scott?"

"No. I will give you a real estate lesson." He took two papers from his pocket. "These are the leases for the cottage, Pam. Read them. Are they correct as to time and price?"

Pamela blinked several times before she came to the place for the signature. He still was interested enough in her to care. She looked up.

"Quite right. Don't think I'm so stupid as not to have tried for a lease, Scott. She just wouldn't agree to one, that's all."

He held out his pen. "Sign. Witness her signature, Terry." He waited for the ink to dry. Folded the papers and slipped them into his breast pocket.

"Mrs. Isabelle Stevens will sign these, hand over a cheque to cover advance payment, or she won't get into the house. She will find me parked on the front steps when she arrives. I have had dealings with her before." He caught Pamela's hands close in his. "For a hard-boiled business woman you need someone to look after you more than anyone I know."

Terrence coughed. Mallory laughed. "Sorry, Terry! It shan't happen again — at present. Good morning. I'm off to hold-up the Tenant on her porch." He paused on the threshold.

"When I come back I will have a cheque for you, or a cottage for you to rent. Guess which, Miss Pamela Leigh."

Chapter XIV

SUNSET in Fairyland, the Silver Moon in the lap of
May, apple trees like gigantic pinky pom-pons.
Lilacs: yellowy whites, purples, dusty maroons and
rosy orchids bordering the picket fence; yellow-
throated vireos, flitting through them, twittering
as they flew; somewhere in the orchard a thrush
singing his heart away.

Seated on the step of the porch Pamela clasped
her hands softly in her lap. Heavenly music. She
might not hear it again this year; it was time for
the singer to fly north. She drew a deep breath of
air freighted with the perfume of lilacs. She looked
from the riot of blossoms to her frock, shaded yellow, orange and flame like the breast of an oriole,
to the sparks in the synthetic topaz in her bracelet.
Her heart spread plumy wings. That streak of
blue through the orchard, the mellow green of the
lawn, the lemon and rose of the afterglow, the lights
like misty opals in the village, the heathery tinge of
distant cranberry bogs, the gold of the star just
above the horizon, the ultramarine sea, the silver of
the dunes, set her pulses thrumming, set her very
soul afire. Curious how deeply color moved her.

She gently stroked the Babe's head as he snuggled his nose against her knee. His eyes closed spasmodically; his body sagged as he succumbed to sleep; he braced, relaxed, braced again. The girl's dreamy gaze was on the purplish column of smoke which spiraled from the cottage chimney. A fire-worshipper with no need to economize on wood, was the Tenant. Was Mrs. Belle Stevens paying her bills in the village? Over a month now since the day Scott Mallory had returned from the cottage to the Silver Moon with a signed lease and a cheque for advance payment on the rent. His eyes and voice had been grim as he advised:

"The next time you rent property consult a lawyer, not an architect."

He had left her staring unseeingly down at the slip of paper vainly trying to think of a reply which would be sufficiently appreciative without sounding as if she were a penitent, prostrate at his feet.

She had not seen him since. From Hilda Crane and her sister, who had discovered a contract affinity in Harold Leigh, she heard that he had been frequently at the Inn in the village, that business had taken him often to New York City.

Had she known that it was Hilda Crane's sister who was hiring the cottage, that she would have the girl whom she thoroughly disliked and distrusted, for a neighbor all summer, would she have leased it to her? Silly question. Of course she would. One didn't permit one's emotions to nuzzle opportunity aside when one had interest and taxes to meet. Besides, the Tenant was a lavish patron of the Silver Moon. Forewarned by Scott, she had firmly, if smilingly, refused credit at Mrs. Stevens' first visit, had explained that she had to conduct her business on a cash basis. The wealthy, but financially skiddy, widow had graciously complied with her terms and had come again and again. Now that Scott had stopped coming, what difference did it make where he went? Each morning when she awoke her first thought was:

"Was I right or have I needlessly sacrificed a friend?"

Right or wrong, Phineas Carr would appear in court for her. The trust and confidence she had had in him when he was her grandmother's adviser, had returned, strengthened twofold during the interviews in which he had instructed her as to her part in the trial. Counsel for the prosecution would present the plaintiff's case first, it was up to the defense to shoot holes through it, he had explained. Leigh vs. Leigh was marked for next week, he had told her this morning. Occasionally, like an echoing step a long way off, would come the remembrance of her impression that somehow, in some way he would change the pattern of her life.

A soft light stole over the apple trees — those beautiful trees on which blossomed the promise of next year's taxes — a light all pink, yellow, amethyst and silver, delicate as malines, colorful as a fairy rainbow, a radiant wash of gold on the tops, flickering, unearthly shadows below.

The letter crushed in her free hand recaptured Pamela's attention. If Scott had not come he had written. The contents pertained to her father's finances to be sure, but he had not forgotten the troublesome Leighs. She spread out the sheets. As she read she could hear the vibrant tones of his voice, see his amused eyes, feel his hand settling the fur about her shoulders. Heart-warming to be near him even in spirit.

No word about the suit—perhaps already he approved the wisdom of her decision—no word except about business until the end. He wrote:

Your father may be interested to know that I attended a stamp auction in New York week before last. Not to buy for myself, in the interest of a client. The place would have provided you with material for an article. Atmosphere to burn. Seats arranged like those in a small theatre, a few prospective bidders scattered about absorbed in catalogues. A black velvet stand illumined by a skillful arrangement of lights. The auctioneer in the shadow, his face a ghostly blur. He seemed indifferent, but he caught every signal almost before it was given. Was it uncanny intuition or years of practice? The room filled for the great smash in the lot. It was an English, 10 shilling, King Edward stamp overprinted I.R. Official.

Sold for two thousand dollars! Tell your father about it. Probably he knows all the royalties in the stamp world and won't be surprised. I'll confess that the value of that small square of paper rocked my mind. Suppose I had dedicated my career to collecting instead of to law? I might have been a millionaire by this time.

                              Sincerely yours,
                                 SCOTT MALLORY.

"Sincerely yours." The stereotyped phrase hurt Pamela even as she assured herself that she had deliberately cut off any chance of a warmer ending. He thought Philip Carr's money would be a lure for her. Better for him to think so. She tucked the letter inside her frock as she gazed across a strip of darkening water to purple blurs which were the sand dunes crouching beneath scooting clouds. Did living up to one's convictions always take the joy out of life?

The auction room would have provided her with material, he had written. Would she ever, ever write again? She bit her lips till she flinched. Quitter! Hadn't she figured that making good as a writer wasn't such a different proposition from making good in matrimony? Both professions were a matter of sportsmanship, of keeping on keeping on in the face of discouragement, of continually giving one's best, and trying, everlastingly trying, to make it better.

A night-hawk shrilled overhead. Eerie sound. From the poultry house came the creak of closing doors. A cloud of swallows fluttered above the barn, darting and soaring like a troop of miniature black witches astride their broomsticks. Terrence's voice rose in the words of Holman Day's verse which he had set to music.

> "'Now when the milkman got to town
>   And opened the can, there lay
> The fool frog drowned; but hale and sound,
>   The kicker he hopped away.'"

Did he keep the legend of the kicking frog always in mind to bolster up his morale? The dog lost his balance as Pamela sprang to her feet; he regarded her with reproachful eyes. She patted his head.

"I'm sorry, Babe. The thought that Cecile might be the 'kicker' who hopped away, upset my repose of manner and incidentally yours."

Was that a streak of pink in the orchard? Milly Pike again? She was making daily appearances on the place, ostensibly for eggs; perhaps she really was curious to see the patrons of the Silver Moon, they would supply her with talking-points for some time. Was Terrence the attraction? Pamela's heart stopped. He would be, he must be immune to anyone so blatantly cheap. Would he? Must he? Who would have thought that fastidious Harold Leigh would have fallen for a woman like Cecile Mortimer?

"Hi Pam!"

She waved in answer to her brother's shout. Her eyes were tender as she crossed the lawn to meet him, the dog close at her heels. How good looking he was! He radiated a sort of mischievous gusto, as if life were an amusing show in which he was cast for the part of comedian. The open collar of his madras shirt set off the fair perfection of his throat which would not tan. Out of school hours he should be enjoying the carefree life to which a seventeen year old boy was entitled; instead he worked on the place early and late, occasionally squeezing in a set of tennis. He no longer waited on table except in a rush. The Academy boys were thrilled to take his place and tips.

Terrence grinned at his sister. "Did you see Milly Pike beating it for the orchard?"

"Then it was Milly?"

"Unless it was her astral personality. If so, it is as pink as those gingham dresses she wears."

"Did she speak to you?"

"Sure. Said she came for eggs."

"Did you give them to her?"

"I did." His lips twisted in his adorable one-sided smile. "The Carrs will have jaundice eating so many eggs, if they don't watch out. Want to know what I think? She's a spy."

"A spy! For whom?"

"That's what I'm trying to find out."

Pamela teased, "You have been over-indulging in talkies, Terry."

"Perhaps I have — but — that case Leigh vs.

Leigh is coming on, isn't it? The second Mrs. Leigh may want to know how many people come here, may want to get a line on what we are making. Lately Milly has been sidling up to Father, talking to him when he has been on the porch."

"To Father! Do you mean that she may have been asking questions about the case? Terry, he wouldn't be so simple as to tell that girl anything, he would snap her head off for impertinence first — but, Mr. Carr warned me not to let him talk with anyone. What a muddle. Weren't there enough complications without having Milly Pike cross our life-lines? She only comes when you are here. I thought — I was afraid —"

"That she hung round here to see me!" Terrence's face crimsoned with amazed resentment. "The female mind sure moves in a mysterious way its wonders to perform! Thought you had more sense, Pam, even if you have an imagination which works overtime. Whatever she comes for, the next time will be the last." He chuckled. Pamela caught his arm.

"Terry! You won't hurt her?"

"I won't hurt her." He grinned as at an amusing thought before he demanded, obviously to switch her train of thought, "Why the evening get-up? Special company?"

"Have you forgotten that the Tenant and Miss Crane are coming to play cards with Father? For the third time in the last ten days he has discarded his lounging robe and is attired like a man and a gentleman in blue serge. He doesn't look in the least like an invalid. Play with them, will you? They don't really want me. Card playing is not my métier. I have no card sense."

"You have but you don't want to play, do you?"

"No, I don't. In New York I never had time, there were so many thrilling things to do and see when I wasn't at work."

"Picking up the little plot germs, I suppose." Terrence's voice dripped mystery as he added, "You don't have to go to the city to get them. This place is squirming with 'em."

Pamela's eyes sparkled with laughter. "Folks is sayin'! You are excited over that spy hunch, aren't you? Hurry and change. Father doesn't like to be kept waiting for his game. I am going to the orchard for one spray of blossoms for the bronze jar in the hall. Japanese effect. I will be back before the guests arrive."

Terrence sighed resignation. "If I've got to play, I've got to, I suppose, though I have plenty of studying to do. I'll change as soon as I've shut the Babe into the barn. I'll leave the door open a crack so he'll see and hear but can't break out."

"See and hear *what*, Terry?"

"Go on, giggle; you think that's another hunch, don't you, Miss Pamela Leigh? It isn't. Someone or ones tried to break into the poultry houses last night."

Concern shadowed Pamela's eyes. "Really! You would better tie the Babe if you mean only to frighten the would-be raiders. Remember his rush at Cecile. He would tear a trespasser to pieces if he caught him."

Terrence grinned. "Chicken thieves would sure be his meat. Come on, Babe."

Pamela's mind was on the card players as she opened a gate in the picket fence. She had a little more card sense than she had acknowledged to Terry, but her playing set her father's always quivering nerves on edge. He had rallied to the stimulus of his contract-avid neighbors. She had doubted her ears the first time he had asked her to put studs and links into a shirt to wear with his blue clothes. He must be better, much better physically, though he never admitted it. Was the day approaching when she would be free, when she would look back upon the Silver Moon experiment with a tolerant smile, when her present feverish determination to keep out of the quagmire of debt would seem fantastically exaggerated?

Petals dropped as softly as snow-flakes as she entered a fragrant lane between gnarled tree trunks. Shadows wrapped her round. They seemed to fill the world, as they lengthened, darkened in the windless hush. Milly had disappeared among the trees. She looked down the blossom-bordered grass path. Her heart stood still. Was it — it was, Philip Carr standing with Milly Pike under an arch of pink and white branches. Was he arguing with her? No, his attitude was more that of a suppliant. Phil and cheap Milly! Unbearable! They looked up. Had she broadcast her concern? The girl slipped away, wove like a pink ribbon through the distant orchard, and vanished. After an instant of hesitation, Philip Carr approached slowly. What should she say? Nothing, unless, he referred to his meeting with Milly Pike.

Even in the dim light she could see him redden to his ears as he looked at her. But, his eyes met hers steadily, honestly. He, stoop to clandestine meetings with his mother's maid? Where had the odious suspicion come from? Eddie Pike's suggestion and her plot-complex, of course. If ever again she had time to harness the last to her typewriter it ought to make her fortune. How could she have been so unjust to a man she liked so much? Yet— he had seemed to be pleading fervently.

"Greetings, Miss Pamela Leigh." The jauntiness of Philip Carr's voice was somewhat strained; beneath the lightness she sensed an undercurrent of excitement. "Came up tonight to talk over a plan for a second cottage. Now that we have one leased and bringing home the bacon, we'd better get another started. You're a knockout in that gown, you flitted into the orchard like an oriole."

It was evident that he intended to ignore the tableau he and Milly had presented in the blossom-scented lane. In that case she must not refer to it,

Pamela decided. Her insouciance matched his as she approved:

"Nice of you to come, Phil, but I can't talk cottage tonight. We have guests. Want to do something for me?"

The arm he slipped under hers twitched as if his nerves were jangling. Was Milly responsible for the turbulence of his body and spirit? It showed in his voice, in his eyes. Was Philip Carr shaken by conflicting passions; was he struggling to prove himself more than the mere puppet of physical attraction? She sensed an implication she didn't understand as he repeated:

"Do something for you! That's why I'm here. If you don't know how I feel about you——" He cleared his voice, steadied it to ask, "What do you want me to do?"

"Take a hand at contract and let Terrence get to his studies." Pamela intended to clear the air of sentiment by her practical tone. She succeeded as thoroughly as a brisk wind clears the atmosphere of fog. His grip on her arm relaxed. She explained lightly:

"I am a total loss at cards. Miss Crane will have a much better evening if you are her partner; she is politely bored with Terry though he plays a fine game."

"What is she doing in this tidepool, Pam? After Scott Mallory? The man who introduced me to

her a couple of months ago at a dance, said that
Mallory was her shadow when he first came back
from South America, then apparently the affair was
off. Now that he is in the public eye — the politi-
cians are after him hot-foot — she wants him back,
I'll bet. Understand he did some week-ending here
for a while. Don't have to tell you that though, do
I? Perhaps she got her sister to hire your cottage
that she might spy — "

"Spy! Good grief! Have you picked up the spy
germ too?"

"What do you mean, 'too'?"

His face reddened, his usually lazy brown eyes
glowed. He was startled, undoubtedly startled.
Why? If she told him of Terrence's suspicion of
Milly Pike he might think that she was doing it
because she had seen him with the girl in the orchard; it might complicate the plot more. Whatever Power was mixing life-lines was getting on ex-
tremely well without help from her.

"Did I say 'too'? My mistake. Miss Crane is
wasting her time if she is expecting to meet Scott
Mallory here. He never comes to the Silver Moon
now that Father's affairs are straightening out. Be
a dear and devote yourself to the snappy Hilda,
will you?"

"Take me for a sheik?"

The protest was denatured; his voice held a hint
of cocksureness; his lips widened in a pleased smile.

The all-conquering male! As they stepped into the open from the dim, weird beauty of the orchard, Pamela encouraged gaily:

"Not a sheik but the very king-ripple on the wave of romance, Phil. You—"

Her voice trailed to a thin whisper as a man stepped from the purple shadow of a lilac bush. Scott Mallory! Why had he come? He was unpredictable. If he had to come, why appear as she was patting Philip Carr's hand? Silly habit she had of patting the hand of anyone whom she happened to like at the moment. As she met Mallory's turbulent eyes a typhoon of emotion caught her, swirled her along while mentally she clutched frantically for a hold on something. Into her confusion broke Philip Carr's voice.

"See who's here! And you said he never came. Mallory will take Terry's place at the card table, Pam. You and I will go joy-riding."

"Sorry!" Scott's curt regret slid down Pamela's spine like a cube of ice. "I can't take anyone's place. I want to talk with Miss Leigh—alone, Carr. Business, important business of—her father's."

Chapter XV

ONE impish eye of the half-moon glimmered through a fluff of cloud as if gloating over the holes it was making, over the strange light it was casting on the faces of the girl and the two men. Philip Carr's mouth was set in a stubborn line, his hands were thrust hard into his pockets.

"What's the big idea high-hatting me, Mallory?"

Pamela could appreciate his mother's sensations when spiritually she stepped between father and son. A "buffer" Hitty had called her. She placated hastily:

"No one is high-hatting you, Phil. You told me that you would take a hand at contract. Please go."

"Oh, all right. I'm going because *you* ask it, Pam, understand?"

He strolled away, as if at any moment he might change his mind and return. Pamela's eyes followed till the front door slammed behind him. The hurt, the sense of loss, the disappointment of the days which had passed since she had last seen Scott Mallory, smoldered as she looked up at him defiantly.

"All the dictators are not in Europe."

His amused eyes tore at her heart. "Was I dictatorial? What's the difference so long as I carried my point? He's gone. Come over to the seat. I have something to ask you."

He laid his hand on her arm. She shook it off even as her whole being responded passionately to his touch. "Are you that kind of a person?" she asked herself. "Lucky, you have found it out in time. Just an aching, spineless jellyfish when he touched you, weren't you?" She was conscious of a nervous break in her flippant protest.

"Sit on that damp, rustic seat in the only evening gown I own?"

In answer, he pulled off his coat and spread it over the rough wood. Before she realized what had happened he was seated beside her. Behind them the drowsy quiet of the orchard was stirred by a plaintive "Whip-poo'-will! Whip-poo'-will!" The moon had withdrawn its watchful eye to sulk behind a silver fleece. Had it not been for his white shirt sleeves she could hardly have made out Scott Mallory's figure in the scented dusk. She could feel his presence. Did little currents of suspense and passionate emotion pass between them? Apparently he was unconscious of the tension. Perhaps it was she who was at once broadcaster and receiver.

"Why didn't you tell me about the Babe's attack on your stepmother?"

Surprise tripped Pamela's breath. How had he known?

"Why should I tell you?" The desire to hurt him as he had hurt her — if that were possible, which it probably wasn't — sent her plunging on. "Expect me to keep a line-a-day book for your perusal? I don't tell you everything that happens in my life, you know."

"I know, all right. I know that a lot is happening you don't tell me. But, he is my dog and I am responsible if he makes trouble."

His anger was masked quickly in well-bred calm. Poise with a capital P. One couldn't imagine Scott Mallory, with his background of good breeding, his cool smile, blowing-up unless under extreme provocation. Even as she acknowledged that, Pamela remembered his passionate fury when she had told him that Phineas Carr was to be her counsel. Nothing calm about him then.

"Did you tell your father about the stamp sale?"

An intuitive flash told her that that question was the real reason for his coming. The give and take about the dog had been but a preliminary. Was that all he had to ask her? Had he no explanation to make of his reason for staying away? No regret to express that he was not to handle her case? Were she submitting her own story for criticism would her instructor point out:

"You have employed a complication here, Miss Leigh, which could easily be unsnarled by a question, a word of explanation. It won't get by as a story."?

Lot that instructor would know about it! As a general theory his criticism was justifiable. As a practice in this case it would not work. Could she say to Scott, "Why haven't you been to see me?" She couldn't, not with Hilda Crane in the offing. She answered his question with another.

"Were you skulking in the shadow like a super-detective in a mystery story to ask me that? I thought you had some dark, dour bit of evidence to contribute to my case. I forgot. You know nothing about it."

He caught her arm as she rose. "Why do I know nothing about it? Why?"

Lordly impatience. Sparks falling on dry grass. Words setting flares in her imagination like little incendiaries out to start a conflagration. Her voice answering flippantly:

"Because, I couldn't afford to retain the rising light of the Massachusetts Bar — my mistake — I should have said, ' risen.'"

He slipped into his coat as he explained irrelevantly, "Thought I heard a mosquito's faint, far song. They are bloodthirsty devils at this time of day."

So easily did he put out the fire, blow away the smoke of battle. He walked beside her toward the house. She stopped at the steps.

"Won't you come in? Miss Crane and her sister are playing contract with Father and — "

"Carr?" He supplied the name quickly, asked

as he had asked weeks before, "Do you like this Carr boy?"

She answered as she had answered then, "Quite mad about him."

Defiantly unmindful of the fact that her flame-color slenderness was visible from the living-room window, he caught her by the shoulders.

"Did he give you that topaz bracelet?"

The touch of savagery in his voice set Pamela's heart soaring like a little balloon which had flung over crippling ballast. Had she her friend back again? Her voice was tormentingly gay.

"Topaz! Don't you recognize one of Mr. Kresge's choicest products? I bought it that epoch-making day in Boston when I lost every shred of sales resistance."

His hands tightened on her shoulders. "Was it epoch-making?" His grip hurt. "We will have another like it. I am only temporarily out of the ring. Temporarily — get that — Pam?"

The front door of the house opened. Mallory stepped back into the shadow of the shrubs. Pamela ran up the steps, slightly breathless. Hilda Crane stood on the threshold, her blonde hair like a halo against the light.

"I came out for air. I'm dummy. Thought I heard voices. Wouldn't for the world barge in on a twosome."

Evidently Scott had seen her and had side-stepped recognition. Why? Didn't he want Hilda to know that he had come to the Silver Moon! Why should she herself care what he did? Why *should* she care? How life tore at one's heart. Was it ever simple? For her there seemed always some crippling complication. Would she go on for years fighting herself? Fighting in a circle? As she entered the house she answered Miss Crane's implication.

"You need not have been so sensitive. A man came—with a message for Father. How is the game going?" She approached the card-table where Mrs. Belle Stevens, the Tenant, was dealing.

She was an ample woman with the back of her plump white neck unmistakably going dowager. Her violet eyes were on her reflection in the gilt-framed mirror as she studied the effect of her long fingers manipulating the brilliant-backed cards. Her small mouth puckered fretfully at the corners—a horrible warning to a person who habitually let her temper get the better of her. Her nose was curiously flat with spreading nostrils. She never looked at one directly but had a way of staring into space as if listening to celestial voices. Harold Leigh was watching her with an annoyed frown. His daughter knew from his expression that he had been losing. He took his contract seriously. He rebuked peevishly:

"We have been waiting for you, Miss Crane."

Philip Carr rose, pulled forward a chair. "Come and be my mascot, Pam."

Mrs. Stevens laid down the cards to direct her whole battery of charm at Pamela.

"Your father tells me that you write, Miss Leigh."

Pamela laughed. "A fact except for the tense. I haven't touched my typewriter for months. Looking back from the 1950s I may sparkle on the pages of Who's Who, but at present my name is not one to be used on a magazine cover to lure subscribers."

Hilda Crane picked up her cards. "Belle has a flair for lions: literary, artistic, musical. Some whom she traps are big ones entitled to roar their way through society, some are little more than tame cats. Look out that she doesn't annex you, Miss Leigh. Three spades!"

Had Miss Crane intended to imply that she was little more than a tame cat, Pamela wondered. Nothing subtle about the suave blonde's methods.

"You never want a thing till you suspect that someone else wants it, do you Hilda? Five hearts!" snapped the Tenant.

As Pamela left the room to prepare a cold drink, voices in a heated game-post-mortem followed her. Philip Carr's whole attention had not been on the cards. She had realized that. He had laughed, then gone suddenly serious as if a shadow had passed over his mood. What had he on his mind? Mephisto removed his head from under his wing as she passed him in the dining room.

"Look who's here!" he croaked, blinked lidless eyes and shivered.

"You are a great little stabilizer, Mephisto. You always get a laugh out of me."

Thoughtlessly she allowed the swing door to strike her heels. The bang wrenched an explosive "Gosh" from the parrot. With the sound came the memory of Thanksgiving Day when, for the first time, Scott Mallory had come to the Silver Moon. A, the advertiser, she and Terry had called him. Sometimes her life seemed like one of her own plot diagrams, criss-crossed with an invisible web, with every contact marked with an ineradicable dot.

She removed a pan of ice-cubes from the electric refrigerator. Lucky Grandmother Leigh had installed it. Her heir might, doubtless would — if that day in Boston was an example of recklessness — have squandered its price on clothes.

What a day! It had left a technicolor memory with sound effects of saxophones whining, piccolos whistling, violins sighing, drums throbbing, voices crooning to voices which crooned in turn:

"'Should I reveal exactly how I feel
Should I confess I love you?'"

She and Scott had been the best of friends then. If only — The Babe! Barking furiously. Chicken thieves? She ran to the foot of the back stairs, called in a voice she hoped was not audible in the living room:

"Terry! Terry!"

Her brother was already half way down. He took the last three steps in a jump. Pamela caught his hand in which something bright glistened.

"Terry Leigh! You're not going out with a revolver!"

"Boy! Don't you know a flashlight when you see one?"

"You mustn't go out, Terry! They might s-shoot!"

"Let me go! The Babe's stopped barking! I'll bet I've lost 'em."

He dashed from the house, his sister at his heels. The world was white with moonlight. At the barn they collided with Hilda Crane and Philip Carr. The Babe was frantically wriggling his head which he had thrust through the opening between the big door and the casing. His eyes were ruby red, he snuffled and whined.

Hilda Crane's blonde head shone like silver in the moonlight, her bare neck and arms were alabaster fair. Carr's voice was curiously shaken as he demanded:

"What started the dog on the warpath? We were in the midst of a rubber when he let loose."

"Chicken thieves, we think," Pamela answered. Her anxious eyes were on Terrence who was making a round of the few poultry houses in use. Suppose it hadn't been chicken thieves? Suppose it were someone spying? "Anything wrong?" she called as he tested the lock on the nearest door.

He joined them, a troubled frown wrinkling his brow. "Everything okay so far as I can see. What was it, young fella?" he coaxed soothingly as he approached the door. The others followed close.

"Perhaps Mallory came back and he heard him," suggested Philip Carr.

"Mallory! Mallory came back!" Miss Crane's repetition was faintly contemptuous. "What do you mean, Phil? Scott left in his roadster — for Boston, I presume — directly after dining with Belle and me. He had planned to spend the evening but he answered the phone and immediately after said he had been called away on important business."

Carr's eyes met Pamela's. He lifted one brow slightly before he acknowledged:

"My mistake."

He spoke in a low voice to Terrence, who nodded before he pushed open the great door, switched on the lights. The dog leaped on him, dashed out to sniff the ground.

Four pairs of eyes traveled over the shadowy barn as their owners remained near the door. The place was fragrantly musty from the hay which fringed the lofts. The old horse scrambled clumsily to his feet, thrust his head over the door of his box stall and whinnied; the cow contributed a soft "Moo!", and went on chewing her cud; the Babe dashed in to snuffle vociferously around a mouse hole.

Terrence whistled to the dog as he flashed the

light along the mows. He tweaked the Babe's ears
as the Belgian thrust a cold nose into his hand.

"You're a false alarm, young fella. You—"
the words trailed off in a faint whisper. All eyes
followed his. In the spot of light focussed on the
hay dangled the sleeve of a yellow slicker.

Chapter XVI

TERRENCE tipped back his chair, clasped his hands behind his head as he frowned at his sister across the breakfast table. Sunshine streamed in at the window. It dappled with gold the gem-like colors in the rare hooked rug, lingered lovingly on the Lowestoft punchbowl which lent superdistinction to the maple lowboy, shot a vagrant ray through the diamond-shaped panes of the corner cupboard to set the Sandwich glass agleam, gently touched the white hair of John Leigh on the wall as he looked down upon his descendant with speculative blue eyes under bushy gray brows. With many shivers, much rolling of eyes, Mephisto on his perch was practising the rising, falling notes of a motor horn. The aroma of coffee, the smell of golden, crisp curls of bacon were in the air.

"How the dickens do you suppose that slicker got on the hay-mow?"

Pamela thoughtfully creamed her coffee. "Perhaps Eddie Pike threw it there, Terry. He was here yesterday dressing chickens."

"Eddie Pike! You couldn't pry him out of that

old army coat if you gave him a dozen slickers. I'll bet there's nothing under it but skin. No sirree! Someone was sneaking round the poultry house and made his get-away when the Babe barked."

"Then I suppose the wearer of the slicker crawled through the loft window, deposited his garment on the hay to give local color and departed via airplane."

"Think you're comic, don't you? Just naturally helpful, aren't you, Miss Pamela Leigh? Oh, shut up that confounded tooting, Mephisto!"

The parrot dodged the muffin the boy flung at him. Head coyly on one side, snickered.

"Bad boy!"

Terrence scowled at his sister's ripple of laughter. "I suppose you think that's funny."

"I do. You shouldn't spend hours teaching Mephisto to talk if you don't care for repartee." She rose and began to clear the table. "Onward Christian Soldiers! I have heaps to do."

Still in the tipped-back chair, Terrence ran his long, capable fingers through his red hair.

"What did Philip Carr mean about old Scott? Did he show up last night."

Pamela paused in the process of placing glasses on a tray. "He did. Just before I went into the house."

"What did he want?"

"To know if I had showed Father a letter he had sent me. He only stayed a few moments."

"That's kind of funny. Miss Crane said he left the cottage after a telephone call to go to Boston. I'll bet he was using business as an excuse to break away from her."

Pamela sternly disciplined an impulse to hug him. "Then you don't think Hilda attractive, Terry?"

"Who me! Nothing doing! I hate a girl who paws. She—I'll answer."

Pamela followed him into the kitchen, set down the tray as he picked up the receiver.

"Silver Moon. . . . She's here. Hi, Pam—"

Pamela answered the call.

"Right here. . . Judge Carr! . . . I know you are not a judge, but I have caught the habit from the villagers. . . . Today! Ten o'clock! I thought it was set down for next week. . . . I'll be there. . . . Yes, I remember. No—I will be glad to have it over. Good-bye!"

She hung up the receiver. Sat back for a moment in the little chair. Terry caught her shoulder.

"What is it, Pam? You're chalky!"

"The trial begins today."

"Thought it was set down for next week."

"It was, but Mr. Carr—he corrected me when I called him Judge—said that the cases ahead of us had gone off the list—if you know what that means —and ours would go on today. He knew it yesterday afternoon but didn't tell me for fear I would lie awake all night thinking about it. Terry, I'm panicky. Suppose Cecile wins the fight?"

Terrence patted his sister's shoulder. "Brace

up! It will be great to have the darn thing behind us. Pull yourself together and don't let the lawyer on the other side get you on the run. His name is Hale, isn't it? I'll bet he's the big-hearted-Otis type. Hale by name and hearty by nature. Watch your step. He'll get you all messed up if he can."

"How can he, if I am telling the truth?"

"What does that guy care about the truth?"

"Mr. Carr said that he had little to lose if defeated, much to gain if he wins; that several times he has been spectacularly successful. Suppose this is another victory?"

"Don't get excited. I don't know anything about him except that he is attorney for the second Mrs. Leigh. That's enough for me. I'll bet 'He's tough ma'am, tough is J.B. Tough and devilish sly.'"

A smile lightened the gravity of Pamela's eyes. "Been reading *Dombey and Son* again, haven't you? I wonder if Cecile will stay at the Inn."

"In our village? Why should she? The county-seat is in the next town. She'd be likely to put up as near the court-house as possible. Wish I could drive you over, Pam, but there'll be the dickens to pay and then some if I don't report at the Academy. The powers that be don't like it much that, with exams in the offing, I have to appear as witness."

"I'm sorry, Terry. Isn't it maddening that our lives can be upset like this by a lie? Put up the 'Closed' sign as you go down the drive, will you? Hitty must call off all reservations by phone. Dis-

appointing people may permanently disable our business, but, Mr. Carr warned me that because Cecile
had been in the talkies and he was appearing in court
again—he looked as embarrassed as if he'd been
caught beating the tom-tom outside his own show,
when he added that—the case would be front page
news and the curious would flock to the Silver Moon
if it were open."

"We've got to lose money, pay out money, hand
the second Mrs. Leigh publicity which will be meat
for her, because she has accused you of something
you didn't do. Ain't law humorous! Wish old Scott
were on the job."

"I don't, Terry. I am thankful that he won't be
in court to hear the bones of our family skeleton
rattled."

"Will Father be called to testify?"

"Only if our side needs him. Phineas Carr wants
to keep him out of it if possible, though he admitted
acidly to me that nothing would please him more
than to force his ancient enemy to the witness stand
and put him through the third degree. He has
warned me time and again not to let him talk with
anyone about the case. Think I'd better tell Father
that it goes on today?"

"Sure, Pam. It will give him time to mull over
his testimony. Maybe the defense will be reached
tomorrow. You'd better get going."

Pamela glanced at the clock. "I didn't realize it
was so late. Good luck to you, Terry."

She hastily changed from her morning frock to her last year's slim little tailored outfit of navy blue crêpe printed with white for jacket and skirt, with a smart sash of green, and a blouse of finely tucked net. She pulled on a hat of knitted straw which matched the sash in color, caught up a green bag. She critically regarded the ensemble in the long mirror. Her navy shoes and stockings might not be the last word in fashion but they were effective.

She was too colorless. Her anxious eyes were like black glassies in her white face. It wouldn't do for the jury to get the impression that the defendant was frightened at the start. She deftly deepened the red of her lips, added a touch of rouge to her cheeks. Better, much better.

She caught up Scott Mallory's letter. Her father was adjusting a stamp in a book as she entered his room. She laid the envelope on the table.

"Here's a letter from Mr. Mallory. He has sold some of your securities for a better price than he hoped. I believe he is getting stamp-minded. He thought you would be interested in an auction he attended where a ten shilling, King Edward stamp — I think it was — sold for two thousand dollars!"

"What!" Harold Leigh's eyes blazed at her from a livid face. What a fanatic he was about stamps! "What did you say it was?"

"Look at the letter. I can't stop to read it to you. I am due at the court-house in fifteen minutes."

"The court-house! Does the trial start today?"

"Yes. I hope, Father, that you will feel able to testify if we need you."

He looked down at the sheet of paper in his shaking hand. There was a sardonic glint in his eyes as they met his daughter's.

"I'll be there, if I never do anything else in my life."

Pamela ran down the backstairs, dashed through the kitchen explaining as she went.

"The case is called for this morning, Hitty. Cancel all reservations for today and tomorrow and don't make any more. Business as usual after the trial. Keep an eye on Father. Don't forget you will be called to testify."

Mehitable Betts wiped her bony hands on a towel as she followed to the drive.

"Forget! I guess Phineas Carr hasn't drilled me in what I'm to say for nothing! If 'twan't goin' to be trouble for you I'd be tickled — "

The engine of the sedan drowned her voice. Pamela waved to her as the car coasted down the drive. She glanced at her watch. What did the law do to a person who was late when summoned to court?

She flashed past charming old houses, glimpsed fragments of gardens: some weeded and ordered, patched with stately tulips, starred with narcissus, bordered with purple, orchid and white lilacs; some as devil-may-care as a village ne'er-do-well, yet with a rakish charm. She passed orchards like great drifts of pinkish snow. A southerly wind sprang up. Petals fell like flakes, platoons of little clouds quick-stepped across the blue infinity of sky. When the breeze was not blossom-scented it was laden with the tang of the sea.

She parked her car in a crooked lane which had strayed from the highway arched with fine old trees. Her breath quickened as she approached the gray stone court-house. What was that across the street? In an interstice between automobiles she made out the letters NEWS. A sound wagon! Phineas Carr had been right. His return to the arena was not only of front-page importance, it was news-reel material. How had she dared ask a man, whose appearance in court started a horde of reporters on his trail, to take what must seem to him a trivial case? What a break for Cecile! She was being handed publicity worth its weight in gold.

"Stts!" A hand jerked Pamela behind a tree.

"Phil! Oh, Phil, I'm so glad you are here."

"Are you, Pam? Then that makes it worth while."

Made what worth while, Pamela wondered, even as she approved the Panama in his hand; it had exactly the right slant to its brim. His gray suit was a masterpiece of tailoring; his shirt, tie, socks, the boutonnière of bachelor buttons achieved a harmony in blue; his brown eyes glowed with a curious light. As she met them, Pamela felt as if she were being swirled along on a tidal wave of excitement, much as she had felt last night when she was with him, only to a lesser degree. What did it mean? Milly Pike couldn't be responsible for this mood.

He caught her arm. "This way, hurry. I'm rescuing you from the cameras. We'll beat it to the rear door."

"I feel like a conspirator sneaking in like this," Pamela protested as they entered an ante-room. "Have they taken any pictures?"

"They snapped Carnation Carr and the plaintiff. Not together, of course. She was keen for it. She would be."

"This trial will be a grand advertisement for her just before she appears in your revue."

"It isn't my revue and she isn't appearing."

"Phil! Did you really turn her down?"

"I didn't, but I made it plain to the producer that he would have to choose between her and me. He cocked his ear to the siren clink of gold, took my backing and my stage sets." His voice broke on the last word.

"Phil! What has happened? Beneath your concern for me you are all twinkle, twinkle. I feel as if I had been dropped into a fireworks demonstration with sparks flying in all directions."

"You won't wonder that I twinkle when you hear. Didn't mean to intrude my affairs while you are so anxious about this infernal case, but I've got to tell you, Pam, I've got to tell you." His breath caught in a gulp. "My work for the revue has gone over big."

"Really! Phil, how marvelous! When did you hear?"

"Phone an hour ago. Show opened out of town last night. Didn't tell you it was imminent, didn't want you to know if it was a flop."

"Last night!" He had known that his work was being tried out. No wonder his nerves had been jumpy. And she had suspected him of being emotionally upset by vapid Milly Pike. Her spirit was on its knees in apology as she demanded, "Why weren't you at the premiere?"

He avoided her reproachful eyes. "Well, you see, I knew this case might be called any minute and I thought — I didn't know but what in some way I might help. Mouse and lion stuff, with Carnation Carr as your counsel, but you never can tell. Mother was there."

"Phil, what a dear you are! Tell me quickly what you heard about your work in the revue."

"One dramatic critic of parts wrote: 'The settings by Philip Carr furnished a sure-fire combination of economy and illusion. That young man will go far.'"

"Isn't it wonderful! Now you will tell your father, won't you?"

"Not until he is through trying your case. He will be too absorbed to take it in."

Her case! Apprehension swept Pamela in a suffocating tide. Phil didn't realize that by his ultimatum to the producer he had strengthened Cecile in her determination to humiliate her stepdaughter.

Oil on smoldering coals! Cecile! She pulled Philip Carr nearer by the lapel of his pocket to prophesy shakily:

"The second Mrs. Leigh will make every man on that jury believe her a martyr. Getting emotional effects is her profession."

"Beat her at her own game. Pack a little IT into your voice and eyes when you face the twelve good men and true."

"When I do that, you may expect to see our sand dunes shed their tin-can fringed petticoats and dive into the bay in a swimming contest. It isn't my line."

The lightness of her tone belied the turmoil within her. Suppose—suppose Cecile won a verdict for thirty thousand dollars? She looked at the gilt lettering on the frosted glass in front of her as she laid her hand on the knob below it.

SUPERIOR COURT
Jury Sessions

Her throat tightened, she moistened suddenly dry lips. Was success or was defeat waiting for her on the other side of that door.

Chapter XVII

As Pamela entered the court-room, Phineas Carr,
with a white carnation in the lapel of his perfectly
tailored morning coat, a lustrous black pearl in his
gray four-in-hand, beckoned to her. His dark eyes
were reassuring, the clasp of his hand was steadying
as he met her at the opening in the railing and led
her within the bar.

She was conscious of the stir, the hum of interest as he pulled out a chair for her behind the table
at which he had been sitting. She swallowed hard,
attempted an imitation of complete indifference to
the human element in her surroundings. Her fea-
ture work had taken her into court but never before
had the Stars and Stripes on the wall above the
judge's bench assumed such dramatic significance.
Her eyes traveled from the flag, past shelves of
books, to the patch of blue sky visible through the
tall window, on to her stepmother, Cecile Mortimer
Leigh, seated at a table, the twin of the one over
which Carnation Carr was bending. With a nice
sense of values the morning sun shot a shaft of light
straight at the plaintiff's face. Her black suit was

lissome, very French and very costly; though the
jury, being men, would think it simple because it was
black.   Her white turban, gloves, bag, were the
latest word in fashion.   Her lips were delicately
accented, her green eyes set in brilliantined lashes
held an appealing hint of wistfulness.   They sharp-
ened as they met Pamela's but only for an instant;
they softened so quickly that the girl wondered if
the flash had been the product of her own tricky
imagination.   Whether it had been or not, the second Mrs. Leigh was a shrewd and dangerous woman.

Terrence's quotation from *Dombey & Son* recurred to her as she studied the man beside Cecile.
He might be forty, he might be fifty; no youth left
in his face.

"He's tough ma'am, tough is J.B.   Tough and
devilish sly."

He shook his mane of black hair as he talked to
his client, gesticulated with a plump hand on which
his glistening nails gave the large diamond on his
finger a hard run in the matter of brilliance.   His
teeth flashed whitely between heavy lips; his eyes
were too small, his nose too large.   He might have
stepped from the Well Dressed Man page, so immaculately and smartly was he apparelled.   Cap'n
Iry Crockett's word, "natty," fitted him as perfectly as did his spats.

A brass-buttoned, blue-coated sheriff rapped with
his striped wand of office, announced in a stentorian
voice:

"Court!"

Attorneys, clients, jurymen, spectators who filled every available seat, rose. The black robed, white haired, fresh skinned judge entered. Pamela regarded him curiously, wondering what a judge thinks when he first steps into the court-room into which virtue and viciousness, crime and expiation, right and wrong, beauty and ugliness, have been pitched for trial.

"Hear ye! Hear ye! Hear ye!" intoned the sheriff and court was open. The jury was impaneled. Pamela thoughtfully observed the men as they took their seats. Strangers to her, all of them. One of the two smoothly, sleekly, conspicuously urban jurors wore an elk's tooth on his chain. They must be city men who paid taxes and kept their residence in the county. She knew by their appearance that they were preordained champions for Cecile. The others were farmers, small storekeepers. Phineas Carr's gray brows almost obliterated his dark eyes as he scrutinized each man as he took his place. The business of impaneling the jury finished, counsel for the prosecution opened his case.

"May it please the Court, Mr. Foreman and gentlemen of the jury." Hale made a few suave comments and explanations before he called the plaintiff.

Cecile approached the witness-stand with the rhythm and dignity fashionable at the moment. Pamela stole a glance at the jury. To a man they were impressed by her pink and white femininity, by the wistful sweetness of her long green eyes. The minor note in her voice was bound to rouse the protective instincts of the male — if he had any. The judge sat with elbows on the arms of his chair, the tips of his long, nervous fingers pressed together. The blue-coated, brass-buttoned sheriffs slumped in their seats on platforms on either side of the room, their red and white striped wands of office resembling nothing so much as lean and hungry barber poles. In their time they had seen too many pink and white plaintiffs and defendants with wistful eyes come and go, to have their spines unkinked by the specimen now before the court.

Under the skillful questioning of her attorney, Cecile told a story of neglect and hardship and shaken nerves — the result of her stepdaughter's machinations — of the effect of a heartless letter on her already bruised heart. Adroit questioning by her attorney brought out the story of the vicious attack of the dog, deliberately set on her by the defendant. Spectators reacted. A murmur of indignation swept the court-room like the preliminary mutter of an oncoming storm. Phineas Carr looked at a sheriff from under bushy gray brows. That dignitary rapped smartly on his desk.

"Order! Order! Order!"

Pamela bit her lips till she tasted the sickish sweetness of blood. Cecile's story would bring an acceptance by wire, were it submitted to a confessional magazine, she appraised bitterly. Cheapness unbelievable. How could the woman — if it were true, which it wasn't — bear to advertise her unhappiness, send the details shrieking across the country by wire, by radio, by the printed page? — Bear it! Wasn't the desire for publicity one of her reasons for bringing the suit?

Hale, counsel for the plaintiff, waved his large smooth hand dramatically in the direction of counsel for the defendant, smiled his flashy smile, patronized in his large smooth voice:

"Your witness, Mr. Carr."

Phineas Carr rose. He touched the carnation in his coat lapel as if to make sure it was there before he looked down at a slip of paper in his right hand. At the first sound of his rich resonant voice, the jury, which had been noticeably lolling, straightened to a man. With counsel-trained expertness the plaintiff answered his questions. Then he seemed to draw himself together like a panther about to spring.

"Mrs. Leigh — you have entered complaint in this court in that name, though outside it you have resumed your maiden name, I understand — you are an actress, are you not?"

"Yes, I have acted." Plaintiff's voice and eyes were wary.

"I understand that you are a most convincing actress."

Pamela choked back an appreciative "Marvelous!" Clever of him to set the jury to wondering how much of Cecile's testimony was real, how much histrionics. Hale fidgeted in his chair. Phineas Carr went on serenely.

"You testified under oath that since you left your husband on June first of last year you have made a bare living, that you had received no money from him."

"I said, except what he sent me a short time ago for an operation."

"And that amount was?"

"I said eight hundred dollars."

Counsel for the defense toyed with the carnation, apparently refreshed his memory from the paper in his hand before he asked suavely:

"Mrs. Leigh, you testified that because of the strain on your nerves occasioned by your husband's neglect you had been unable to earn money for some months. My brother Hale will correct me if I am wrong."

As his "brother" merely answered with a glare, Phineas Carr continued:

"Yet, two weeks ago, you bought stock and gave a check for seventeen hundred and fifty dollars in payment, did you not?"

The plaintiff gave an excellent imitation of a victim contemplating a yawning trap. Her counsel blinked as if from a knock-out blow. Was he surprised? Through Pamela's mind echoed Scott Mallory's words:

"That client is a menace who, before trial, wil-

fully or in ignorance, withholds facts from his lawyer which are brought out in cross-examination."
It was quite evident that Hale had not known of the
seventeen hundred and fifty dollar payment. The
effect was but momentary. He was on his feet with
a catlike pounce.

"Your Honor, I object. The fact that my client
bought stock has no place in this evidence."

"Your Honor, considering that the plaintiff has
testified that she has been almost in a state of destitution because defendant wilfully and maliciously
diverted the flow of money from husband to wife, I
insist that the fact that Cecile Mortimer Leigh had
seventeen hundred and fifty dollars to invest, has a
place in this evidence."

"The question stands."

"Your Honor —"

"Sit down, Mr. Hale."

Hale sat down. Phineas Carr patiently repeated:
"Mrs. Leigh, two weeks ago, you bought stock
and gave a check for seventeen hundred and fifty
dollars, did you not?"

The green eyes wistfully sought the jury as if im-
ploring them to observe one poor little woman being
heckled by a big strong man.

"I think I —"

"I don't want to know what you think. I want
to know what you did."

The judge reminded patiently:

"Answer yes or no, Mrs. Leigh."

"Yes."

"That will be all."

Phineas Carr sat down. Pamela's thoughts sifted and resifted like the golden dust in the shaft of sunlight as she looked at him in consternation. Did he intend to ignore Cecile's accusation that her stepdaughter had — with malice aforethought — set a dog on her? Would he ask no questions about the letter which counsel for plaintiff had read with such devastating effect?

Hale, who had gripped the edge of the table as if ready for a spring, stared at counsel for the defense; his lower jaw sagged. The jury registered disappointment, for all the world like small boys who had gathered for a fight only to see the champion walk out on them. Pamela caught a twinkle in the judge's eyes, a twitch at the corner of his lips. Had he seen Carnation Carr in action before?

Hale summoned witness after witness to testify to the state of destitution and nerves to which the plaintiff had been reduced through the machinations of her stepdaughter. He was prodigal with his smile, suave to the women, impassioned at strategic points. He pulled out the *simpatico* stop in his voice organ at the dramatic moment and set his listeners sniffing. A high-voltage advocate, indubitably.

Only once he seemed perturbed. After the noon recess, pink-frocked Milly Pike slipped into a seat left vacant by a witness. He scowled at her inquiringly for an instant before he returned to the matter at hand. Pamela looked quickly at Philip Carr where he sat on the front bench reserved for spectators. His eyes were on Milly, his lips were tightly compressed.

Phineas Carr's cross-examinations were superficial, quite as if having established the two facts, first, that Cecile Mortimer Leigh was an actress, second, that she had paid out seventeen hundred and fifty dollars for stocks, nothing else really mattered to him. Nevertheless, by questions and pleas for exceptions, he managed to keep the plaintiff's witnesses on the stand, Hale jumping up with objections, until the afternoon session closed. Why, Pamela wondered impatiently, why didn't he push along and get it over with? Was he stalling, waiting for certain evidence? The case had come to trial a week before he had expected.

"Hear ye! Hear ye! Hear ye! All persons having anything further to do before the Honorable the Justices of this Court, at present depart and give your attendance at this place tomorrow morning at ten o'clock, to which time and place the sitting of this court is now adjourned.

"God save the Commonwealth of Massachusetts."

The judge left the room. The jury filed out their special door. Spectators whispered, looked back curiously as they straggled to the street.

"Be on hand promptly tomorrow morning, Miss Leigh. Hale says he has one more witness to present. After that — we'll mop 'em up," with which prophecy Phineas Carr picked up his papers and departed.

Pamela's courage trailed its wings as she left the court-house. It seemed as if Cecile and her attorney had stolen the show. As she hurried toward the lane where she had parked the sedan, a sarcastic voice drifted back to her.

"Thought you said Carnation Carr was a fire-eater? A spell-binder?"

The second voice was distinctly apologetic. "He is usually. Don't know what cramped his style to-day. Perhaps he's got notional."

"Perhaps 'twas the plaintiff. She's a honey. Like to see her on the screen. The jury just lapped her up."

"The defendant was more my style. She's got class. She was as white as a dead girl but she sat with her hands quiet. Notice how the other one was twisting her beads, or jingling her bracelets, or straightening her hat, or arching her neck like a bird looking for a worm? Every minute on the move. If I'd been her lawyer I'd have knocked her one over the head — as you do a drowning person when they struggle, so you can save them. That plaintiff needs to be rescued from herself."

Philip Carr was waiting for Pamela beside the sedan. His eyes were brilliant; he pulled at his slight mustache. He was taking this case hard. From time to time she had glanced at him in the court-room. His expression had been tense. Had he doubted his father's skill?

"What was Carnation Carr saying to you just before you left, Pam?"

"That the plaintiff's counsel had but one more witness to put on in the morning, then it would be our turn. Don't worry, Phil. I have absolute faith in my attorney."

She knew that he watched her as she drove away. Something was on his mind. Doubt of his father? Doubt clutched at her own heart. Carnation Carr had seemed so — so casual.

As she drove up to the Silver Moon, Mehitable Betts, gray hair streaming like the witch of Endor's, rushed out before she could stop the car.

"Pamela! Pamela! Your Pa's gone!"

"Gone!"

The girl slid out of the seat. Caught the woman's bony shoulder.

"Gone where?"

"I don't know. He flew off in a plane!"

Chapter XVIII

PAMELA stared at Mehitable Betts with the incredulity she would have felt had the gaunt woman announced Harold Leigh's departure for the moon.

"How did he get to the field?"

"Now don't take it so hard, Pam, he'll come back all right — if he don't, I don't know as 'twould matter. Eddie Pike was here working over the chickens. I nearly lost my mind when your Pa walked into the kitchen — though I know he'd been talking excited over the phone; the minute you left he put in a long distance call — he pushed me aside when I would have stopped him, just as though he was lord of the universe and I a laborin' ant in his way, and announced he was going out. He was dressed fine. 'Course Eddie hasn't any mind to lose, but, I thought his lower jaw had come permanently unhinged when your father stood over him and ordered him to take him to the field in that old flivver of his — somehow Eddie's got the front wheels on again — he kept looking over his shoulder as if he thought a goblin'd got him."

"Do you suppose Father ran away to avoid testifying in the case? The defense begins tomorrow."

"Land's sakes, does it? Glad I know so I can put my hair up in curlers tonight. How did it go? Did Phineas Carr lay 'em all out flat?"

"No, he didn't. He was as mild as cream cheese." Pamela's eyes were troubled as she remembered the comment of the stranger. "Don't know what cramped his style today." And yet the way in which her counsel had seared into the jurors' minds the fact that Cecile was an actress, that it was her business to get her effects across, had been masterly.

"Any telephone calls, Hitty?"

"Six for reservations. I turned 'em all down. You'd thought I was talking a lollipop away from a baby, they were so resentful. Seems restful, doesn't it, not to have a lot of cars tooting up the drive, and folks walking all over the house as if they owned it, and wantin' to buy the furniture? Later, Terrence is going to have supper with one of the Academy teachers. When it's time I'll bring you something to eat in the living room on a tray."

"Will you really, Hitty? It would be marvelous." Pamela's voice was unsteady. "I am tired. Not physically, but tired of turning things over and over in my mind, wondering what is the best thing to do in the extraordinary complications of my life. Things were in a mess before, but with this queer get-away of Father's I don't know what to expect —but," she added loyally, "of one thing I am sure, had he thought he could help me he would not have gone."

With an angular, work-worn hand Mehitable Betts awkwardly patted the girl's shoulder.

"Keep on keeping on, Pam. Things will straighten out. Things have a cur'ous, unbelievable way of straightening out. When they get so 's it seems as though you just couldn't bear 'em another minute, something breaks to clear them up. I've seen it happen over and over again. 'Fair tomorrow!' your Grandma used to say. Stop worrying about your Pa. He'll land on his feet like a cat. You go change your clothes — 'twill rest you."

In her own room Pamela thoughtfully regarded the telephone. Any chance of reaching Scott Mallory at his office? Even if he were not interested in her, he would advise her what to do about her father. She glanced at the clock. Not too late to try.

She put in the call, drew a bath, recklessly emptied into it the perfumed crystals she had been hoarding, laid out fresh lingerie as she waited for the telephone to ring. She eagerly answered the bell.

"Mr. Mallory's office? . . . Gone! . . . Out of town! For two weeks! . . . No. No message. Good-bye!" That was that.

She was about to slip her frock over her head — the georgette frock the color of orangey-red zinnias which always buoyed her spirit — when she heard a commotion. She dropped the filmy thing as she ran to the window. Milly Pike was at the gate of the

White Hope's yard! Her head was superciliously
tilted as if challenging doubt of her courage. Coral
comb and wattles twitching, the great rooster was
preparing to charge. Didn't the silly girl know
better than to go near that fighter?

Pamela bolted down the back stairs, dashed
through the kitchen to the accompaniment of Hitty
Betts' shrill protest.

"For the land's sake! Where you goin'——"

As she sprinted from the door, Milly was shrieking toward the drive with the infuriated rooster on
the hop, skip and jump after her. Pamela ran after
them calling as she went:

"Terry! Terry! Terry!"

Milly looked over her shoulder. Strategic error.
She stubbed her toe, fell. With a victorious squawk
the rooster pounced. Pamela grabbed for the bird's
legs. He pecked at her as she caught them. She
held the heavy, flapping creature at arm's length.

"Get up, Milly. Quick! Run. I can't hold
him."

The girl scrambled to her feet. She sobbed,
panted, gurgled. "Terry said he bet I wouldn't
dare go into the rooster's yard. I'm not afraid of
anything but——he flew at me and——"

"Run, Milly, run! I can't hold him much longer
if he flaps like th-this."

The girl shot down the drive.

"Hi, Pam!"

Breathless, crimson-faced, Terrence erupted from

nowhere. He was in the throes of mirth as he grabbed the rooster. Indignation crowded at the heels of Pamela's relief.

"Terrence Leigh! What did you mean by daring Milly to open that gate? The rooster might have injured her seriously. Want another law-suit on our hands?"

"I was watching." The youth's jaw tightened. "She's been sneaking round here long enough. Either she's spying for the second Mrs. Leigh or she's in league with chicken thieves. Haven't decided which. She pretends that she likes me. Hooey!" He grinned. "I told her that the White Hope after this would be on the loose, he needed more exercise. She—"

"Pamela, what you doing prancing round here in your underclothes?" Hitty Betts' shrill protest drowned Terrence's explanation.

"In my what?" Pamela looked down at her slim body simply and revealingly attired in a pink crêpe step-in. Terrence checked an hilarious shout, to tilt a lance in his amazed sister's defense.

"Don't get excited, Hitty. Pam's bundled up compared to most of the girls when they go swimming." He chuckled infectiously. "Just the same, you'd better beat it, woman. There's a car shooting up the drive. One of the Academy teachers coming to take me off to supper."

Pamela shot for the house with Mehitable Betts breathing hard at her heels. Safely in the kitchen, she explained:

"I saw Milly fooling with that gate. Forgot I hadn't my gown on, forgot everything but that she was in danger of being spurred."

"Serve her right if she had been. She comes hanging round here every day — hmp, she wouldn't have so much time if M's Carr was at home. She comes poking her nose into what I'm doing, asking questions about the folks who come. Yesterday, she sat on the porch rail for almost ten minutes talking to your Pa. I told Terrence about it. Says she comes for eggs. Eggs! It's Terry she's after. She's boy and clothes crazy. You better go put something on or you'll catch cold."

Had she done everything she could do to locate her father, Pamela asked herself, as after supper she curled up in a corner of the swing couch on the porch. She missed him, missed the feeling that he was in his room, missed the murmur, the music, even the static of the radio which so often had exasperated her. Heavenly night. Not too cool for a thin frock, not too warm. A spatter of pale stars, a gay old-blade of a moon, if the come-hither glint in the one eye visible, the quirk of the corner of a mouth, were a token. A pink glow in the west, sleepy chirps from the orchard, a mint-scented breeze, satin-fingered, on her lids when she closed them.

She kept the seat gently in motion with one foot. In the excitement of the rooster's attack on Milly she had forgotten to ask Terrence if he knew of his father's mysterious departure. She would not worry about him. He had been gaining steadily in health and strength. The fact that he was able to dress and walk through the kitchen " as if he was lord of the universe," proved that he was infinitely better. She should be grateful for his desire to get away, not alarmed by it. Perhaps she had needed this anxiety to make her realize how much, deep in her heart, she loved him. Flying! Where? He still kept his box in a Trust Company's vault in New York. She knew because she had typed an order for certain securities to be sent to Scott Mallory. Brown of Boston! The name boiled up from her subconscious. Had her father gone to confer with the man with whom he had been in correspondence? If so, Brown would undoubtedly notify his family if he showed signs of dementia. Dementia! That hectic suggestion helped. She would not worry about him. She would drop responsibility on the broad shoulders of Brown; somehow she was sure they were broad.

Several times she had assured herself of the absurdity of worry about a man of the world like her father before a light swept up the drive. An engine purred softly as a car disappeared behind the house. Only two persons she knew drove a high-powered roadster. Philip Carr and Scott Mallory. Could it be Scott? His secretary had said that he was out of town. Gone for two weeks. Had he purposely planned to be away during the trial? She waited on the steps. Two coming. Terry's whistle. A laugh, Philip Carr's — not Scott's. She had the sensation as of a non-stop drop from the top floor of a skyscraper. She heard Terrence say in a high, excited voice:

"Hitty reported that yesterday she cornered Father again. I tell you, Phil—we've got to—"

"Sssh, not so loud, boy—oh, there you are, Miss Pamela Leigh." The change in Philip Carr's voice from mystery to simulated casualness would have been funny at any other time than at this, Pamela reflected.

"How'd you make out today, Pam?" Terrence chuckled reminiscently. "Your appearance at the ringside at the White Hope's little bout, in your pink undies, knocked the trial clean out of my head."

Pamela smiled at young Carr. "Greetings, Phil! Counsel for the prosecution got his testimony in except for one witness, Terry. He will put him or her on first thing tomorrow, then we present our side. You were there all through it, Phil. Who else can that man Hale produce? It seems tragically possible that he already has put in an unbeatable lot of evidence. Of course, it wasn't true, but, what have you?"

Carr dropped to the steps beside her. "I think I know whom he's got up his sleeve—if he can catch her—him. Cap'n Iry Crockett's testimony that, 'It looked as if Pam-ee-lia had set the dog on her stepmother,' was a bomb. I thought you and he were great pals."

"We are. He was under oath. He had to tell the truth. He said the same thing to me here."

"Did Carnation Carr know that?"

"Yes. After our first interview I felt as if I had told your father everything I had thought, done, or emoted since I left the cradle."

"He knew also about the letter you had written your stepmother?"

"Boy! Did the second Mrs. Leigh's lawyer lug that in?"

"He not only lugged it in, he read it to the jury, Terry. Such passion. Such fervor. It certainly was good. As a piece of creative literature I was proud of it. It would have taken a prize in a hew-to-the-line contest."

"I'll bet it would. You can sling a mean typewriter when you get started."

Philip Carr observed thoughtfully: "I followed the testimony as close as a trailer hitched to a fliv. That man Hale handed out some body blows which seemed as if they must knock the stuffing out of the defense. I thought Father would start out on high and smash through their evidence till the plaintiff's counsel would be put to it to scoop up the splinters. He didn't. He just sat there and took them. As a parent I may not be crazy about your attorney; but, as a lawyer I've thought there was nothing bigger, better, bull-dogisher in the world. This time he's got me guessing."

His voice was troubled. Pamela took up cudgels in defense of Carnation Carr. There was more assurance in her voice than she felt.

"He is doubtless saving his ammunition — including a few poison-gas bombs — for tomorrow. You must be on hand, Terry. Get excused from the Academy."

"That'll hurt. Will our invalid be able to testify?"

For the first time since their arrival Pamela's thoughts reverted to her father.

"He's gone!"

"Gone! What d'you mean, gone? Passed out?" The boy's face was pale with surprise.

"No, Terry, no." Swiftly she repeated Mehitable Betts' story of the departure. "At first I was stiff with anxiety; then I got hold of myself, tried to get hold of myself — I'm still panicky inside — argued that if he were able to carry-on like that, he was able to see the project through."

"Perhaps he shot for the promised land to side-step testifying."

"Meaning New York City, Phil?"

"What else could I mean? If I'd been caught in this tidepool for months and a nice big wave of energy washed me out, I'd keep going till I reached the white lights."

"Where do you suppose he went, Pam?"

"I am as stumped as you are, Terry. It costs heaps of money to fly. I don't believe he had enough to go far. He might think we were treating him like a child and be furious if we try to find him."

"Might phone old Scott and set him detecting."

Pamela felt her color deepen. She was glad that the gay old-blade of a moon had hidden its light as well as its come-hither eye behind a cloud.

"I — I thought of that. Called his office. He is out of town for a few days."

"Then I guess you have done all that is possible. Father has played us a low-down trick, after the months we've been waiting on him hand and foot, to step out without an explanation. I hope he does get lost. I hope he spends the night in the hoose-gow."

"You don't mean that. You are as anxious as I am in your heart, Terry."

"Perhaps I am, but he might have had the decency to let you know after the way you've coddled him." Terrence unfolded his long self like an extension ladder from the chair in which he had been slumped. He stretched his arms and yawned. "Don't you worry, Pam, he will come home when he is hungry and his money gives out. His get-away shows that he's a lot better, doesn't it? And so to study. First, though, I'll go out and tuck in the hens and kiss the cow and horse good-night. Do you know the first thing I'd do if I came into the money — I'd go the rounds and thumb my nose at every item of live-stock on our ancestral estate; then with an incubator full of eggs to draw on for balls, I'd practise my curve on the barn windows. That's how crazy I am about the poultry business. Where's the Babe?"

"Hitty shut him in the barn and left the door partly open."

"I thought the old girl was frightened to death of him?"

"She is. That act was a triumph of affection over fear. I must have seemed a little low when I came from the court-house. She did everything she could to help." Pamela was indignantly aware of the unsteadiness of her voice. Terrence awkwardly patted her shoulder.

"Looks as if you had managed to chip her granite heart. Don't worry, Pam. Everything's going to be all right. Nightie-night."

The light of Philip Carr's cigarette glowed and faded as his eyes followed Terrence on his way to the barn. Came the sound of the great door being pushed open, the joyous yelping of a dog, the fragrance of hay, the warm, sickish scent of animals."

"That boy is pretty well fed up on farming, if you ask me. Don't blame him," he sympathized.

Pamela bit her lips furiously to steady them. What had happened to her tonight? She was all shaky inside. Was it the shock of her father's sudden departure? She should be happy that he was well enough to go. Had she lost grip on her courage because she had stopped work for twenty-four hours? Had she lost faith in her attorney? He had seemed horribly casual. She tried to speak lightly.

"Terry is a dear. He is the sweetest, bravest boy. I—" Her voice broke. Philip Carr flung his arm about her and pulled her head to his shoulder. She tried to draw away, relaxed against him.

"I—I—don't know what is the m-matter with me. Things are in s-such a m-m-mess." The last word was a sob. He laid his head against her soft hair.

"Cry it out, dear. You've had this coming to you. You know I love you, don't you? I've been waiting to hear from the settings before I told you. I wanted to have something of my own to offer you. You know—"

A light swept the steps. Pamela jerked her head from the comforting shoulder. A roadster. A soundless roadster! A high-powered roadster! Scott's? Had he seen the tableau on the front steps? Of course, unless he was blind. Served her right for being such a weak sister.

Voices in the house. To whom was he talking? She ran into the hall. Scott Mallory, his face colorless, and her father were at the foot of the stairs. Harold Leigh, pale, but defiant, forestalled his daughter's protest.

"Now, don't make a scene, Pamela. I had business in New York. I flew there and back to Boston. Had a conference with Mallory and he drove me down. That's all." He gripped the rail. "Hang these confounded stairs, must have been designed for a chamois."

Scott Mallory caught Pamela's hands as she took a quick step toward the door.

"Wait. Was Carr kissing you?"

Her temper flamed in one of its periodic reactions to his authority. "And if he were? Would you have me go to my grave unsung and unkissed? How dare you come into this house and ask questions? You haven't been here for weeks and now you — you —" her voice broke. Try as she would she couldn't piece it together.

Mallory looked up at the man who was just disappearing in the hall above, before he caught her in his arms, held her so close she could hear the heavy pounding of his heart.

"Go unkissed? Not so long as I'm on earth." He crushed her closer. "You've got to listen, Pam —"

"Sitting alone in the dark, Phil?" Hilda Crane's voice on the porch outside. "I thought I heard Scott's car. I phoned his office and Miss Cryder told me that he was on his way down. I —"

With extraordinary agility Mallory kicked the door shut. From the floor above drifted the sound of strings, deep and full, high and shining, in forward marching rhythms. Tightly as she was held, Pamela managed a shrug of disdain.

"Philanderer!"

His laugh was reckless. "Am I? Well, if that's what you think of me I'll take some of the perqs that go with the title." He crushed her mouth under his, lingeringly released her only to snatch her close again, his eager, ardent lips on hers.

He let her go as the knob of the door turned. Pamela caught at the newel post to steady herself. She was half way up the stairs, Scott was lighting a cigarette when Hilda Crane entered the hall. In spite of her thrumming pulses she managed her voice creditably.

"I will give your message to Father, Mr. Mallory, it will not be necessary for you to wait."

His eyes met hers. How dared he smile? Hilda Crane linked her arm in his.

"Scott, take me home, will you? I came up to make a reservation for tomorrow, Belle wanted to entertain a party at luncheon, but Phil Carr tells me that the Silver Moon won't be open for business. Is that true, Miss Leigh?" Her voice was aggrieved.

Pamela resented her tone. "It will be closed until after the trial."

Miss Crane clasped a hand over the one already on Mallory's arm. "I spent the day in court. I was thrilled. Of course, I don't know anything about it, but it seems to me that Mr. Hale's argument was unanswerable."

"He hasn't argued yet, Hilda." Mallory's interruption was curt. "Though I haven't a doubt he attempted it."

"How do you know, Scott? You weren't there."

"Didn't have to be there to know that counsel do not argue until both sides have put in their evidence."

"Why, oh why didn't they go? Was each one waiting for the other, Pamela protested mentally. She couldn't bear looking at them another instant. With an attempt at gaiety, she suggested:

"Would you mind finishing the discussion of the case on the way home? Phil asked me to go for a drive — and —"

Face darkly red, eyes black with anger, Mallory opened the door wide.

"Our mistake. Profuse regrets for having detained you."

Philip Carr entered, blinking at the light.

"Just came in to say good-night, Pam. Got to call a man I know on long distance. May I take you home, Miss Crane?"

There was a note in Scott Mallory's laugh which tightened Pamela's throat unbearably.

"Too late, Carr. I am already elected for the honor."

Chapter XIX

OBVIOUSLY Phineas Carr was uneasy. He kept glancing at the clock on the court-room wall as he sat behind the table with his client beside him. He was as immaculately apparelled as yesterday except that there was no flower in his coat lapel. Five minutes before ten. The spectator benches were packed, the jurors were in their seats. Cecile and Hale were conferring. Pamela's courage mounted as she watched them. The plaintiff was maddeningly complacent but her counsel was unmistakably disturbed. Had he discovered a weak link in the evidence for the prosecution?

In spite of her effort to keep her attention on her surroundings, Pamela's thoughts persisted in slipping back to the scene in the hall last night. Scott's face had been colorless, his voice icy when he had bade her a formal good-night. Of course, he had known that she had had no date for a drive. Why had she thrust Phil Carr between them? Because she had been unbearably hurt that Scott's secretary had told Hilda Crane where he was — under instruction doubtless — and had put her off with, "Away for two weeks." That was the answer.

If he cared so little for her that he kept away from the Silver Moon, why had he kissed her? What was one kiss in this age of promiscuous kissing? She closed her eyes, every pulse in her body quivered, her lips still burned from the pressure of his. Of course he had seen her head on Phil's shoulder as the car lamps had spotted them; equally of course, being a man, it wouldn't occur to him that she might be so low in her mind after a day in court, that any masculine shoulder — it didn't matter much whose, so long as it was a sympathetic one — would be a comfort. She had been too fiercely hurt to explain.

Phil had stood beside her on the porch as Scott Mallory's roadster coasted down the drive; moonlight had turned the hair of the girl beside him on the seat to silver-gilt. Carr had whistled.

"Something tells me I made a break somewhere? What set Mallory on his ear? Did he think I was trying to cut in on him when I offered to take Hilda Crane home? He needn't worry, I don't want her. You asked me to be nice to her and I was doing my darndest."

"Let's forget them. Will you be at court tomorrow morning for the opening, Phil?"

He had deliberated before answering. "Can't tell yet. I may — be called away on business."

She must stop looking back, hadn't she enough in the present to think about? She glanced around the crowded court-room. Philip Carr had not come. She missed him.

A chauffeur in navy blue uniform with brass buttons — such as the old-time coachman used to wear — his face red, his breath short, hurried into the court-room. He spoke to a sheriff who nodded affirmatively. The man entered the bar and laid a small package on the table behind which sat Phineas Carr.

"Sorry to keep you waiting, sir, but the mail was late."

He opened the package, removed a perfect white carnation. Phineas Carr fastened it in the lapel of his coat. The chauffeur picked up the box.

"All right now, sir?"

Carr's face relaxed in a whimsical smile. "Quite. Now the trial may go on. Take care of those flowers."

"Yes sir."

The chauffeur departed. Pamela looked after him, then at the man beside her. He had stopped fidgeting. Was it possible that a flower in his buttonhole could work that change?

"Court!"

The occupants of the room rose as one. The sheriff intoned. The judge took his seat. Hale put his witness on the stand, a witness who merely corroborated what those before had testified. Phineas Carr waved away cross-examination. He spoke to the girl beside him.

"It is your turn now, Miss Pamela. Nothing to

be afraid of. When you go on that stand say to
yourself, 'I am right! I am right!' You'll get that
across to the jury. Tell the truth and stick to it, no
matter what Hale asks you. Answer my questions
as I have coached you. Answer his with 'yes' or
'no' when you can get away with it."

The room whirled before the girl's eyes as she
stepped to the witness stand, steadied at the first
word of her counsel. She felt as if he had gripped
her hand tight in his. By question after kindly question, he led her on till she had told the story of her
father's financial and physical crash, of his wife's
desertion, of her utter bewilderment at the sudden
turn in their fortunes, of the decision of Terrence
and herself to take the invalid to the Cape. She
touched on the necessity of selling her jewels to pay
nurses and doctors. Counsel for plaintiff sprang to
his feet, roared objection. The judge ordered the
evidence stricken from the records, Hale resumed
his seat obviously exultant.

The defense attorney smiled. The bit of testimony had been indelibly recorded in the minds of the
jury. He touched on the dog episode, emphasized
his client's statement that the animal never before
nor since had shown antipathy to a visitor on the
place. Wasn't that a slip, didn't that play into
Cecile's hands, Pamela wondered nervously, in the
instant before he passed on to the next question,
quite as if the little matter of the dog were unworthy
of his valuable time.

"Your witness, Mr. Hale."

He sat down. Counsel for the prosecution rose. Pamela's heart threatened to choke her with its clamor, she gripped the rail in front of her. Hale smiled suavely. His smug satisfaction at her evident perturbation steadied her as nothing else could have done. She slipped the betraying hand into the pocket of her jacket and returned his smile. He was plainly disconcerted. He pushed the papers about on his table, as if undecided, before he asked his first question. Strategic blunder. It reminded Pamela of Phineas Carr's command:

"Say to yourself, 'I am right! I am right!' You'll get that across to the jury."

Hale, counsel for the plaintiff, shook out his whole bag of tricks; he smiled, he insinuated, he accused, he roared. He assumed a ponderous solemnity, he set traps. He featured the letter she had written to her stepmother, in which she had refused to give her sanctuary in time of need. He went dramatic over the attack of the dog. Phineas Carr interrupted in the midst of a heart-shaking peroration.

"Your honor, may I remind my brother that this is not the time to argue his case to the jury?"

"Keep to the cross-examination of the witness, Mr. Hale," rebuked the judge dryly.

Pamela found herself anticipating Hale's questions. "I'll wager he has taken the same plot-construction course I took," she reflected with half her mind, while she fixed the other on the prosecuting attorney. She returned to her seat as limp as if she had been put through a wringing machine. Phineas Carr approved:

"Well done, my dear. Horace Hale didn't advance plaintiff's case by so much as the fraction of an inch."

One after another Phineas Carr examined his witnesses. Pamela listened tensely. She forgot that she was being sued for the alienation of a husband's affection, forgot that a verdict against her might mean the loss of the home Grandmother Leigh left her. Her attorney was superb. He experimented with his witnesses as a master-scientist might with potent, inflammable chemicals. So much of this, so much of that, a suave reminder here, a flick on the raw there, never enough to precipitate an explosion nor cause collapse into a dud.

Terrence's tenure of the witness-stand was brief. Pamela's heart thumped with pride as she looked at him. He was so loyal, so clean, so boyishly honest, the jury could not help but be impressed by his testimony for the defense.

Intermission followed. Brother and sister drove in the sedan to the shore. In the shadow of a bath-house Pamela spread out the tempting luncheon Mehitable Betts had provided.

"Better take it," she had insisted. "You may not want to go to the Inn today, you an' Terry can picnic somewhere. 'Twill do you good to get away from people."

"Wise Hitty," the girl thought as her spirit quickened to the beauty, the mystery beneath the rippling cobalt sea. She shook her head as Terrence offered sandwiches, temptingly thin ones, suggestive of crisp lettuce, and olives and cream cheese. She sifted white, shining sand through her fingers.

"Couldn't swallow. I — I — have a horrible premonition that something will break this afternoon."

Terrence filled a cup with steaming coffee rich with cream from the thermos, added sugar with a lavish hand.

"Something will break, all right, if you don't eat. What can happen to us — unexpected, I mean. Counsel for the prosecution has put his case in, hasn't he?"

"Yes — but I can't explain the curious feeling. Perhaps it is the effect of the strain. I missed Phil Carr in the court-room. He said he might be away on business."

Terrence threw a pebble with practised skill at a gull soaring and dipping overhead.

"Phil's a good scout. Was Hale broken up when his witness wasn't on hand at the opening of court this morning?"

"Wasn't on hand? What do you mean? She was there. Just another sob-sister for Cecile."

Terrence's eyes, big and velvety and black with surprise, were in striking contrast to the snowy hunk of angel cake in which he had set his teeth. He swallowed convulsively.

"She was *there?* Sure, Pam?"

"Sure? Of course, I am sure. What are you talking about?"

He rolled over in a paroxysm of mirth. "Now what do you know about that?" He shouted again.

"Terrence, if there is anything funny in this awful case, sit up and tell me about it. I'd like to see a joke, if there is one."

His hand shook as he refilled his cup. "Can't tell—now!" He choked over the coffee, dropped his head on his arms folded on his knees and shook with laughter.

His sister maintained an ominous silence. He raised his head, wiped his eyes. With a too evident attempt to divert her attention, he pointed excitedly toward a husky, smartly designed cruiser driving at full throttle, churning snowy fountains of spray as it hit the high spots.

"Watch her bank as she turns at full speed! Turning in her own length! Cutting through the water at a sixty-mile clip—if it's an inch! What a boat!"

"She is a beauty. Her nickel bright work glitters in the sunlight like diamonds."

"The glitter would catch your eye. You're a North American Indian, Pam, when it comes to color and sparkle."

"I'll be as bronzed as an Indian if I sit here in the sun and wind much longer." She drew a deep breath of the soft, briny air. "I feel made over. The breeze has blown the cobwebs from my mind."

"Sure you won't eat anything? All right, let's go." Terrence collected the remains of the luncheon. Pamela glanced at her wrist watch.

"There is still half an hour before court opens."

"I know, but I must go for Hitty," he gurgled irrepressibly, "*et als.*"

"You're all gales and giggles inside, aren't you, Terry? What others?"

"Did I say 'others'? Just a figure of speech, woman." He chuckled again: "Come on, let's get going."

Mehitable Betts was the first witness called at the afternoon session. Lucky Terrence had started when he did. What had sent him into such paroxysms of laughter, his sister wondered. She would make him tell when she reached home.

An iron-gray frizz fringed the brim of Miss Betts' pansy-laden hat — a hat unquestionably of the vintage of the merging 'twenties. Her slinky drab dress accentuated her height and angularity. She was primed for combat, as spiked with aggressiveness as a hedgehog with quills.

Phineas Carr had her confirm two of Pamela's statements before he turned her over for cross-examination. Without rising, Horace Hale waved a plump hand.

"No questions."

Mehitable's jaw dropped. She blinked incredulously. She stared truculently at counsel for the prosecution before she turned to the judge. His lips twitched.

"That will be all, Miss Betts. Step down."

His Honor had a nice sense of humor, Pamela told herself, in the midst of her own suppressed, nervous laughter. Hitty was a pricked balloon if ever there was one. Minutes on end, while at work in the sunny kitchen, she had rehearsed the incontrovertible evidence she would present under oath, which would leave the "actress woman" and her lawyer "without a leg to stand on between them." Poor, disappointed Hitty, the great moment of her life gone flat.

"Scott Mallory."

The name crashed into Pamela's sympathetic reflections. It unseated her heart. Scott a witness in this case! Why? To what could he testify? Not once in their conferences had Phineas Carr mentioned the possibility of his appearance. What had her counsel up his sleeve? How good looking Scott was! How clean-cut! Was his fine, lean face less colorful than usual or was her imagination playing tricks? She especially liked that blue serge suit. He was the only man of her acquaintance whose taste in ties she approved. How could she sit here appraising him when her whole financial future was at stake? Without looking, she sensed the consternation of plaintiff and her counsel, a tightening of the spinal vertebrae of the jurymen, concentration on the part of the judge.

Phineas Carr settled the white carnation in his coat lapel before he began the examination of this witness. For the rest of her life the spicy scent of a pink would project this court scene on the screen of her memory, Pamela predicted.

"Mr. Mallory, you own the dog known in this case as the Babe, do you not?"

"Yes sir."

"Will you tell the jury where and why you bought him?"

Mallory's voice produced an instant emotional effect. No wonder he was a successful advocate, he had fire and personality plus. No editor would blue-pencil that story, Pamela thought as he answered the question. His evidence was boiled down to essentials. He told of buying the dog of a fisherman who sold him because his son, a fisherman, hated and abused the animal. Counsel for plaintiff, eyes wary, waived cross-examination.

Phineas Carr rose. "I present my next witness, your Honor. The Babe."

A chill of excitement cavorted up and down Pamela's spine as the Belgian police dog dashed through the jurors' entrance dragging Eddie Pike at the end of his leash. Was it Eddie Pike? Gone was the rope-belted army coat. The man's clothing screamed. Checks. Stripes. Dots. A blinding rhinestone horseshoe in his tie. A huge ring shot passionate purple lights. There was a hint of frightened vacancy in his eyes, on his sagging lips. The jury grinned to a man, the spectators tittered, the sheriff rapped for order.

Noble tawny, proudly conscious of his swankish

new breast-strap, the Babe stood with forepaws on the rail of the witness-stand. Head cocked, ears pricked, he regarded the faces bent eagerly toward him. Without warning he yelped joyously. With a leap he jerked the leash from the lax hand of his keeper and cleared the shoulders of the clerk of the court by an attenuated inch. With forepaws in Pamela's lap he snuggled his cold nose into her neck. She smothered her laughter against his shoulder as she encircled him with her arms.

With a cry of well simulated terror Cecile clung to her counsel's arm. Pandemonium. Laughter. Shouts. Raps! Raps! Raps! The sheriff's stentorian command.

"Order! Order! Order!"

Phineas Carr caught the dog's leash, dragged him to the stand.

"Take him in there again, Pike, and *hold on to him*. Understand me? *Hold on!*"

Eddie gasped like a codfish out of water as he gripped the leash. With forepaws on the rail, mouth open as if in hilarious appreciation of the riot he had staged, tawny eyes snapping, red tongue dripping, the Babe surveyed the court-room. His Honor covered the betraying twitch of his lips with a transparent hand. Counsel for the plaintiff seemed in a daze. One of the jurors indulged in a nervous chuckle. Phineas Carr addressed the judge.

"May it please the Court, I have put this witness on the stand to account for his attack on Cecile

Mortimer Leigh, alleged to have been promoted by the defendant in this case."

"Ready!"

At the quick command a sheriff opened the jurors' door. Someone in a yellow slicker backed into the court-room. The dog turned. He stiffened. The hair on his neck ruffed. He glared at the oilskin clad figure with eyes gone red. Ears laid back, ivory tusks gleaming, he strained at the leash. Eddie Pike turned as purple as his ring from the strain of holding him. The dog snarled, growled, barked, bristled; his jaws dripped. Phineas Carr snapped his fingers. The figure turned, peeled off the slicker. Terrence! Pamela went limp as her brother laughed, inquired soothingly:

"What's it all about, young fella?"

Except for the growl rumbling in his throat the dog might have been turned to stone. Then with an apologetic "Whoof!" he extended a placating paw. Terrence accepted it with grave ceremony. At a word from Phineas Carr, youth, man and dog departed.

Hale shook his black mane and shot up.

"I object to this melodrama, your Honor. It is irrelevant to this case. I move that it be struck off the record."

Counsel for the defense suavely addressed the Court.

"Your Honor, you heard Mr. Mallory's testimony to the effect that he bought this dog from a fisherman, whose son, also a fisherman, abused the animal. Fishermen spend much of their lives in oilskins. Would that not account for the Babe's yellow-slicker complex? You saw what happened when his young master — whom, it must be evident to the least intuitive person in this room, he loves — appeared in a yellow slicker. Does that not explain to any intelligent person the attack on Mrs. Leigh when she appeared at her stepdaughter's residence attired in Iry Crockett's oilskins which she had borrowed? After this demonstration, is it not rank nonsense to claim that the dog's attack was instigated by this defendant?"

The judge scrutinized a paper on his desk. Peered over the rims of his horn spectacles at Hale.

"On the testimony in this action so far presented, I rule this evidence admissible. Motion denied. Proceed, Mr. Carr."

"I have but two more witnesses, your Honor. I may need but one." He cleared his throat. Was the pause due to nervousness or his appreciation of the dramatic value of suspense?

"Brown of Boston."

Chapter XX

WHAT possible connection could the man on the witness stand with a large loose-leaf book in his hand, have with this case, Pamela wondered. Brown of Boston. She had imagined him broad of shoulder, ruddy, a balloon-tire sort, who would ride lightly over the ruts and bumps of life. On the contrary, he was tall, hawk-faced, with large eyes magnified by the strong lenses of horn-rimmed spectacles; he suggested a wire-spring quality of mind. His well-tailored clothing needed pressing.

She glanced at the plaintiff and her attorney. Unless their expressions belied them they were as much at a loss as she to account for this witness.

Phineas Carr tenderly fingered the petals of the carnation in his coat lapel. The room was uncannily still, the atmosphere pulsed with suspense. Motes of golden dust coasted down a sunbeam. Outside, the trip-hammer tap of heels in the corridor; somebody whistling "Kiss Me Again" from Victor Herbert's *Mlle. Modiste;* the bang of a door. Inside, the montonous tick-tock of the wall clock.

"Mr. Brown, you are a collector and dealer in stamps, are you not?"

There was a sharp jingle of bracelets. Pamela looked swiftly at Cecile. She was colorless. Her counsel's expression remained faintly puzzled. One of the two urban jurymen leaned forward eagerly. The witness attested:

"I am a philatelist, sir."

Phineas Carr smiled, explained suavely: "I used the simpler term for the benefit of my brother advocate. Of course his Honor and the gentlemen of the jury understand the more technical name."

His brother advocate audibly snorted but let the gibe pass while he watched warily for a chance to jump into the ring.

"Mr. Brown, a short time ago, you purchased at auction a rare stamp, an English, 10 shilling, King Edward stamp overprinted I.R. Official, for the sum of two thousand dollars."

A murmur of incredulity rippled through the court-room.

"Order!" rapped the sheriff.

"Will you show that stamp to the jury?"

Brown of Boston removed a leaf from his book. Counsel for the defense waved away the Clerk of the Court when he would have taken it, himself held it before the twelve men. The urban juror with the elk's tooth on his watch chain lost his balance in his eagerness to see. Counsel for the plaintiff appealed to the judge.

"Your Honor, I protest against the holding up of this case for irrelevant testimony."

"Your Honor, the testimony is not irrelevant."

Phineas Carr's contradiction lashed. "I propose to show that this plaintiff, who claims that the defendant did wilfully and maliciously poison her husband's mind against her until her nerves were so shaken that she was unable to fill her theatrical engagement, sold this rare stamp for two thousand dollars, less commission."

Counsel for the prosecution sprang to his feet, shook his mane, bowed formally to the judge.

"I move that that statement be stricken from the records. The sale of that stamp has no bearing on the question before this jury, which is, did the defendant or did she not influence the plaintiff's husband against her? The introduction of this stamp act is a ruse to rouse the sympathy of the jury."

"This is not the first time a Stamp Act has roused the sympathy of citizens of this Commonwealth, your Honor," Phineas Carr reminded dryly.

The gentlemen of the jury smiled broadly, the spectators tittered, the sheriff rapped. The judge fitted finger-tips together and deliberated.

"I agree with counsel for the defense. The sale of the rare stamp has a bearing on this case. Motion denied. Proceed with your witness, Mr. Carr."

Counsel for the defendant stood tall and straight. The fingers of one hand gripped the carnation-decked lapel of his morning coat, the other held a slip of paper. Color burned in his high cheek bones, his dark eyes were smoldering coals.

"Mr. Brown, how did you know that this rare stamp was to be sold?"

"Collectors and dealers are usually notified of sales, sir; besides, there's a sort of wireless over which news spreads when a rarity is about to change owners."

"Were you surprised when this specimen was offered for sale?"

"Yes sir. Right off the reel I had a hunch——"

"Just a moment. Aren't rare stamps constantly coming into the market?"

"Yes sir."

"The collecting of stamps is a costly fad, is it not?"

"I would rather call it an investment, Mr. Carr. I have several clients who spend between twenty-five and thirty thousand dollars a year for contemporary and rare stamps. Of course, during the late depression, values shrunk — except in outstanding rarities — as in everything else."

Was Carnation Carr dragging this out to create suspense, Pamela wondered. If he were he was succeeding. She was on the edge of her chair, there wasn't a person in the room who wasn't listening avidly — except counsel for the plaintiff who was whispering to his client. Thirty thousand dollars a year for postage stamps! Unbelievable.

Counsel for the defense continued: "You spoke of a hunch, Mr. Brown. You mean, I suppose, that you were suspicious that something was wrong about this sale. Explain to the jury what you mean by hunch."

The plaintiff's attorney sprang to his feet. "I object to that question, your Honor."

"Objection overruled. Proceed, Mr. Brown."

Hale had the temerity to glare at the judge before he sat down. The lips of his Honor set in a straight line. Brown looked at counsel for the plaintiff over the horn rims of his spectacles before he explained:

"I had a hunch there was something irregular, because when the owner of a stamp like that had bought it of me he said, 'It has been one of the ambitions of my life to own this. I'll starve before I part with it.' He is a philatelic fanatic. I felt sure that if he were to sell it, he would offer it through me."

"Any other reasons for suspicion, Mr. Brown?"

"Yes sir. From time to time, previous to this, to be exact since last July, several rare stamps were sold which I knew to be from this same collection. I began to suspect they had been stolen."

The judge bent forward. "How did you know they were from that collection, Mr. Brown?"

His voice was drenched with interest. Had he also collected stamps as a boy? Pamela glanced about the court-room. If his Honor's expression was a test, every person present had at one time or another been bitten by the stamp-bug. Absorption unbelievable. The witness smiled indulgently.

"Just as a collector of works of art knows where

to locate a Rembrandt, a Corot, a Daubigny, or any one of the great masterpieces."

Hale rose. "If these stamps were such rare treasures, how could they be so easily stolen, may I ask?" His amused skepticism was well done.

"You may not ask." Phineas Carr's protest was a roar. "Your questions are in order when this witness is turned over to you for cross-examination, not before." Counsel for the plaintiff dropped to his chair somewhat heavily.

"Did it occur to you to query the owner of these stamps as to the reason for their sale, Mr. Brown?"

"It did. Then I heard that he had lost his fortune and was up against it. Thought it might hurt his pride if I seemed curious. He had been doing a little exchanging of stamps with me to keep him amused, he wrote."

"But you did finally question him? Why?"

"In a registered letter he sent a mint block, which I had bought for him, with instructions to sell it."

Pamela remembered her father's wail: "My mint block! My mint block!" And she had thought it might be a rare print!

"Please explain to the jury what a mint block is, Mr. Brown," Phineas Carr requested.

"The term is borrowed from the numismatists — coin collectors. It means a block of six or more unused stamps with the original gum." Witness opened his book, extracted a leaf. "You will notice on this example of twelve stamps that the perforation between the two rows is missing."

The judge leaned far forward, there were red spots on his cheek bones, his eyes shone boyishly eager. Brown indicated a place on the page.

"Here is the lot I bought. A mint block of twelve stamps of the partly perforated six-cent 1894 issue. It is one of the largest blocks of its kind known Notice the sheet-number in the margin. I ordered it put up at auction. Bid it in for $1000."

The concerted "Oh!" of the spectators passed without rebuke from the sheriff. He was pop-eyed with amazement. Phineas Carr returned the precious leaf to its owner and inquired:

"It was after that sale that this English stamp came on the market?"

"Yes sir. I bought it. I was so keen to get it — stamp collecting is just as exciting as horse-racing at times — that I didn't think where it came from. It isn't the only example of its kind. When I came to I began to wonder. Yesterday morning, the man whom I had thought might be the owner, phoned me. He had just heard of the sale of a stamp like his. I told him of my suspicions, with the result that I picked him up in a plane. We flew to New York, checked up on his stamps and found that several were missing from one of the most famous collections of English stamps in the country — in the world."

"Did you inquire of the bank officials if anyone but the owner had had access to that box?"

"We did."

"And the answer?"

The ticking of the clock boomed through the silence. A bee buzzed in at the open window, realized its intrusion and buzzed out. Someone caught his breath in a nervous gasp. Phineas Carr fingered the petals of his carnation. His face was quite white as he repeated:

"And the answer?"

"Mrs. Harold Leigh."

Counsel for the prosecution pulled his client back to her chair when she would have risen. His face was patched with purple, his voice was shaken as he demanded:

"Your Honor! Do you realize that witness has intimated that an innocent woman stole and sold those stamps?"

"Sit down, Mr. Hale."

The plaintiff's attorney swayed for an instant as if debating the wisdom of obeying the judge's command, before he resumed his seat. Phineas Carr addressed the Court.

"Your Honor, before I turn this witness over for cross-examination, I wish the jury to understand our claim, which is: that the plaintiff has not been without funds; that she sold rare stamps to the amount of ten thousand dollars, which she took from the safety-box of her husband without his knowledge or consent."

Cecile Mortimer Leigh sprang to her feet. "Suppose I did?" Her voice was shaken, her green eyes were wistful. She was attempting to charm, less obviously than on her appearance on the witness-stand, but with deadlier purpose. "Hadn't I a right to support from the man I married? His daughter had turned him against me —"

"If counsel for the prosecution does not restrain the plaintiff I will fine her for contempt of court!" Thus the judge. The spectators showed symptoms of applause.

"Order! Order!" The sheriff was crimson from the volume of his roar. Horace Hale caught his client's arm. His face was expressionless as he talked with her in a low tone. A playful breeze danced in at the window, cut antics with the pages of the stamp book of Brown of Boston on the witness-stand, before it danced on.

Phineas Carr addressed the Court. "Your Honor, the plaintiff has by that last admission substantiated our claim that she has been far from destitute during this last year." He waved a transferring hand. "The witness is yours, Mr. Hale."

The face of counsel for the prosecution was livid as he rose. His contemptuous eyes rested for an instant on the plaintiff before he spoke.

"May it please the Court, Mr. Foreman and gentlemen of the jury, I find that this case has been falsely represented to me by my client. I withdraw."

He swept up his books. With elaborate formality he bowed to the judge, to the jury, to opposing counsel. Head high, with catlike tread, he left the bar.

Phineas Carr fingered his white carnation.

"'*Te morituri salutamus!*'" He delivered the gladiatorial salute in a voice, which, though low, must have been audible in the most remote corner of the weirdly still court-room.

Chapter XXI

HER father owner of one of the most famous collections of stamps in the world! Pamela's mind steadied from the shock of Brown's statement. It must be worth thousands if that King Edward specimen was a sample. He had owned them when his daughter had sold her jewels to pay his bills and those of his wife, when she had given up the chance to make good in the profession she loved, Terrence the school in which he was happy, to carry on the Silver Moon that he might have proper food and care. She tried to excuse him. He had been ill then, prostrated, hadn't realized conditions. But the months since? Had Scott Mallory suspected that he had concealed assets? Of course. Hadn't he asked her for the address of the stamp firm? Brown of Boston!

Phineas Carr returned from a conference with the judge. Pamela sensed the tense concentration of jury and spectators. What would happen now that counsel for the plaintiff had withdrawn from the case? His client had been close on his heels as he left the court-room. Carr swept up his papers. Smiled his whimsical smile as he said in a low voice:

"That will be all for the present, Miss Pamela. Went off with a bang, didn't it? Hale justified my belief in his flair for theatric values. Pretended that his client had not told him all the facts — probably she hadn't — and walked out of the court-room with the sympathy and admiration of every spectator in it. This case will bring him business. Unless I am mightily mistaken — and I'm sure I am not — that is the end of the suit for alienation of affection."

The kindly words with their tinge of humor smashed Pamela's self-control. Her body shook, her voice caught in a sob when she tried to speak, her breath came in gasps. Phineas Carr laid his hand on her shoulder.

"Take your time, take your time. Stand up, my dear. His Honor is leaving the court-room."

He waited for the echo of the sheriff's proclamation to die down. "You are coming home with me. I shan't allow you to go back to the Silver Moon till you get your grip. Your father might be — well he can be very unpleasant. Mrs. Carr has returned. She told me to bring you for tea no matter which way the verdict went, said she had some wonderful news to tell you. We will slip out the rear door and dodge reporters. I told your brother not to wait, that I should run away with you."

He nodded to a sheriff. The brass-buttoned one cleared the way to the door by which the judge had departed. A chauffeur in a white linen duster with

cuffs and collar of the deep blue of the shining town
car, at the door of which he stood, touched his cap
as they approached. Phineas Carr seated himself
beside her on the broadcloth cushioned seat. He
folded his hands on top of the curved handle of his
cane. Apparently unmindful of the curious crowd
which had collected or the fact that she was shivering from reaction, he observed as the car shot
forward:

"Of course, Miss Pamela, that stamp testimony
had no legitimate right in this trial." He chuckled.
He was boyishly exultant, not so unlike his son when
he was pleased with an achievement. "But we took
a chance on it. I happened to know that the presid-
ing judge was a stamp addict. I recognized the
Elk juror, when he took his seat, as a plutocrat and
a philatelist. We got by."

We! It was the "we" of a crowned head or an
editor, Pamela thought, as she tried to control her
shaking body.

Mrs. Carr met them on the threshold of the Ship
Room. Even in her turmoil of mind Pamela paid
tribute to the lustre of her pearls, the exquisite
amethyst frock, the sparkle of excitement in her
lovely eyes. Her husband tenderly patted her
shoulder.

"We licked them, my dear. Let this child cry it
out for a few minutes, then bring her in for tea."

So he had observed her reaction. Pamela pulled
off her hat in the charming yellow and lavender room

in which Mrs. Carr had left her. Cry it out! Not
she. She sopped her face and throat with cold water
until they glowed. Dusted her skin with powder.
Her pulses steadied, her heart quieted, gay courage
got the upper hand of taut nerves. Her eyes shone
like dusky brilliants as she pulled her green hat over
her dark hair before the mirror. She nodded to her
reflection.

"Ashamed of you for going to pieces over good
fortune. What would have happened had you lost
the case? If you knew the relief I feel—"

"Should I reveal exactly how I feel—"

The song rose in her heart. The tightening lips
of the looking-glass girl warned her. With a stifled
exclamation she turned away.

On the threshold of the Ship Room she para-
phrased gaily:

"See the conquering heroine comes! Sound the
—" The sentence thinned into a mumble as Scott
Mallory looked up from contemplation of the fire
which, even on this spring day, flickered and faded
on the hearth. Where had he come from? Why
was he here? Was that her father talking with
Carnation Carr over by the window? Her father?

The stiffening went out of her knees. She sank
into a chair beside the tea-table. Mrs. Carr smiled
at her as she sugared the rare cups as richly, darkly
red as the carnations in a tall slender vase on the
table. The fat Georgian tea-kettle snorted a white
puff of steam, rattled its silver cover.

"I thought we would wait tea for Phil, Phin. He—he has something wonderful to tell you." Mrs. Carr's voice shook with eagerness.

Her husband's face darkened. "He doubtless is still engrossed by the business which kept him away from court when I was trying a case. I had hoped he would be sufficiently interested to hear it through. Wait if you like. Mr. Mallory has something of importance to tell us." His eyes cleared of annoyance, his voice was almost boyish as he amended:

"But, before he begins, I want you to know that the sudden termination of the alienation suit—don't interrupt the Court, Mallory—was due to him. He worked up the defendant's case; I merely presented it. Day before yesterday when I found that it would come up for trial the next morning, I phoned him. At the risk of being chewed to pulp he experimented with the yellow slicker and the dog."

The mysterious appearance of the oilskin sleeve on the hay-mow was accounted for. Pamela's first reaction was relief; she hadn't cared for the possibility of skulking chicken thieves in this era when automatics were as easily acquired as a daily paper. Terrence was so careless of his own safety. So had Scott been when he had angered the Babe. The evening she and Philip Carr had met him in the orchard, he must have been lingering about for a chance to get to the barn unobserved. Why couldn't Phineas Carr be friendly with his son as he was with others? Was he jealous of his wife's affection for the boy? He was too big a man to be so small. It was abundantly evident that he had been hurt that Philip had not been in court to witness his victory. What would he say when he heard Phil's grand news? Father and son were playing at cross-purposes.

"Miss Pamela! Miss Pamela, you are not listening," Phineas Carr reproached. "The stamp business was all Mallory's idea. I stalled yesterday at the trial to give Brown of Boston and your father time for their investigation. The case was sprung on us a week earlier than we had expected, we were not quite prepared. Brown spent last night in this house, Mallory and I the evening working up his testimony. I waive my claim to the old maple, Miss Pamela. Settle the question of fees with my associate. I merely served as senior counsel. Now, Mallory, it is your turn."

Then she was still head over ears in debt to Scott? Pamela's heart stopped and raced on. What next!

Scott Mallory stood back to the mantel, hands thrust hard in his pockets. He shook his head. "Not my turn. Mr. Leigh's."

Harold Leigh left the window. The skin over his knuckles was strained shiny as he gripped a chair-back. He seemed years younger than before his air trip. There was about him a trace of the gay and gallant man who had won the adoration of his small daughter. Pamela steeled herself against him, kept her eyes on the fantastic pinkish shadows the firelight cast on her crêpe jacket and skirt, as he explained:

"Of course, when the right time came I intended

to make up all you had spent for me, Pamela, but this last year of depression has been a bad time to sell stamps. I have traded under an assumed name always. Saves publicity. Cecile had a duplicate key to my box—it had not occurred to me that she would use it after she left me. They knew her at the bank. When we were first married she went there with me several times—I was fool enough to take the box in both our names and more of a fool to leave some of my valuable stamps there in a sealed package." His eyes were as anguished as might be those of a parent parting with an adored child. "Brown sold the mint block for me and sent the cheque directly to Cecile. I told you that I wouldn't let you mortage your property for her; besides, I was afraid she would come after the money. I didn't want her poking into my affairs." The slow color rose under his waxen skin. "She has an infernal way of getting what she wants."

His daughter looked at him steadily. "What is the value of one of the most famous collections of English stamps in the country—the world perhaps?"

He cleared his throat nervously. "That is no one's business but mine, now." He drew two cheques from his pocket. "Mallory has advised me that as Cecile will undoubtedly win in her proceedings for an allowance, I would better give you and Terrence what I owe on the legacies your mother left. I had intended to make good when prices went up. I may be a stamp fanatic but I am not a thief. When the crash came and my wife deserted me, I was too numb mentally to realize what my collapse was doing to your life and Terry's, Pamela. Then, then somehow I didn't care. I never would have lost that money nor my own had I stuck to the business I know, but Cecile was all for speculation. I am not afraid to stack thousands on my knowledge of philatelics. These are Brown's cheques for a portion of my holdings. He was only too eager to buy what it was like tearing my arm off to part with."

Irritated resentment in his voice, the furtive gleam Pamela had seen before in his eyes. She felt as if she were looking on at a play with the lead acted by a stranger. Even as she told her father that she was happy that he was well again; that she was glad for Terrence, more than for herself, that he was able to make good on the legacies; she was hurt, intolerably hurt, that he had hoarded when he might have helped. Her voice sounded in her ears like that of an automaton. To Harold Leigh it must have seemed as usual for he approved:

"Glad that you are facing the facts without a fuss, Pamela. Mr. Carr has agreed to act as guardian for Terrence, it is the arrangement your grandmother wanted. The income from fifty thousand dollars, augmented by some of the principal if necessary, will see the boy through college."

He dropped a cheque into his daughter's lap. "Here is the same amount for you. Mallory has fought tooth and nail to get it for you. I would have preferred to wait until prices went up before I turned some of my holdings into cash, but he is so — so unflinching. I hope he will show as much fight for me when Cecile comes after that allowance. May I commandeer your limousine, Carr, to take me home? I notice it is at the door." He coughed hollowly. "I am beginning to feel the nervous strain of the last forty-eight hours."

Pamela sat stiffly erect listening to the departing purr of the motor. Had that touch of exhaustion in her father's voice meant that he was returning to his role of invalid? She looked at the slip of pink paper. Fifty thousand dollars! Scott had practically forced that money from her father. He had been working for her all the time she had thought him indifferent. He and Phineas Carr were conferring. Would he give her a chance to thank him, to explain that she liked him more, infinitely more than she liked Philip Carr? A voice crashed into her repentance.

"I don't care if they've got the judge of the court in there! I'm goin' to see his folks. I'll tell 'em!"

Eddie Pike! Eddie in his variegated court costume on the threshold! What had happened now? His ready-to-wear bow tie was under an ear, his china-blue eyes bulged, the rise and fall of his lurid plaid waistcoat registered turmoil, his slack mouth gaped.

"Say, Judge, I want to know about my sister."

Phineas Carr scowled at him, growled, "Inquire of my wife. She hires Milly."

Mrs. Carr smiled at the belligerent intruder, said soothingly:

"We don't know where Milly is, Eddie. Cook says that at about nine o'clock she saw her meet someone — a man, she thought — outside the back gate. She hasn't come home."

Pike took a step into the room, his face worked horribly. With an unconscious sense of dramatic values he paused long enough for suspense to get in its nerve-tickling work.

"Course she hasn't come home. She's run off with your Phil in his slick roadster!"

Mrs. Carr swayed, steadied. "Have you lost your mind, Eddie?" Her fixed smile never wavered as her eyes met her husband's. Face ashen, he looked back at her.

How ready he was to doubt his son, and how it hurt him, Pamela thought as she met his tormented eyes. Phil and Milly! Memory projected a picture of the two under an arch of apple blossoms, the man apparently pleading. Hateful suspicion. She wouldn't believe it.

"Where did you pick up that crazy idea, Pike?" Scott Mallory's coolly amused question snapped the tension.

Eddie blinked vacant blue eyes. "You're the lawyer fella that got Terry and me to take the dog to court, ain't you? My idea ain't crazy. I've watched 'em. I've follered 'em. This mornin' I see 'em start off. Milly and a suitcase."

"A suitcase!" Mrs. Carr's repetition quavered.

"Yes sir — ma'am. An' if Phil Carr's run off with my sister — "

Scott Mallory caught his shoulder. "Go slow, Eddie!"

Pike waved a wild arm. "You can't softsoap me. I say he's got to marry — "

"Who's got to marry who? What's all the shouting about?" demanded Philip Carr from the threshold.

Chapter XXII

YOUNG CARR grinned engagingly as he asked the
question, but the lighter he held to his cigarette was
not quite steady. In his effort to produce a voice
Pike gasped like a goldfish snapping at food in the
water of a crystal bowl.

"What did you think of my coup, Judge? Masterly, what?"

His son's question brought a faint color to Phineas
Carr's cameo-like face. Was it generated by relief
or anger?

"Not knowing to what you refer I can't express
an opinion."

"Phin! Don't be so hard!" pleaded his wife.
She smiled at her son through a mist of tears.
"What was the coup? Tell your mother, Philip."

That "mother" contracted Pamela's throat.
She had not known that a word could sound so like
shaken music. Pike recovered his voice to demand,
with that brand of truculence which only the drunk
and the mentally retarded achieve:

"You tell me what you done with my sister! Ran
away with her, didn't you?"

Philip Carr deliberately turned his back on his father to smile boyishly at his mother. Her eyes responded with a lovely light.

"Sure, I ran away with her — in a sense. Didn't Terry tell you of our scheme, Mallory?"

"No."

Scott was as unsympathetic as Phineas Carr, Pamela thought indignantly. There were little flames in the dark grayness of his eyes, a tenseness of jaw which she had come to recognize as steel against which it would be futile to batter.

"Tell me what you done with my sister, you—"

Philip Carr roughly interrupted. "Shut up, Pike. Cut out the whine. Your sister is in the kitchen. I promised her that if she would tell me something I wanted to know I would take her to a city shopping and pay the bills — the girl is clothes mad. She was canny enough to withhold the information I was after until we drove into the yard here a few minutes ago. Now you know the truth, fade-out. You smell horsey."

"He is on the level. Go, Eddie." Scott Mallory answered the question in the troubled china-blue eyes interrogating him.

Pike loped to the threshold, stopped to wag a threatening head. "I'm goin'. But if it ain't true, if Milly ain't in the kitchen, I'll be back. I'll be back!"

His mutter thinned into the distance. A girl's shrill exclamation was shut off by the slam of a door.

Philip Carr drew a long breath. "That's that!"

His father crossed the room to stand beside Scott Mallory before the fire. Two powerful, forceful men. The same fairness of spirit—except in the elder man's attitude toward his son—the same sincerity and competence in their profession. Would they have been sympathetic as father and son, Pamela wondered, or were they too much alike?

"What's this about a coup?" The elder Carr's voice was as implacable as when he had a witness writhing under cross-examination, his fingers tightened on the lapel of his coat under the white carnation.

His son chuckled boyishly. Phil was *sweet,* Pamela told herself; most men would have furiously resented that tone.

"It was this way, Judge. Terrence and I got a hunch that Milly Pike was in the pay of plaintiff's counsel. No family the size of ours could possibly consume the number of eggs she personally conducted from the Silver Moon—you will find them all charged on your bill, Mother. We didn't know what she was snooping for but we were convinced that she was spying. Remember the time you caught me talking to her in the orchard, Pam? I was trying to make her tell me what she was up to."

"Why didn't you tell me your suspicions?"

"Don't bite, Mallory. Who knew that you were interested in the case? Each time I met you in this tidepool you were zealously preferring a blonde. Thought that was why you came to the village."

From under her lashes Pamela observed the

tightening of Scott's lips. Why didn't he deny that implication about Hilda Crane? Only one answer to that,—he couldn't, and tell the truth.

"Why didn't you tell me? You knew I was counsel for the defense."

Philip Carr abandoned boyishness as he might an outgrown garment. His face was colorless, his eyes were hotly indignant as he answered his father.

"Can you see me coming to you with any confidence? Honestly now, can you? You would have made me feel that I was a fool. You may be a demon at law with an uncanny nose for scenting out the truth in a case, but you go blooey when it comes to knowing your own son."

"Phil!" Mrs. Carr protested faintly.

He pressed her hand against his cheek. "It's all right, Mother. He's had it coming to him for some time."

He smiled at his father; Phineas Carr's fingers clinched on his coat lapel. "Now that is off my chest I will proceed with the saga of the kidnapping of the fair Milly, if you can call it kidnapping when the victim is rarin' to go. When Hale said at the close of court yesterday that he would present one more witness in the morning, Terrence and I were sure he meant Milly Pike. I had seen him scowl at her when she came into the court-room. Hitty Betts had reported that the girl had been talking to Mr. Leigh. That didn't look good to us. We didn't know to what she was prepared to swear, but we determined to put her where she couldn't swear to anything — unless at me."

"Do you know the penalty for tampering with a witness?"

Philip shrugged. "Don't roar, Judge. Of course I do. You understand, don't you, Mother? I wanted to help Pamela, the girl I am going to marry."

Pamela's senses whirled like a merry-go-round gone mad, steadied. Her eyes flashed to Scott Mallory. Had he exclaimed before he turned to stare down into the fire, or had she imagined it? With a joyous croon, Mrs. Carr flung her arm about her.

"My dear! My dear! Is it true? I am the happiest woman in the world. Now I have someone to whom to leave my pearls!"

Pamela's tongue clove to the roof of her mouth, her throat dried, her eyes were drawn to Phineas Carr as by a magnet. His seemed to bore into her soul before he looked at his son. He understood, thank heaven! He knew that Phil was taking her love for granted.

"This is joyous news, Philip — but, don't misunderstand me, my boy, when I ask you to finish the saga of the fair Milly, before we — we — offer our sincere congratulations — if — they are in order."

His voice was affectionately friendly. His wife regarded him with wistful radiance, his son, incredulously.

"I can't believe it is you, sir, speaking as one

gentleman to another. There isn't much more to it. Terry and I had sniffed smoke where there was no fire. When I pinned the girl down to confession she admitted brassily:

" 'I've got a crush on Terry Leigh. All the girls in the village got their Academy boy-friend. They bet me I couldn't get him. I bet I could. Only excuse I had to go up to the Leigh place was to get eggs. I talked to his father when I couldn't see him.' Her tone was nasty as she added, 'I'm off him for life. He set the rooster on me. Anyway, there's someone else I like much better.' So there you are! I'm a flat tire. I spent my day kidnapping a witness who wasn't a witness after all. If you had needed more proof that I was not cut out for the legal profession, Father, you've got it in the way I dug for evidence where there wasn't any. Now, we'll talk about Pam and me — and the stage settings."

Scott Mallory abruptly flung his cigarette into the smoldering wood-coals. His face was white, his smile twisted.

"Then this is where a mere outlander makes his exit. I'm off to New York tonight for a few weeks, Mr. Carr. Upon my return we will settle up the details of this *cause celebre*."

"Just a moment, Mallory. I've been unjust so many times to Philip that I'm afraid he'll misunderstand me now." Phineas Carr steadied his voice. "Happy as I would be if it were true, Miss Pamela has not yet corroborated Philip's statement. For a recently engaged girl she seems singularly disturbed."

Pamela was only dimly conscious of Mrs. Carr's shocked, "Phin!" She looked at Scott Mallory. His expression was cold as the Arctic pole and about as remote. A lot he cared if she were engaged to Philip Carr. Hadn't Phil said that he had been preferring Hilda? She could change the pattern of her life by accepting Philip — his mother's pearls — but, she didn't want a man, any man, in her life. Fifty thousand dollars of her own! She had forgotten that, forgotten that there need be no more cooking or catering or serving for her. She smiled at Philip Carr as she shook her head.

"I am sorry. I —"

"Hi, Pam!"

Terrence hailed her from the threshold. "I told Mr. Carr at the court-house I'd come for you at five. Phil, I nearly laughed my head off when I found you'd lit out with a witness what wasn't a witness. We were some little detectives, been over-feeding on mystery stories, what? I hear the second Mrs. Leigh's counsel walked out on her. Been hanging round the post-office to get the dope on what people were saying. They are strong for you, Pam."

Pamela linked her arm in his. She blinked furiously to keep back tears as she looked up at him, he was such a dear.

"Terry — Terry!" She swallowed a sob of

sheer excitement. "You may practise your curve! You may fire every egg through the barn window! Father has deposited fifty thousand dollars with Mr. Carr for you."

Her brother flung a protecting arm about her shoulders, his eyes were terrified, his face colorless.

"Pull yourself together, Pam! I knew this strain would get you if you didn't have a change of scene. Father's crack-up, Cecile's get-away, creditors hounding, patrons fussing. Cooking! Cooking! Cooking! Keeping the old frog kicking! Round and round. It's the treadmill that gets the farmers' wives. Cheer up, Pam, everything's going to be all right. Mr. Scott, you tell her!"

Scott Mallory put his hand on the boy's shoulder, his eyes were unashamedly full of tears, his voice husky.

"Steady, Terrence. Your sister is stating facts. Evidence at the trial brought out the fact that your father has been hoarding a fortune in rare stamps. Today his agent, Brown, bought enough of them to enable him to repay you and Pamela the money your mother left you."

Terrence went limp. "Do you mean it! Do you mean that Father will go on his own again?"

No thought of what the money would mean to him, merely an overwhelming sense of freedom from his father's incessant fault-finding. Pamela herself knew that sense as of a spirit uncaged.

"Milly Pike, who be you, to tell me whether I

can come into this house or not? Get out of my way, an' stay there."

With the last word Mehitable Betts appeared on the threshold. Her pansy bonnet was awry, a gray shawl dragged from one shoulder, she gripped a straw suitcase. Mrs. Carr nodded dismissal to the angry-eyed, pink-frocked maid, who hovered behind her. Phineas Carr pushed forward a chair.

"Come in, Miss Betts. We must have been waiting tea for you."

The gaunt woman straightened like a martinet. Sniffed.

"I won't take tea. I came to give notice to Pamela."

Again! Pamela sighed, remembered that it didn't matter. Every reservation had been cancelled. The "Closed" sign would remain out until one-time patrons forgot the Silver Moon. She was sorry in a way, making good had been thrillingly interesting. Quite from force of habit, not because she thought it of importance, she inquired:

"What is the matter now, Hitty?"

"Matter!" Miss Betts dropped her suitcase with a thud, the better to hitch her spectacles into place. "Matter! Your father's second wife's up at the house with him!"

"What!" Pamela and Terrence united in the exclamation.

Miss Betts' lips puckered satisfaction. "Land's sake, I thought you'd be surprised. They're up there on the porch. That smart parrot knows something irregular's going on. When he isn't tooting like an auto horn, he's shivering and ruffling his feathers and croaking 'Goo'bye! Goo'bye!'"

"Are — are they talking together — like friends?"

"Well, I wouldn't call her conversation friendly, Pamela, I'd call it mushy. He didn't look's though he was considering poisoning her, either. She's trying to get him again, I guess. I heard her say, 'Motoring in England would set you on your feet, Harold. Let's go.' You ought to see that dog of yours, Terry. Lying on the grass, head on his paws, dejected like, as though he couldn't bear life another minute."

Terrence chuckled. "It sounds domestic enough, Hitty. What sent you flying off the handle?"

The glare of outraged Miss Betts should have withered him.

"Domestic! Your Pa comes to me and he says, lordlike,

"'Mrs. Leigh will be here for supper, Hitty. Serve it on the porch.' I looked at him an' I says, 'I *was* working for Pamela. I'm *leaving* this minute.' He just raised his brows in that way he has and walked out. As I was reaching for my hat I heard him say,

"'Pamela'll be here soon and she'll get supper for us, Cecile.'"

For one terrifying instant Pamela thought her

mind would snap from fury. Every ship in the room seemed to be flying along under bellying sails. She struggled to piece her voice together, it came raggedly.

"I get supper for them! With a cheque for fifty thousand dollars in my pocket! I won't go back to Grandmother Leigh's house while Cecile is there. She can cook. I'm through! Terrence, go to the Inn and stay until you hear from me. I'm going away by myself to—New York—I'll stay with Madge Jarvis! No, Phil, don't touch me! I haven't gone crazy, though I may sound so. Your father understands. Ask him. Don't be afraid of him. Tell him at once what a hit your settings have made. He will be so proud of you. I don't love you. I'm sorry. I don't love anyone except—except Terry." She stopped at the door.

"Thank you all for what you have done for me. I—I've just got to get away!"

Her heart was pounding, her breath came as if she had been running as she jumped into the sedan. She threw it into gear and sent it roaring along the drive.

Chapter XXIII

THE road stretched ahead, silken smooth, between spreading fields already slumbering in the rosy afterglow. On the crest of a miniature hill Pamela stopped the car. Over the tops of a clump of scrub oaks she could see the dunes, humped like *papier mâché* shapes against a darkening sky, with foaming shallows at their bases. Houses, which looked for all the world like gigantic marshmallows scattered in a genie's flight, dotted the foreground. A lovely village, a village to return to, not one in which to spend one's youth.

She drove on. A rim of burnished copper hung on the far horizon for an instant before it dropped out of sight. With its passing, familiar objects and sounds took on an unexpected strangeness. She passed the court-house. How gray and stolid! What stories it could tell of the meting of justice, perhaps the defeat of justice. Lengthening shadows, unearthly flickers where gold-washed leaves stirred restlessly under a caressing breeze. Murmur of little night-prowlers awakening in wood and field. Carpets of moss. Maze of willows. Paths through lush meadows worn by plodding feet. Darting birds. Munching cows gazing with ruminative eyes. Old horses going coltish in their hind legs. A church bell summoning the faithful. Happy-go-lucky cedar fences neither knowing nor caring whither they straggled, unmotivated as she was now.

The road proved not so straight as she remembered. Was it because she was alone? Now that the tumult and the shouting within her had died down she would better check-up emotionally, her life seemed all loose ends. Where was she going? To New York, she had said. A frenzied determination to escape had shaken her when Hitty had reported Cecile's presence at the Silver Moon with her husband. Had it been caused by jealousy? No. She still loved her father but she would rather not see him again until the memory of these last months had dimmed.

A quick thinker, Cecile. Doubtless she had figured that as she had been discredited in the trial her best move was to be reinstated as Harold Leigh's wife — now that she knew that he had money. They were waiting for Pamela to return to get supper for them, were they? If they waited for that they would starve! Oh, but they wouldn't starve. Cecile could cook. And then — and then her husband could turn a postage stamp or two into a magic carpet to transport her to England. Steady! Why boil-up over something which had passed?

What had the Carrs thought of her outburst?

With the question came a picture of the room she had left. Against a background of ships of every conceivable type and material, she visualized Mrs. Carr's wistful face; Philip tugging at his small mustache, his expression crestfallen; Phineas Carr with fingers clutching his flower-bedecked lapel, watching his son with sympathetically understanding eyes; Terrence crimson with indignation; Mehitable Betts, her grim mouth clamped with satisfaction at the reaction to her announcement; Scott—

At the imminent risk of ditching the car Pamela closed her lids tight. Even that didn't shut out his eyes, they burned into her soul. Where had she taken the turning which had smashed their friendship? When Hilda Crane's sister had dotted her life-line with an offer for the cottage? The plot-complex again!

She forced her attention to her surroundings, glanced at the speedometer. She had driven fifty miles! She would stop for the night at the first attractive inn. She could make New York tomorrow. She had twenty dollars, some change in her purse and a cheque for fifty thousand. She must spend the cash carefully. Fifty thousand! Unbelievable! No more catering at the Silver Moon. In retrospect, even that didn't seem so hard; hadn't the Chowder House brought Scott into her life? She had liked her patrons, most of them. Nothing now between her and her chosen work. Life, liberty and the pursuit of plot-germs! At present her mind was as empty of ideas for stories and articles as a squeezed orange was of juice; but once she touched her typewriter they would come trooping along, she knew from experience. She was approaching a village. She looked at the gas-gauge. She would better stop and have the tank filled.

A pleasant street. Gardens bordered and starred with spring flowers colorless in the twilight, filched of their fragrance by a moist breeze which scattered it prodigally. Nice old houses, their ancient glories mellowed by time and the absence of fresh paint. A little white church with presumably a dove-gray parsonage beside it. Its familiarity had a dreamlike quality. A garage!

A man in greasy overalls hurried from the dark interior before she stopped the sedan. He touched a lock of rough hair, sunbursts of fine lines crinkled about his eyes as he smiled.

"How much, Miss?"

"All the tank will hold."

He disappeared behind the car. As she waited, she watched a brilliant star prick through an indigo sky, impale itself on the church spire where it hung like a bit of glittering tinsel on the top of a Christmas tree. Lovely night! Freakishly unreal, though; were it not for the odor of gasoline she would think she was living a dream, nothing unreal about the smell.

The garage keeper's concerned face appeared at the car window.

"Say, Miss, yer tank's leaking something terrible."

Existence shed its dreamlike quality to bump into
facts.

"How can it leak?"

The man's smile revealed teeth startlingly white
in contrast to their begrimed setting.

"I don't know how it can, Miss, but it does."

"How quickly can you repair it?"

He scratched his head contemplatively. "Run
her into the shop. I'll take a look."

Pamela regarded him thoughtfully. If she were
a judge of human nature — she flattered herself that
she was — the man was honest and respectable. He
hadn't discovered the leak merely to give himself
work. She drove into the garage.

From the top of a packing-box she watched him
as, flat on his back, he poked around under the car
with his flashlight. It was evident from his absorption that he was an engine addict.

Her glance traveled round the dusky shop. One
shelved wall was entirely given over to what might
be generically termed "parts." There were bunches
of waste by the oily dozen; a gas-tank on wheels;
grease and tire-rim machines; a battery-charger in
the act of transfusion; new tires, a squad of them
in a corner; boxes of tubes; a wrecked flivver, a
complete and perfect thing of its kind. On a bench
near the window reposed a pile of thick sandwiches
and a steaming cup. Pamela's eyes came back to
the prostrate figure on the floor. Tank conditions

must be serious to keep the mechanic there all this time. Lucky he had discovered the leak; else she might have been hung up between towns without food for man or beast, figuratively speaking.

The thought set hunger gnawing. She had been unable to so much as taste the luncheon Hitty had provided. With the thought came the remembrance of Terrence's laughter. What wonder he had "laughed his head off" when he visualized Philip Carr speeding away with a witness who wasn't a witness? Later, Eddie Pike's melodramatic accusation had entirely submerged the tea-party. She had been driving at supper time. She was hollow to her toes. She was entitled to be low in her mind; hunger set Terrence and his father prowling for someone to bite, it reduced her spirit to its lowest denominator.

She slid from the box, circled a puddle of gasoline, jumped a water-hazard. She gently nudged the mechanic's boot, shouted to make herself heard above his pounding and tapping.

"How long will it take?"

The man wriggled out, sat up. He wiped his hot face with a hand which left a sardonic streak from eye to nose. Not so good. After all, he didn't look so dependable as she had thought.

"Can't tell yet, Miss. You'd better sit down an' take it easy."

"But, I am starving. Any place near where I can get something to eat?"

From the hoplessness of his expression she deduced that eating wasn't being done this month in the village. Or — eyes narrowed, she regarded him speculatively — was he trying to keep her here?

He scratched an ear, jiggled the tools in his hand. He was stalling. What would she better do? Insist upon driving out, leaky tank or no leaky tank?

"Let me think — Car just stopped outside. Excuse me, Miss; can't afford to lose a sale."

He hurried away wiping oily hands on oilier waste. Pamela heroically turned her back on the sandwiches. Even if she did suspect the man of double-crossing her, it would be like stabbing him in the back to snitch any part of his supper. She looked at the clock. Getting late. She was strong for adventure but this one lacked a sense of timeliness.

Was the tank really leaking? She doubled like a jackknife in an attempt to look under the car. Her hat fell off. She caught it before it reached the floor. Gas would be dripping if the leak were as serious as the man had intimated. She couldn't see a drop, there was no puddle visible. He had tricked her —

"To get the proper perspective you should be flat on your back."

"Scott!"

Pamela straightened. The suddenly right-side-up shop whirled. She backed against the bumper of her car, clenched her hands behind her.

"I'm not going back! I am not going back!"

Mallory's face, which had been a ghostly blur,

took on form and color, dark color. He caught her shoulder.

"Come away from that dirty car! You will spoil your clothes." He drew her forward. "I am not here to drag you back. The mechanic says it will take time to find the leak. If you want to go on tonight you'd better come with me."

"When did he tell you that?"

"When he was filling up for me. Said he had a job inside which might take a couple of hours."

"Oh, he did! What communicative souls men are. Babbling brooks have nothing on them. I suspect he is trying to put something across."

"Mike Shaughnessy wouldn't do that!"

"Mike? You know him then?"

"I — I usually stop here on my way back and forth. Remember I told you I went to the parsonage across the street once with a wedding party? Mike and I got rather fratty then so I buy gas here on my way up and down."

Pamela listened with her ears, not with her mind. She remembered his story on the way home from Boston about the eloping couple. She had been half asleep which fact accounted for the dreamlike quality of the church and dove-gray house when she had passed it a while ago.

"Pam!" Mallory's voice, the grip of his hands on hers shocked her back to the present. "What has come between us? You know that I love you, don't you? You know that yarn of Phil Carr's about

Hilda Crane and me was straight fiction, don't you?"

She kept her eyes on his hands. She hadn't known that a gassy, oily garage could seem so like heaven. She lingered outside the gates.

"Why should I know?" She steadied her traitorous voice. "I am not a mind-reader. You came to the village often, but not to the Silver Moon."

His grip tightened. His voice was husky from repression.

"The day I went to warn Carnation Carr to keep his hands off my client, he showed me the risk if I tried your case, said that I would be vulnerable because — because I loved you. He's a prince! He advised that I keep away from you until after the trial. I had told him about meeting Cecile in New York and of her evident suspicion. My calls upon Hilda were a smoke-screen — I couldn't hurt her heart, she hasn't any — an excuse for being in the village to consult with him."

He tilted her chin. "Look at me, Pam. You believe me, don't you?"

Her eyes met his. "Yes, I —" He pressed his lips hard on hers. Her hands clung tight about his neck, he loosened his arms only to crush her close again.

"Say, Mr. Mallory —"

Scott held Pamela as in a vise when she would have slipped away.

"I will be out in a minute, Shaughnessy. Put —

put in a quart of oil—and—and see if the tires need air."

"I get you!"

The mechanic's words were curiously choked. Was he laughing as he bolted from the shop? Pamela looked accusingly at the man who still held her as if he never would let her go.

"Scott!"

"I know what you are going to say. Guilty! Terrence phoned Mike to keep you here until I came. We knew that my roadster would cover the ground in half the time it would take the sedan."

"Suppose I hadn't stopped?"

"Your brother knew the amount of gas in the tank, figured from your hasty departure that you wouldn't stop until you had to."

She tilted her head back against his shoulder.

"Scott, are you sure I am not dreaming?" Her laugh was shaky as she laid her hand on the face swooping to hers. "You needn't kiss me again to make me realize that you—and—I are not a dream. I meant about Father. Is it possible that a collection of stamps can mean so much money?"

"Several years ago one sold for a million and a half. Count Ferrary's netted three million."

"Not dollars!"

"Dollars. Your father's must be tremendously valuable. When you first told me that he was interested in stamps, I wondered. His insistence that his new wife should not be told of his hobby was suspicious. I began to investigate. I knew that you would not listen to me if I told you that I loved you, while you felt you must make a home for him. Right, wasn't I?"

She nodded. "I suspected before that you were a mind-reader."

"I didn't dare trust myself with you — much — it tore me to pieces to be with you and not tell you that I loved you — have you in my arms. Nothing for me to do but find a fortune for him. I found it. He was furiously angry, but, he got over it. Brown was shaking with eagerness when he paid over those two cheques. I doubt if what he bought made much of a dent in one of the most famous collections in the world."

"How did you persuade him to pay Terrence and me?"

"I didn't have to do much persuading. As he improved in health his conscience began to prick. I just encouraged him to make good. I was bound to protect your interests. You were my first Leigh client, you retained me to fire S. Linsky before I talked with your father about his bills."

"Father is right. You are an unflinching person."

He drew her hands to his lips.

"I mean to be now, then never again with you. Marry me tonight, will you — Gorgeous?"

"Scott! Are you mad?"

"Come back! I can argue more eloquently when I have you in my arms. By your own admission you don't care for a wedding splurge. You say that you won't return to the Silver Moon while your stepmother is there — from Hitty's account it looks as if she intended to stay for a while, till she gets that allowance — at least. I must be in New York tomorrow night for a conference with clients from the Argentine, will be there two weeks. After that — well, I have an option on a penthouse for the winter. You may have it all silver walls and eggshell lacquer if you like."

"That is a shameless bribe." In spite of the turmoil within her, Pamela smiled at him. He kissed her.

"Don't do that again. I — I can't think."

"Why think?"

His shaken whisper drew her heart to her throat. She struggled for composure, mocked gaily:

"One can't get married without a license, can one?"

He tapped his breast pocket. "What do you think I was doing while Terrence sneaked in the back door of the Silver Moon — with the almost ex-married close together in a secluded corner of the porch — and packed your suitcase and picked up your top-coat? I was at the house of the town clerk getting a special license."

"Did Terry know that — that —"

"We were to be married? He did. When I told him, he grinned that one-sided smile of his and said, like the soldier he is:

"'Tell Pam that it will be a relief to me to have her away from that cook-stove at the Silver Moon. Tell her to think of me in the stilly night practising my curve with the prize Plymouth Rock eggs.'"

Pamela brushed her eyes against a blue serge breast to clear them of tears. Was that Scott's heart pounding?

Mallory gently smoothed back her hair. "Carnation Carr helped me get that special license."

"Scott, I had a premonition the night I met Mr. Carr in his Ship Room, that he would change the pattern of my life."

"Your departure from that same room this afternoon was a smash. Philip started after you. His father caught his arm. Said with a tenderness of which I did not believe that juggernaut of an advocate capable:

"'That is Mallory's job, Phil.'"

"How did he know?"

"Know! He knew in our first interview. Everyone knew I was mad about you."

"I didn't."

"Your mistake." He laid his cheek on her hair. "Coming with me?"

"To New York?"

"To the parsonage across the street first. Your senior counsel attended to that bit of business for me too. Great things, telephones."

She regarded him with mock gravity. "Do you

know, Scott, it is being borne in upon me how terribly afraid Carnation Carr was that I would marry his only child."

"Don't get him wrong. He would have adored you for a daughter, but — you won't like this — he said that the first time you mentioned my name, he knew you loved me. His assurance was all that kept me going, these last interminable weeks."

His eyes darkened. Pamela was beginning to know that look.

"Coming?"

"Yes."

He raised her hand to his lips. Slipped a ring on her finger, a blazing planet of a diamond set in a twinkling constellation of lesser stars. "I came prepared to make you wear this the moment the trial was over. It will have to serve for a wedding ring too. Like it?"

She looked at him in answer.

Perhaps in time, the haze, behind which lurked the past fifteen minutes, might lift and she would remember clearly the sequence of events, Pamela thought as she followed the stepping-stones from the parsonage door to the shining roadster. She had only a confused sense of a kindly white-haired clergyman with a book; of a placid woman with a mammoth cameo pin at her lace collar; of an amber-haired school-girl; Scott's eyes glowing through the fog; the pressure of his hand, the uneven richness of his voice answering,

"I do."

Mallory pulled her coat from the car. "Better put this on." He drew it about her shoulders with disturbing care. He observed casually as he started the roadster:

"Mike Shaughnessy will take the sedan back to Terrence."

"Was there really a leak in the gas-tank, Scott?"

A note in his laugh set her pulses rioting. "He seems like an honest man."

Moonlight softly blurred the world. Silver dews shimmered on the meadows. The roadster skirted a produce-laden wagon; the lumbering farm horses pricked dejected ears, shuffled hairy fetlocks and relapsed into a plod.

"We'll have a fine day for the trip tomorrow."

Fair tomorrow! Terrifying and disillusioning much of the year behind her; but fair tomorrow and all the tomorrows so long as she and Scott were together, Pamela told herself passionately.

Down the road the lights of a long building twinkled invitingly. Mallory drove more slowly as he asked:

"Hungry?"

"Starving. I had just realized when you crashed into the garage, that I had eaten nothing since breakfast."

"We will stop somewhere for supper at once." He threw a newly possessive arm about her shoulders. "Suppose we stay at that inn ahead tonight? It is a good one."

Pamela kept her eyes on her locked fingers. "You mean — stop here and — and go on to New York tomorrow?"

"Yes. Don't you intend ever again to look at the man you have married — Mrs. Mallory?"

Pamela's lashes swept up. The unguarded, passionate light in Scott Mallory's eyes softened.

"Sweet child!" he whispered tenderly and kissed her gently on the lips.

At the hospitably open door of the inn he caught her hand, drew her into the shadow.

"Happy, dear?"

The hint of remorseful anxiety in his low voice, the husky break in the last word, gave wings to her heart. After all, it was Scott, who, since the day he had stepped into the green and white kitchen had been unfailingly tender; Scott, who loved her, with whom she was crossing this strange threshold. Her radiant eyes confirmed the lilt in her voice as she answered:

"Happy? Top of the world!"

